# DOG COLLAR CRIME

## THE LUCIE RIZZO MYSTERY SERIES

### ADRIENNE GIORDANO

## THE LUCIE RIZZO MYSTERY SERIES

Dog Collar Crime

Knocked Off

Limbo (novella)

Boosted

Whacked

Cooked

*Romantic suspense books available by Adrienne Giordano*

## PRIVATE PROTECTOR SERIES

Risking Trust

Man Law

A Just Deception

Negotiating Point

Relentless Pursuit

Opposing Forces

## HARLEQUIN INTRIGUES

The Prosecutor

The Defender

The Marshal

The Detective

The Rebel

Dog Collar Crime: A Lucie Rizzo Mystery
Copyright © 2013 by Adrienne Giordano
ISBN: 978-1-942504-23-8
Cover Art by Lewellen Designs
Editing by Gina Bernal

# DOG COLLAR CRIME

A Lucie Rizzo Mystery
by
Adrienne Giordano

# 1

On a lovely March day—if such a thing existed in Chicago—Lucia Rizzo led Miss Elizabeth, a Yorkie possessing the confidence of a runway model with a good boob job, across State Street's lunchtime traffic and was nearly pancaked.

"Slow down!" she hollered at the errant driver.

A terrified Miss Elizabeth cowered on the sidewalk and Lucie scooped her up for a nuzzle. "Poor baby. I'm so sorry."

The dog sniffed, then licked Lucie's chin. "You're a sweet girl."

Another lick.

Maybe this dog walking thing wasn't so bad. Heaven knew the investment bankers in Lucie's old office never got their faces licked during the workday. And if they had, surely a sexual harassment suit would follow.

*Speaking of investment banking...* "Okay, girl, playtime is over. You need to poop so I can get home and look for a job."

She glanced at her watch. No time for delays in an already packed schedule.

The sound of heavy breathing pelted Lucie's ears and

she glanced over her shoulder to see a man on her heels. Some people had no respect for personal space. She gave him the Lucie Rizzo version of the narrow-eyed back-off-bub look. When the man didn't respond to her obvious warning, she darted ahead, but Miss Elizabeth flopped to the ground with an effort that sent her sequined barrette dancing in the sunlight. Fabulous.

Lucie stared at the dog. "Get moving, girl."

The dog could have been a statue.

A man wearing a red warm-up jacket strode toward them, his eyes focused on Miss Elizabeth in a way that caused a prickle of unease to snake up Lucie's spine. Another space invader?

She reached for the dog, but hands clamped on her shoulders from behind and shoved her sideways. Her heart jackhammered, and the shove carried her step by step by step until the side of a red Camry loomed in her vision. *Uh-oh. Incoming.* With the force of a line drive hitting a windshield, Lucie plowed headfirst into the parked car.

"Ow!"

Pain slammed into her as she landed on all fours, her right knee taking the blow from the pavement before she rolled to her back. Swirling white birds flapped above. She blinked, realizing they weren't birds but white spots from the whack to her head.

Had she been mugged? Couldn't be. She didn't have a purse.

Panic forced the hour-old kraut dog to lurch up her throat. She shifted to her knees, propped her hands under her and waited for the evacuation of her lunch. She let out a slow breath and stared at her hands.

No vomit. Good.

No leash. Bad.

No dog. Very bad.

She turned her head to where Miss Elizabeth should have been. Nothing. Could the dog have been under her when she fell? She hadn't felt anything or heard a yelp. *Please don't let me have fallen on her.* Lucie might be petite, but her hundred and ten pounds could still take out a three-pound dog. An image of the beloved Yorkie—lifeless—gripped her mind.

The sounds of traffic and car horns nearly blew Lucie's aching head apart, but she peeked all around. No dog. At least she wouldn't have to live with knowing she'd crushed Miss Elizabeth. A moment of relief sparked and disappeared.

The jerk that knocked her over had vanished and sent poor Miss Elizabeth into hiding. She couldn't have gotten far. Her legs didn't move that fast. Lucie dropped to the ground and checked under the cars. Nothing.

She ran to the corner, where a dark-haired man wearing a red jacket bolted through heavy traffic on State Street. She squinted hard and focused on a flash of glitter in the man's arms. Miss Elizabeth's sequined barrette.

"Help!" Lucie's voice carried the high-pitched panic storming her body. "Stop him. He stole my dog."

She stepped off the curb, but a middle-aged man in a business suit heaved her backward before a speeding cab tattooed her to the pavement. "Are you okay?"

"He stole my dog! That guy." *Dammit.* The thief had turned the corner.

"What guy?" the man asked in a this-chick-is-nuts tone.

For a change, she didn't care what anyone thought of her. All she cared about was losing Miss Elizabeth. "The one that's gone."

Fifteen minutes later, Lucie sat on a broken curb while

the biting edge of anger and guilt morphed into emotional sludge.

Yes, at certain times in her life, she needed to maintain absolute emotional control.

This was not one of those times.

She drew a deep breath of Chicago's eau de diesel fumes as a fresh line of cars turned off State Street. The rubber-neckers, apparently fascinated by flashing lights on a police car, slowed to barely moving. Lucie dropped her head into her hands. Hiding would be the best way to limit eye contact with the gawkers.

The cop finished his conversation with dispatch and came around the back of the car.

"Okay, Ms...." He checked his notepad... "Rizzo. Lucia *Rizzo.*"

Lucie's gaze drifted to the name on the uniform that had seen one too many washings. The broken-in look suited the man—this Officer Lindstrom—who kept his dusty blond hair buzzed into a crew cut that accentuated his thick neck and linebacker build. A big boy.

The man's blue eyes drilled into her. She recognized the narrow-eyed fascination that came with wondering if she was Joe Rizzo's daughter.

Her father, being the accused in a long string of criminal trials, left the distinction of 'mob princess' sitting on her like an overweight elephant. This cop was probably judging her as a lowlife. She should be used to it by now, the presumptions about her heritage and character made by people who knew nothing of her work ethic. All because of her last name. All because of her father. The jailbird. Regardless, she was a citizen who had been wronged and deserved respect.

"He's my father," she said.

"Joe Rizzo?"

"Yep."

Lindstrom cocked his head. "*That's* gotta be interesting."

With that, Lucie snorted a half sob, half giggle. *What a lovely sound.* "You have no idea."

"I'm sure. Anyway, we put out a BOLO. It's still early so we might get a quick response."

Lucie glanced up and squinted against the bright sun. "What's a BOLO?"

"Be on the lookout. The BOLO is for a Yorkie wearing a rhinestone barrette."

At least he didn't laugh when he said it. Lucie closed her eyes, felt the swell of bubbling tears and let them fire down her cheeks. Crying. Just great.

"Ms. Rizzo?" Lindstrom said. "You still with me?"

With a vicious swipe, she swatted her cheeks and saw his face soften in a way that offered understanding. *He must be a dog owner.*

"I don't know how it happened. We were walking along and—*bam*—I was on the ground and some goon was taking off with her."

The panic rushed back, clawed at her for being so irresponsible that she'd lose a dog belonging to her most high-strung client. Well, she hadn't actually *lost* the dog, but Lucie took the safety of her charges seriously, and this would certainly be her fault. What if the thieves hurt Miss Elizabeth? Lucie rubbed at a fresh batch of tears. *Idiot.*

Officer Lindstrom went back to his notes. "Ms. Rizzo, your dog's name is Miss Elizabeth?"

"Call me Lucie. And she's not my dog. I'm the walker. Tom Darcy is the owner."

"Miss Elizabeth and...*Mr.* Darcy?"

5

Lucie, awed by the fact that he appreciated *Pride and Prejudice*, glanced up. "You're a Jane Austen fan?"

He winced. "Not me. My wife. I've seen that damned movie six times."

His wife. *He's married.* Not that Lucie was looking, considering she had Frankie, but—*wow*—a guy who'd sit through *Pride and Prejudice* six times. "It's still impressive."

He shrugged, tapped his pen on his notepad. "Is Miss Elizabeth a show dog?"

"No. Why?"

"There's a dog theft ring operating in the city. They steal show dogs for ransom."

Oh, no. Poor Miss Elizabeth. "She looks like a show dog. She's impeccably groomed."

Lindstrom's radio crackled and he spoke into the microphone on his shoulder. He finished the radio call, pulled a card from his pocket and wrote something on it. "I need to run, but here's my card and your case number. If this is tied to the theft ring, the case will go to a detective. If not, it'll come back to me. Either way, someone will follow up."

Lucie took the card. "Thank you. I appreciate your help."

He jerked his head, started for his car, but turned back to her. "Is there someone you can call for a ride?"

A nice guy. Her father would never believe it of a cop. "That's okay. I have my scooter at Mr. Lutz's place."

"A scooter?"

Lucie nodded. "I use a scooter to get around the city faster. My old boss lets me store it in his garage."

"Nice former boss."

"He's trying to help. I was laid off six months ago. The dog walking helps pay the bills while I'm job hunting."

Which was the reason she was sitting on this blasted curb wanting to skewer the bastard who stole Miss Eliza-

6

beth. Lucie mentally settled the queasies plaguing her belly. Maybe the whack on the head was messing with her stomach.

Lindstrom's feet shifted in front of her. "You sure you don't want to go to the hospital?"

As if this wasn't embarrassing enough. "No. Thanks."

"You should get that head checked out. At least go to your regular doctor."

That was doable. "I will."

Lucie watched him jump into the car, flip on the lights and drive off. Part of her wished she could join him, because she now had to inform Tom Darcy his beloved pet had been snatched.

She slid her phone from her pocket. What would she even say? *Gee, Mr. Darcy, you still have a slew of* Pride and Prejudice *characters to choose from for the name of your next dog.*

With that, she ran to the garbage can on the corner and lost the kraut dog.

## 2

———

Lucie stepped through the front door of her parents' Franklin, Illinois home and dropped her duffel at the base of the stairs. The entryway of the shoe-box-sized living room closed in, the nearness suffocating her, while the pungent aroma of her mother's garlic-infused roast beef filled the air. Lucie's tender stomach seized. *Oi.*

Most of her twenty-six years had been spent trying to escape this place, but six months ago, she had moved back. *How did I get here?*

Voices from the kitchen sparked a memory. The Falcone's were here for dinner. Her mother had mentioned it that morning. Terrific.

She shifted to see Joey, her ape of a brother, sprawled across the sofa watching a March Madness basketball game. Frankie, her currently off-again-in-limbo-fiancé-slash-boyfriend—heck, she didn't know what he was anymore, sat in the green wingback chair next to the sofa. For weeks, she'd managed to avoid him. Now, seeing him in his favorite chair, so comfortable in her mother's home, the ache from missing him, the one she had learned to compartmentalize, broke free and cut off her air. "Hey," she said.

Joey craned his head in her direction and a slow, filthy smile seeped across his face. He'd better not start with the poop scooping jokes. *Not today.* She squinted and tried to put a little nasty into it. Not easy for a girl known as the good one in the family. But if she stared hard enough, maybe her older brother wouldn't start. "Don't say it, Joey."

In typical Joey fashion, he remained stretched on the sofa. He ran his tongue along his perfect top teeth—a total giveaway of the act of terrorism to come—and Lucie squeezed her butt cheeks together.

He could be a real hater.

Frankie stood and moved toward her with his hands extended. "Luce."

*No.*

"How'd it go?" her brother asked, his voice light and menacing. "The poop scooping?"

And there it was. His ever-present need to goad her into a fight.

The cackle erupting from Joey's wide-open mouth banged around inside Lucie's already pummeled and aching skull. She scrunched her nose so hard the pain shot through her cheeks. *Be strong.* But after the day she'd had, the screeching laughter pounded at her.

"Luce," Frankie said again, but Joey's laugh burned her like a hot pipe. Suddenly she was eight years old again, when he'd left her hanging from a tree branch after challenging her to a pull-up contest. Even at eleven, he'd been a jerk.

*Be a big girl, be a big girl, be a big girl.*

Frankie stepped closer. "Don't snap."

Forget snapping. The thing going on inside her was an

implosion. A veritable war between her crazy and *uncrazy* self. At this moment, crazy had superior firepower. Even with Frankie's family sitting in the kitchen.

*Better luck next time, Uncrazy.*

Lucie launched herself across the back of the sofa and landed on Joey. She might have been screaming. She wasn't sure because all she heard was the cackling. That cackling, mixed with the increasing closeness of the walls, ignited her.

What did it matter? After this rotten day, all she wanted was to punish someone. That someone happened to be her brother.

Joey put his hands up to protect his head, but his laughter continued. *Kah-kah-kah-kah-kah-kah.*

Such a bastard. A bastard with a stupid, stupid laugh.

Plus, he outweighed her by a good hundred and thirty pounds—why did she have to be the petite one? He could easily toss her off, but this was his demented idea of fun.

She feinted right, went left and whopped him on the side of the head.

"Ow!" he hollered, half-laughing.

He made a move to harness her wrists in his giant hands, but she swatted at him and dug her knee into his thigh. He winced—success—and she bared her teeth at him.

Then she went airborne, her legs bicycling as Frankie hauled her backward. "Easy, killer."

Her breaths came in halting, rib-fracturing bursts, but she kicked out one last time and missed. "You're an idiot, Joey."

She squeezed her eyes closed and concentrated on the feel of Frankie's steadying arm. His calming presence poured into her, settled her rioting brain. Even now, after all this time, she loved it when he touched her. When his hands were on her, she came alive, every nerve ending exploding with a fierce pleasure and longing to get closer.

Thank God for the magic of Frankie.

After a minute of prepping to face her brother, Lucie exhaled and opened her eyes. "I'm okay. You can let go."

"Hmm. Too bad," Frankie whispered in a way that meant he was feeling frisky.

And wasn't it typical of him to be thinking about sex at a time like this? Although, he pretty much thought about sex every ten seconds, so why would this moment be any different?

"You are a freaking lunatic." This from her brother still sprawled across the sofa.

Mom stepped into the room with Frankie's mother and father trailing. "What is all the yelling?"

Joey picked up the television remote and flipped the channel from the basketball game. "Your daughter is a whack job, Ma."

"Joseph, that's not nice."

Not. Nice. Her mother was clueless when it came to Joey. And of course, this scene unfolded in front of Frankie's parents.

Mom came closer, brought Lucie in for a hug, and the smell of her almond shampoo penetrated the wall of anger and humiliation. Theresa Rizzo, at fifty-five, despite her cluelessness concerning her son, was an excellent candidate for sainthood. Always home. Always consistent. Always available.

Unlike Lucie's other parent.

Lucie pulled back and stared at her mother. For years now, she'd worn her chestnut hair shoulder length with wispy bangs to hide her wide forehead. Her heart-shaped

face held hard fought frown lines, but her mother's eyes...
they were special. Not brown, not green, but something in-
between, and when she turned them on someone, her mood
wasn't hard to distinguish. Those eyes now held concern.

"Are you all right?"

"I'm fine, Mom." Finally, Lucie faced Frankie's parents.
"Hi, Mr. and Mrs. Falcone. Sorry about that."

"Eh," Mr. Falcone said. "It wouldn't be the first time
we've seen siblings fight."

Frankie rolled his eyes as his parents headed back to the
kitchen. "Nice, Pop."

"Dinner in ten minutes," Mom said. "Why don't you go
get cleaned up?"

An escape. Sainthood for Mom. Stat. "Good idea. I'll be
down in a few minutes."

Mom started to turn, but stopped. "By the way, I spoke to
your father today. He put you on the list for next week."

The list.

"And if you don't visit him," Joey said. "He's gonna
fry you."

Frankie and Lucie both spun on him. "Shut up."

Mom, as usual, ignored Joey and leveled her gaze on
Frankie. "You're on the list, too."

"Uh-oh," Frankie said.

Lucie grinned. "Looks like he heard."

Joey laughed. "I didn't tell him."

Probably true. Joey never seemed to care whether
Frankie and Lucie were broken up. Frankie had been his
friend all their lives and that would never change. That
friendship sat at the root of why Lucie kept ending things
with Frankie. He couldn't tear himself away from the life she
so desperately wanted to leave.

The break-ups never lasted though. There was this

pesky thing called love between them, and she could never completely let him go.

Lucie brought her eyes back to her mother. "Does Dad know we broke up?"

Her mother shrugged. "This falls into the what-he-doesn't-know-won't-hurt-him category. That category seems to be expanding rapidly."

No joke there. They'd been hiding a lot from her father since his incarceration almost two years ago. Despite living in a conservative home and not throwing money around on flashy cars and clothes, her father had long ago drawn the interest of federal prosecutors. They wanted Joe Rizzo, mob boss, but they couldn't get any organized crime charges to hold and settled for a minor tax problem involving the three Italian beef restaurants he owned. Most people would have walked away with a fine, but not her father. The government wanted Joe Rizzo to pay for his sins. Whatever they were.

Lucie shook off thoughts of explaining to her father why she wouldn't marry Frankie, whom her father adored, mostly because Frankie's father was her father's closest friend. Thus, the reason the Falcones came for dinner twice a month even though her father was locked up. Lucie also suspected these family dinners meant her mother received an infusion of cash—her father's cut of whatever nefariously raised money the mob guys came up with—from Mr. Falcone to help with expenses while her father was away. Talk about a tangled web.

She walked to the stairs where she'd left her duffel. "I'll deal with visiting Dad later. I need to get this stuff unpacked before it wrinkles."

Frankie sidled next to her. "I'll take that up."

No. Last thing she needed was to be alone with Frankie. In her bedroom. "I've got it."

He leaned forward, wrapped his hand around hers on the handle of the bag and the heat from his palm seeped into her. Hoping he wouldn't move, she stayed there for a second. With Frankie around, the speed of her world slowed and reminded her of summer strolls on the lakefront. The Frankie Factor.

A crooked grin spread across his face. "I'll take care of it."

No sense arguing with him. He'd just do it anyway. "Thank you."

She marched up the worn carpeted stairs, mentally groaning over the red and green floral wallpaper dating back to the eighties. She spied a streak of black that had become part of the décor twelve years ago when she had tumbled down the stairs with a permanent marker in her hand.

A noise pulled Lucie from thoughts of adolescence, and she looked over her shoulder to find Frankie staring at her butt. What there was of it anyway. Too bad some of the flesh in her ginormous boobs couldn't have landed on her rump.

"Stop looking at my butt."

"Can't help it. It's in my line of sight."

The trademark Frankie smile appeared, the one that could put General Electric out of business. Who needed light bulbs when Frankie smiled? Even his presence illuminated a room. He kept his dark hair short, but with enough length that it curled around a face full of yummy angles. When he chose to pleasure a woman with a look from his coal-black eyes, he did it with a focused intensity that made her feel like she was the only one in the county.

Unfortunately for Lucie, Frankie's massive good looks left people wondering what he was doing with *her*, Miss Completely Average. She wasn't ugly, for sure. Her blue eyes were a plus, but her drab brown hair and lack of hips didn't usually attract hotties. Nope. The only curves Lucie had were in the chest area. Luckily, Frankie was a boob guy. Then again, she hadn't met many men who weren't.

They reached the top of the stairs and she made a left into the first doorway into her childhood bedroom. The curtains had been changed, but the white swirly-cornered furniture and light green wallpaper still remained, somehow, in pristine condition.

She hated that wallpaper.

Franked nudged her. "Are we going to stand here all day?"

"Uh, sorry." She stepped into the microscopic room and he pushed by her to drop the bag on the bed. The two of them, in there together, made the room beyond small. It didn't help that Frankie wore her favorite faded Levi's that clung to his lean body as if they were tailor-made for him. The Levi's did it for her every time.

"Are you okay?" he asked. "You've been edgy since you got home."

Edgy. Good word for it. With his protective nature, he'd love this one. "After my trunk show, I had a couple of dogs to walk. One of them got stolen."

He abandoned the duffel and spun to her, his face turning to stone. "What happened? Are you hurt?"

She waved off his concern. "I'm fine. I was walking Miss Elizabeth and some goon knocked me over and grabbed her. I hit my head, but it's not bad."

"Why didn't you call me?"

He stepped toward her, but Lucie held out her hand. "I called 9-1-1 and they sent a squad. The cop said there's a dog theft ring operating in the city. It could be related." Lucie pressed her palms into her forehead. "God, Frankie, that poor dog. I'm so scared for her. Plus, Mr. Darcy was bawling when I told him. He adores her."

"Screw the dog, Luce. You should get checked out. You could have a concussion."

He extended his arms to wrap her in a hug, but hesitated before folding them across his chest. She blew air through her lips. They simply stunk at being in limbo. As much as she wanted to draw comfort from him, it wouldn't be fair. To either of them. "I don't think it's a concussion, but I made a doctor's appointment. The cop said they'd call me if they find Miss Elizabeth. I'll have to wait. I keep having visions of that dog being tortured. She was in my care and I let her get taken."

"It's not your fault. They'll find her."

He knew her too well. *So not going there right now.* "Anyway, the trunk show went well this morning."

He unzipped the duffel and opened it. One of her hand-made dog collars caught on the netting inside the bag and Lucie gently pried it loose. "I sold all the rhinestone studded items. The coats with the fur collars also went. Otis loved the camo shirt."

"He tell you that?"

She smacked his arm. "I could tell."

Of course, Otis was a dog. An Olde English Bulldogge to be exact. Lucie had been walking him for five months and understood the flow of his moods. The dogs, with their unabashed love for her, had become the bright spot over these past months. Keeping on schedule with dogs wasn't easy, but she looked forward to walking them each day. With the winter months over, she found joy in the crisp spring air, cleansing her of the negativity that surrounded her current life situation. The dogs had become her sanctuary.

She held up the paisley collar still in her hand. "It's

unbelievable how much these rich people will pay for dog accessories. I sold that pink triple rhinestone deal for a hundred and fifty dollars."

Frankie whistled. "Who needs investment banking when you've got Coco Barknell?"

"Coco Barknell?"

"That's the name I thought of for your company."

Oh, no. She wasn't starting a company. She was an investment banker. Four years at Notre Dame and an MBA said so. Unfortunately, the banking industry didn't agree and when her company merged with a larger one, she'd been *rightsized*. And here she was, back in her old room. Gone was the Chicago loft with the corner window that gave her a six-inch view of the lake. That view might not have been much, but to her, it was the wide-open space of freedom. But freedom had a cost, and the lack of income forced her to rely on unemployment benefits and her savings, which wouldn't go far. Being a fiscally responsible girl, Lucie chose to move home and regroup.

She stared at herself in the bedroom mirror and imagined herself shrinking, her body closing in from the pressure of the miniscule room. Miss Rise-Above-Being-A-Mob-Princess was busted back to her old life.

"Coco Barknell," she said. "That's got a ring to it. Banking is where I belong, though."

Frankie shrugged. "You're good at this crafty stuff."

Lucie glanced at the princess desk that had been a mainstay since her twelfth birthday. She'd set up a card table next to the already cluttered area, and it held stacks of plastic storage bins stuffed with dog collars, shiny colored beads, rhinestones and rolls of fabric. It didn't leave much room to maneuver, but she needed a workspace.

Coco Barknell. Maybe she'd fiddle with a business plan in her down time.

"I was quite the Bedazzler in high school."

"You still are."

Frankie grinned, but it wasn't about dog accessories. This was the grin of lust and long nights, when Lucie thought her body would never get enough of whatever he offered.

Oh, boy. She blew out a breath and sat on the bed only to have him drop beside her. The sag of the mattress rolled her in his direction and their shoulders bumped. She scooted away. No sense in torturing herself.

"I *did* make good money at the trunk show today."

"I'm telling ya, Luce, Coco Barknell."

"I got lucky, Frankie. Mrs. Lutz recommended me to a few of her wealthy friends and it started this whole thing."

"And here you are with a regular gig. That's what I love about you. You never let anything hold you down."

A burst of pride swelled in her chest. He loved her. She knew it, but hearing his approval gave her a boost. This was the gift of Frankie. And the reason women always got caught in his gravitational pull. They wanted to sleep with him, sure, but at his core, Frankie cared about people. He was also a guy's guy who loved any form of sports. Yep, Frankie appealed to the masses.

She glanced around the cramped room. *How did I get back here?*

He nudged her with his elbow. "Where'd you go, Squish?"

Her childhood nickname capped it. Tears threatened and she blinked to clear the haze. Such a long day. "I guess I'm officially back if you're calling me Squish."

He rolled his lips together and popped them open again. "It slipped."

"It's okay. This time." She bumped him with her shoulder and the familiar heat that came with touching him made her want more. For that reason, she didn't object when he slid his arm around her and pulled her close.

"Luce, moving home is a setback. It's not permanent."

"I keep telling myself that."

"I said you could move in with me."

She curled her lip. "That might be a tad awkward, being that we're broken up."

"That was your doing. And we can fix it lickety-split. All I asked was for you to give me a break about moving away from my family. It's not a lot to ask."

"We want different things."

Frankie grunted, the sound packed with dynamite. He pulled his arm away and stood to swat the door closed. "That's crap."

"It's not crap. The gossip doesn't bother you." She cupped her hands around her mouth. "Ooh, there's that Falcone boy. His father is mobbed up. Don't mess with him."

"I can't control what people whisper about. I like my life. I know who my friends are, and they don't say crap like that. By now, you should know who *your* friends are. Our *friends* are the ones who know we're more than what our fathers do for a living. They understand that you have an MBA, and I got a free ride to LSU. They get that, Luce. Screw everybody else."

"You have to admit, it was different when I lived downtown. You came and stayed with me and we were nobodies. We were just a couple of up-and-comings out for dinner. Nobody whispered. I liked *that* life."

Frankie shrugged. "So, we'll go downtown for dinner.

Why do I have to abandon my family for that? They're important to me. This town is my home. It's what I know and you want me to walk away."

"All I want is boundaries. The thing I love most about you is your sense of loyalty. But that loyalty blinds you and it suffocates me."

He closed his eyes and his lips moved in a silent three count. A Frankie Zen moment. A few seconds later, he opened his eyes. "*Suffocates* you?"

"You know what I mean."

"I could turn this around and ask where *your* loyalties are, but I won't. I respect *your* feelings."

Lucie leaped off the bed. Nowhere to go. The blasted room was so small she couldn't move. "You don't understand."

"Is this about moving to New York again?"

She spun away from him, took two steps and bumped the card table. Dammit. She turned back. "What's wrong with moving to New York? I could get a job there. You could work anywhere as a sportswriter. Plus, if you want to be at a network, New York is the place to make that happen."

The room went silent. Frankie stared at her and she wondered if she'd hit pay dirt. He worked for the *Chicago Herald* as a sportswriter, but he had bigger dreams and wanted to be behind a microphone calling a game. A flash of hope wound through her.

"My family is here. I may not agree with what my father does, but he's been there for me. Supported every decision. How do I turn my back on him?"

*Somebody get a mop because my flash of hope just got doused.*

She sat back on the bed, let her shoulders slump forward. "It gets old doesn't it? This argument?"

Frankie dragged his hands through his hair. "I can't do this anymore. I want a life with you, but I won't walk away from people who have been good to me. You know where I stand. When you figure out what you want, let me know."

Frankie pulled the door open but shifted back to her. She looked at him. He looked at her. Nobody moved. The stillness said it all.

---

THROUGHOUT DINNER, LUCIE KEPT HER FOCUS ON HER PLATE while chatting with Frankie's sister. Why not? She'd always liked Angie and it kept her from having to talk to Frankie's father. By the way he kept looking at her, he had something on his mind. Eventually, he'd come out with it. She'd just have to wait.

Frankie leaned back and patted his inflated belly. "Nice work, Theresa. I'll be in the gym for hours tomorrow."

"Well, thank you, Frankie."

His mother, Giovanna, with her newly colored reddish hair—odd, that—turned to his father. "Al, that's why I love this boy, he's so polite."

Lucie nearly coughed up a piece of meat. Somehow, this conversation would come around to her not marrying him.

"I taught him well." Mr. Falcone clapped Frankie on the back and glanced at Lucie. "Where are we on this break-up?"

So predictable.

"What break?" his mother asked. "You two take more breaks than any couple I know."

Frankie held up his hands. "We'll work it out."

"Joe isn't happy," Mr. Falcone said.

Lucie bit down. Hard. The spy had been revealed. No shock there.

"Pop," Frankie said, "Did you have to mention it to him? Lucie has a lot on her plate. She doesn't need her father pressuring her."

How many dinners had she sat through as this argument raged on? Lucie waited for the remainder of the show. What was the point? No one ever listened. She simply sat while the crazies took it upon themselves to decide her future.

"Pressure?" Mr. Falcone said. "Seems to me *someone* should pressure her."

"If she doesn't want to be with me, I'm not forcing her."

Lucie glared at him. "When have I ever said that?"

Mrs. Falcone slammed her hand on the table and the wine glasses jumped. "Why wouldn't she want you?"

Lucie sighed.

"Of course she wants him," Mom said. "Don't be ridiculous. Nowadays young couples take their time. You two need to get into this century and leave Frankie and Lucie alone."

*Thanks, Mom.*

Frankie laughed. She knew he couldn't help it. Things got nutty when the topic of their sometimes-impending nuptials came up. She glanced at Frankie, but he remained quiet, absolutely refusing to tell his parents to butt-out.

And wasn't that part of their problem? His total failure to take up arms against his parents and tell them to stop harping on the marriage issue? Or about anything for that matter. He never went against his folks. Never. And if they got married, Lucie would endure a lifetime of his family's interference.

But she loved him.

Angie waved her fork. "Leave the poor girl alone. She lost her job. Let her get her head together. I give her credit for starting her own business with those dog accessories." She poked her fork at her son across the table. "Paulie, eat your string beans."

Angie gave Frankie the do-something look. He crossed his eyes at her and she bit her bottom lip to block a smile. The magic of Frankie. Having received the result he wanted, Frankie turned to his nephew. "They're good, Paulie. You'll like 'em."

Paulie started on the beans, chewing at the pace of a geriatrics ward. Since the boy's father was never around, Frankie got to be the hammer. Someone had to do it.

"Are you still looking for work, Lucie?" Mrs. Falcone asked.

"Every day. The economy isn't helping. The dog walking keeps money coming in."

Frankie smiled at her. "And she's doing great with the accessories. She unloaded a rhinestone collar today for over a hundred bucks."

Angie's enormous brown eyes took on the wild look of one of those old cartoon characters under hypnosis. "Stop it!"

"Honest to God. I've been telling you guys about the trunk shows. And get this, she had a show this morning, then she went to walk one of the dogs and the mutt got stolen."

Lucie shot Frankie the hairy eyeball. Not that it seemed to be working on anyone today.

"*What?*" his father yelled.

Mom snapped her head in Lucie's direction. "Why didn't you tell me? Did you get hurt?"

"I'm fine."

"Liar. You whacked your head. You need to get checked out."

Not only did Frankie refuse to take up arms against his family, he was sometimes a traitor. This time the result was his father's face twisting into a ball of rage. Lucie knew exactly where this was going. He'd go right to her father, who would blow an artery over someone laying hands on his daughter.

On and on it went. Her dad was already on a tear about her wasting her MBA. As if it was her fault that her company merged and she'd been *rightsized*. Add this to the mix and she might as well curl into a fetal position.

Angie cleared her throat, the universal signal she was about to change the subject. "I want to hear about these trunk shows."

"She's got another one tomorrow," Frankie said.

Lucie fiddled with the stem of her wine glass. "Frankie thinks I should start a business. Coco Barknell."

Mr. Falcone held his hands out. "Two weeks ago it was a hobby. Now you're starting a business?"

Mrs. Falcone stood to collect empty dishes. "That is the silliest thing I ever heard."

Lucie helped stacked plates. "Not really. At the height of the recession, pet accessories had huge profits."

"I think it's a wonderful idea," Mom said.

"Sit, Mrs. R.," Angie said. "Lucie and I will do the dishes while Frankie takes Paulie outside to work on his swing."

Paulie swiveled his head, his droopy brown eyes looking encouraged. "How about it, Uncle Frank?"

Frankie wouldn't say no to baseball. Considering he'd gotten a full college ride on a baseball scholarship, only to suffer back-to-back concussions that ended his shot at major league ball. That didn't keep him from enjoying the game on a recreational level, or coaching Paulie's team. The poor kid's idiot father only knew how to handle a bat when it was connecting with someone's skull.

"You got it, pal. Let's see what you've got. Season opener is next week and you gotta be ready."

Frankie turned to his father. "What do you say, old man? You wanna hit a few with me and the squirt?"

Mr. Falcone perked up. "Old man? I'll knock your lemon in, kid."

"So you say."

"I'll be right there. I forgot to make a call."

Mr. Falcone dug his cell phone out and headed toward the front door in search of privacy. She'd been around this bunch long enough to know that meant *business*.

God help her if that business meant him spewing in someone's ear about her dognapping. Mr. Falcone's interference would only cause problems between her and Frankie. And they had enough of those.

# 3

The next morning, Lucie parked her car two blocks from the Lutzes' and made her way to the house for Otis's ten o'clock walk. The routine always started with Otis on the north side in Lincoln Park, where the brownstones sported oversized windows and elaborate brick facades. The cheapest pair of shoes in this neighborhood ran six hundred dollars. Living here took a stuffed wallet.

Lucie passed patches of green grass tucked under aged oak trees while her dream of being a respected investment banker whirled in her mind. Being known for more than her father's illegal activities was what Lucie craved. Living in one of these lovely brick homes wouldn't be bad either, but the professional respect would always come first. She could still have that dream. Things would turn around.

Aretha Franklin's *Respect* rang from Lucie's cell phone and she pulled it from her pocket to check the screen. Tom Darcy. *Oh, boy.*

"Hi, Mr. Darcy."

"Lucie, my baby is home. It's a miracle."

The day-old tension rooted inside shattered. Miss Elizabeth was home. "Really? She's okay?"

"She looks perfectly fine."

"But how?"

"I don't know. I heard her bark and thought I'd imagined it, but then it got louder. I opened the front door and there she was, sitting on the steps. It's a miracle."

*Enough with the miracles, nutball.* Still, what a relief. Lucie dropped to a cross-legged position on the sidewalk. Horrendous thoughts of doggie torture drifted away, and she stretched on the sidewalk. It had been one hell of a night. "Maybe she found her way home? Could that be?"

"All I know is she's home. I'm so relieved. Unfortunately, I won't need your services any longer. After all, you did let someone kidnap her."

Nutball or not, he had a point and it stabbed at Lucie like something out of a bad horror show. Her breath hitched and her eyes filled with tears. She'd been fired. Again. This time, it truly was her fault. "I understand."

At least the dog was safe. "Miss Elizabeth is a great dog, Mr. Darcy. I'll miss her. I'm so sorry about what happened. I hope you know that."

She clicked off and slapped her hands over her face. Was there anything worse than getting fired? But wait—she'd forgotten to ask Mr. Darcy if he'd called Officer Lindstrom. No matter. She would do it.

Still on the ground, paying no mind to the curious stares of drivers cruising by, she retrieved Lindstrom's card from her messenger bag. A minute later, an operator informed her he was on patrol. She left a message, took a breath to clear her head and made haste to the Lutzes'. Ten minutes lost with that break. She'd have to make it up.

She punched in the garage code and watched the door

roll up. Her scooter sat in its normal spot in the extended space of the one-car garage and Otis, hearing the door moving, howled. He knew what time it was. Lucie time.

Getting into the house took precision. Otis was a jumper. If she threw the door open, he'd fly through the air and flatten her. Being stuck under seventy-five pounds of fur wouldn't be the worst of it. After losing Miss Elizabeth yesterday, Lucie couldn't risk one of her charges escaping.

"Off, Otis," she said in her I'm-the-big-cheese voice. "Off!"

The frantic scratching from the other side of the door ceased and Lucie, holding one hand in front of her, eased the door open while Otis sat patiently, his tongue flapping. The little turkey was catching on. Good for him.

"Good job." Lucie kept her voice neutral. No sense exciting him and causing a meltdown.

With that, he wrapped his front paws around her leg and started humping. This is what her MBA got her. A bulldog working her leg like a horny frat boy. With the humping complete, Otis dropped to the ground and rolled to his back. A laugh burst free and Lucie took a second to enjoy it. How she loved these dogs. Somehow, they always managed to make her smile. "It's a good thing you're cute, Otis."

The dog let out an enthusiastic *woof*.

"Yeah, your life is good, boy." She bent low, brushed a hand down his belly and he licked her shoe. Maybe this dog walking thing wasn't so bad. Unconditional love, fresh air, no late nights.

*Coco Barknell.*

Perhaps the accessory line could be more than a side job. After the weekend sales, it certainly appeared so, but she would have to run some projections and check out the competition.

Otis stood and gave the leash a tug. "I know. You're ready."

After Otis, Lucie hit the Bernards'. They lived in a high-rise with a doorman named Lenny and two Shih-Tzus short on stature and big on attitude. Josie and Fannie liked Lucie, but the neighbors often rushed into their apartments to avoid the mini-tormentors. Lucie, having always been on the petite side, liked the girls' spunk.

Once in the apartment, she grabbed the rhinestone double leash from the hook by the door, bent to snap a clip to each dog and spotted the collars she had sold to Mrs. Bernard. "Look at you guys with your bling on. Such pretty girls."

Josie's red leather collar held a single row of rhinestones while Fannie's white one had red stones. The collars looked lovely against the white of the girls' hair. *Hmm.* Lucie might need business cards in case someone wanted to know where the collars and leash came from.

*Coco Barknell.* Damn that Frankie.

"Okay, girls. Let's hit it. I'm having lunch with my man today and he doesn't like to be kept waiting." A sudden punch hurled into Lucie's chest and she closed her eyes until the beating passed. She'd never get used to Frankie not being hers. If they didn't work things out, she would have to move. Despite being the one who broke things off, she simply couldn't stand the idea of him being with someone else.

"Well, he's not my man right now, but I'm hoping that's short-term because he is pretty darn special. We're just in different places right now...wait, why am I talking to you? You don't care."

She grunted and opened the door. The middle-aged man across the hall had just finished locking his door, and his look of slack-jawed terror made Lucie chuckle. She gripped the leash when Josie and Fannie lunged like a couple of ravenous tigers. "Girls, knock it off."

The man reeled back and wagged his finger. "Keep them ninja bitches away from me."

The girls—with a combined weight of fifteen pounds—went wild, growling at him, baring their teeth and tugging on the leash as the neighbor jumped beyond their wrath.

Lucie contemplated letting the girls loose on the guy. But she'd be a grownup and let it go. "Don't listen to him, girls. We'll just wait for the next elevator."

Once on the street, the distant whooshing of Lake Shore Drive traffic drifted toward them and the girls, accustomed to the route, turned left and went the opposite way to an area that gave them wandering room.

Rays from the late morning sun fell across the sidewalk and Lucie tilted her head back, letting the warmth caress her cheeks. This would be a good day. "Make a right at the corner, girls."

She stopped and pushed the walk button on the light pole. A white van made a right on red just as the light changed and Lucie was glad she'd waited. "Come, girls."

The smell of brewing coffee and frying bacon from the corner coffee shop sent her stomach into a frenzy. She was so ready for lunch. She'd lost five pounds since becoming a dog walker and she wanted those pounds back.

A young man approached and stared down at the dogs. Lucie gripped the leash.

"Nice looking dogs. Can I pet them?"

A pulsing blazed up her arms. Hadn't her father taught her not to trust strangers? She should keep walking. Particularly after yesterday's dognapping.

*Deep breath. Calm down. Focus.* The guy looked harmless

enough, mid-twenties with curly dark hair and twinkling blue eyes. Any normal woman would love to chat him up. Not Lucie. Dognapping paranoia aside, Frankie had ruined her. *Ruined.* He was so damned good looking that she tended to grade all men on his curve. The Frankie Factor.

Her teeth throbbed and she lightened up on the gnawing. She couldn't live in fear. What were the chances she'd get dognapped again?

Minimal.

She was sure of it.

Risking her face breaking apart, she smiled at him. "The girls are friendly." *Most of the time.*

Mr. Cutie squatted and—*holy smokes*—rather than attacking, the girls nuzzled into his legs. They must have sensed kindness in him. He rubbed both hands across the dogs, and Lucie resisted telling him the girls didn't like to be patted on the head. This was surely a self-esteem issue due to their miniature size.

When he tickled under Josie's chin, she nearly swooned. *For goodness sakes, at least play hard to get.*

But then the guy unclipped Josie's end of the double leash and yesterday's dognapping flashed in Lucie's mind.

Someone pushed her from behind, tossing her against the brick front of the coffee shop. The thought of landing on top of the girls sent stinging jolts up Lucie's neck. She let go of the leash and crashed into the wall, her shoulder taking a direct hit.

"Ooof."

The searing pain shot the length of her arm and the tips of her fingers tingled. A rush of air filled her mouth and she puffed it out. *Not again.*

An El train rattled overhead and the sound ricocheted inside her skull. Lucie covered her ears and scanned the area. *There they are.* Three men ran down the street. Two of them had Josie and Fannie under an arm.

"Hey!" Lucie gave chase. She had to save the dogs. A car turned onto the street and the driver glanced at her, but her mind failed and she missed the opportunity to yell. She ran harder, her feet slap, slap, slapping against the sidewalk as her lungs heaved with the effort. If she were in better shape, she'd be able to catch them.

The pain in her shoulder ebbed to a dull ache, but she kept running. *A little farther. That's all.*

The men jumped into a white van sitting at the curb. Was it the one she'd seen turning the corner? Had to be. She reached it just as the door slid closed. The *kuh-klunk* of the latch catching exploded in her ears.

"No." She grabbed the door handle and yanked. Nothing. *Please open.* The van jerked forward, nearly pulling Lucie with it. She let go before she lost an arm.

The van turned left on the next block. Gone. With Josie and Fannie. Gone.

"Ohmygod, ohmygod, ohmygod."

With quivering fingers, she pulled her phone.

"9-1-1, what's your emergency?"

"Help me. Please. My dogs have been stolen." Tears slid down her throat and she coughed them away. *No tears.* "Send someone, please."

"What is your location?"

Lucie spun, checked the address of the building behind her and gave it to the operator.

Five minutes later, a Chicago P.D. squad pulled to the curb. Lucie ran to the car, hoping to see Officer Lindstrom behind the wheel. No Lindstrom. Typical of her luck.

"Please. I'm Lucia Rizzo. They took my dogs. Two Shih-Tzus." Lucie tapped her hand against her nose. "White with little black noses. They each had a fancy collar on. The van went that way," she pointed down the block. "It turned left. Please. Help me."

The officer on the passenger side of the vehicle eased out. What was wrong with him? Didn't he understand a crime had been committed? That Josie and Fannie were missing? Dognapped!

"Tell me what happened, Ms. Rizzo."

He looked impossibly young, with cherub cheeks and the same uniform as Lindstrom. His clothes looked newer though, and he carried a fresh-out-of-the-academy attitude. Superiority. Just what she needed.

She shook it off and gave the officers a description of the van. No, she hadn't gotten a plate number. Yes, she was sure it was white. How would she miss that?

The young officer jotted a note while his partner scanned the sidewalk. "You said they shoved you into the storefront?"

"Yes, I crashed into the wall."

"Are you injured?"

"My shoulder hurts. It doesn't matter. I need to find the dogs."

The second officer, the older one, spoke into the microphone on his shoulder and gave dispatch a description of the van. He looked back to Lucie. "We'll do a BOLO—"

Again with the BOLO? Not that it did any good with Miss Elizabeth. "And that's it? What about the dogs? We have to get them back. They could get hurt."

A second squad pulled up and out stepped Lindstrom. She rushed to him, her fists clenched in the air. "It happened again. Someone stole my dogs."

"I heard." He turned to the other officers. "I handled her call yesterday. Ms. Rizzo has been hit twice."

"Are they show dogs?" the older cop asked Lucie.

"No. But they look like it."

Her cell phone rang—what now?—and she pulled it from her pocket. Frankie. *Shoot.* Late for lunch. If she didn't answer, he would worry. She always called if she would be late. "Hi. I'm sorry."

He laughed in that way that typically made her smile, but not today. "Is this what it has come to? You're blowing me off?"

"Josie and Fannie were stolen."

"*What?*"

She nodded as though he could see her. "I was walking them. A guy came up, started talking to me, then two other guys pushed me over and grabbed them. Just *bam.*" Her voice caught and she sucked in a breath. "Oh my God, Frankie. What if they're hurt?"

"Are *you* hurt?"

"No. Well, I crashed into the building and my shoulder is sore, but the dogs—"

"I'll be right there. Where are you?"

She gave him the address and hung up. Lindstrom finished talking on his radio.

"Okay, Ms. Rizzo. We have a detective on the way. He'll be here in a few minutes. Meantime, we got a description of the van. Maybe we'll grab these guys fast."

Lucie nodded. They had to find the dogs. She glanced at her watch. With every minute, they got farther away.

Another call came in and the two new officers left.

"I can't believe this." *Two days in a row.* Tears moistened her eyes and she blinked a couple of times.

"Lucie," Lindstrom said, "can you think of anyone who might want to do this to you?"

"No. Why would someone do this to me?"

"It could be the show dog thing. Could also be rotten luck you got hit twice. Or, these guys might be following you."

"*Following* me?"

He shrugged. "Maybe they've seen you walking the dogs."

A gray Crown Victoria with a missing front hubcap and dented back quarter panel pulled behind Lindstrom's squad. A tall, lanky guy with short strawberry blond hair got out. *Must be the detective.* He reached into the back seat for his suit jacket—a navy pinstripe—and slid it on.

Lindstrom wandered over and conferred with the detective before they made their way back to her.

"Ms. Rizzo," strawberry blond said, "I'm Detective O'Brien. Are you all right?"

His deep green eyes focused on her and she shifted under his scrutiny. He had a smattering of freckles across his cheeks and a crooked nose—probably broken a couple of times. From this proximity, she noticed the crispness of his white shirt and suddenly felt underdressed in her jeans, long-sleeved T-shirt and jacket.

"We need to find the dogs," Lucie said.

He smiled, one of those killer smiles she imagined could make all sorts of things go his way. Frankie smiled like that when he humored people.

"We're working on it, Ms. Rizzo." O'Brien glanced at his notepad then back up. "Your first name is Lucia?"

"Yes. Everyone calls me Lucie."

And then she saw it, the flicker of recognition in those sharp green eyes. The wondering. The judgment. The disgust.

"Yes," she said. "Joe Rizzo is my father. Can we move on?"

Lindstrom suppressed a smile and O'Brien inclined his head. "Of course. You filed a report yesterday about another stolen dog."

"That one was returned this morning," Lindstrom said. He turned to Lucie. "I got your message. Didn't have a chance to call you back."

Lucie nodded. "Mr. Darcy said Miss Elizabeth was on the porch this morning. He doesn't know how she got there."

Lindstrom and O'Brien exchanged a look.

"Do you have any idea who might have taken the dogs?" This from O'Brien.

"No."

"You didn't have an argument with anyone? Any kind of misunderstanding?"

"No."

He raised his eyebrows. Expecting him to believe Joe Rizzo's daughter could actually be an innocent victim would get her nowhere. Lucie tamped down the tirade spinning inside her. *Concentrate on the dogs.*

"According to the officer, you're the dog walker?"

"Yes."

"Luce!" Frankie's voice boomed and an instant feeling of calm hit her. She turned and he was there, his arms open.

"I'm okay." She hugged him then slowly backed away. "This is Detective O'Brien and Officer Lindstrom."

Frankie held his hand out to O'Brien. "Frank Falcone."

The two men shook hands and the detective eyed Frankie for a minute longer than necessary. "Falcone?"

This must look like the annual meeting of Mob Kids of America. Lucie made a show of rolling her eyes and Lindstrom grinned. "Yes. His father is Al Falcone. Can we move on? Please?"

"Sure," the detective said, but he was still looking at Frankie, and Lucie was about done with this cop and his curiosity. Once again, her father's lifestyle had caused her embarrassment. This O'Brien guy was lumping her in as a lowlife, someone he could laughingly dismiss because of her family. *Not today, pal.*

The reality was, based on who they were, O'Brien could be dreaming up some convoluted scheme where she and Frankie were involved in stealing the dogs.

With her back to O'Brien, Lucie faced Frankie and hoped his mob-kid radar got it that the detective was distracted by their lineage. "Would you mind waiting over there?"

The flash of understanding, that language she and Frankie had perfected over the years, sparked in his dark eyes and he squeezed her hand. "I'll wait by that sign."

---

FRANKIE STOOD BACK WHILE THE DETECTIVE DID HIS THING. Mystified, he shook his head. Why was someone stealing Lucie's dogs? And would she get hurt because of it?

With her pinched mouth, she looked like she'd run a few hard miles. The mouth thing was her tell. Every time things got dicey, there it was.

The cops appeared to be finishing, so Frankie dialed Joey.

"Speak."

"Lucie got dogjacked. I need you downtown."

Joey laughed. "Get outta here."

"I'm not kidding. Three guys boosted those pains in the ass Shih-Tzus."

"Get outta here."

"Get moving. She's a wreck and there's no way she can drive. I have an editorial meeting at two. You need to pick her up at the Bernard place. I'll get the scooter back to the Lutzes' and deal with her car, but you gotta get her home. And don't be a meathead about it."

Frankie glanced up and saw the detective handing Lucie a business card. "Hurry up. And don't expect to be home too soon, because you know she'll want to finish walking the rest of the dogs."

"Ah, crap."

Frankie disconnected and strode toward Lucie. "You okay?"

She nodded yes, but he knew everything about that nod was a lie. Showing weakness in Lucie's family was worse than death. From an early age, the Rizzo kids had been conditioned to survive, but Lucie loved these dogs, and having this happen while they were in her care would devastate her. Frankie kissed the top of her head. "We'll find them."

Damn straight. He'd ask his father to get his crew on it because the stupid sons of bitches who stole those dogs didn't realize they'd crossed Joe Rizzo's daughter. Dumb schmucks.

Lucie clutched his shirt in her hand. "What am I going to tell the Bernards?"

It had to be a rhetorical question, right? He didn't answer. Besides, what could she tell them other than the truth?

"Frankie!"

He stepped back and looked down at her. "Did you want me to answer that?" Her eyes nearly bulged and he backpedaled. "I thought it was a rhetorical question."

In addition to the bulging, she blinked. "Are you kidding?"

He squeezed her arms. "Tell them the truth. This isn't your fault. It could have happened to anyone."

"After what happened yesterday, I should have been more careful."

"How the hell could you have known these guys were going to grab the dogs?"

"I knew I shouldn't have trusted that guy when he wanted to pet them. They're just innocent little dogs, and I didn't fight for them."

The truth of it was, whoever took those dogs would get a whiff of the crap involved with dealing with them and would return them before nightfall. How Frankie would explain that to Lucie without her blowing a fuse on him, he didn't know.

"I called Joey."

"Oh, no."

"You shouldn't drive. He'll come and get you. I'll take care of the scooter and your car."

"I can't leave. I have work to do."

"He knows that. He'll go with you and then take you home."

"I'm going to have to spend the next two hours with *Joey*? We'll kill each other."

He held his hands up. "I told him not to be a meathead."

"Good luck with *that*."

"I have an editorial meeting I can't miss, and I don't want you to be alone."

Frankie pulled her in for a hug and she burrowed into his chest, swinging her head back and forth. "I have to get those dogs back, Frankie. I have to."

"We'll get 'em back."

*With my father's help.*

---

THAT EVENING, WITH STILL NO SIGN OF THE GIRLS, LUCIE SAT in her micro-bedroom distracting herself with a spreadsheet.

The whirring of her laptop filled the silence as she perused her financial report. Two trunk shows had netted three thousand dollars. Three thousand smackers peddling *dog* accessories? It sounded crazy, but the weekend total on her spreadsheet said so, and the stack of cash sitting on her battered card table wasn't a hallucination.

*Coco Barknell.*

Maybe Frankie had something there.

Just because she'd gotten laid off from her banking job didn't mean she couldn't use her skills elsewhere. No *right-sizing*, not to mention being a target in a dognapping scheme, would bring her down. If there was one thing the Rizzo family had, it was stamina. Years of watching her father go through legal troubles had conditioned her for life's ups and downs.

She brought her gaze back to the spreadsheet.

Coco Barknell could be her side business while she hunted for a real job. Heck, it could get her out of her parents' house and living on her own. That was a plan she could work with.

She leaned forward to the pile of printouts on the desk and rifled through them. What did she do with that list of doggie clients?

More paper shuffling. Not here. Dining room table?

She wandered downstairs and the quiet of the house set her on edge. The only thing that would account for the quiet was Joey either being out or lining up a juvenile ambush.

Lucie peeked around the banister. No Joey. Just her mother standing in the dining room. Light from the brass fixture bounced off her hair while she steamed dog coats hanging from an old clothing rack Lucie had found in the basement. The garment rack sat wedged between Grandma Rizzo's walnut table and breakfront, the only place it fit without Joey, the one who would never move out of his parents' home, throwing a tantrum. The house just didn't have room to spare for a rolling closet.

Mom wore a pair of gray cotton pants with a thick-seamed pocket across the side of the thigh. A modern cargo pant. She paired the cargos with a snug white T-shirt and a light pink cardigan. When had her mother become hip?

Lucie ran a hand over the coats that had already been steamed and the softness tickled her hand. She *made* these. Producing dog accessories might not be a global initiative, but losing her job would not define her. She'd bounce back.

"Mom, I'll do that. I didn't leave it there for you."

Her mother turned, steamer in hand, and smiled. "I don't mind. It's fun. Reminds me of my days as a seamstress. When I worked in that men's store on Franklin Avenue, your father used to buy clothes just so I could alter them."

Lucie laughed. "As Dad always says, he laid eyes on you and that was the end of it." She'd heard the story a hundred times and never tired of it. One thing about her father, he had the single-minded fortitude to complete a job. Whatever that job might be.

"Do you miss doing alterations, Mom?"

"Sometimes." She turned back to the steaming. "I miss the interaction."

Lucie shoved a few scraps of fabric, a tape measure and

a box of beads around the table, but didn't see her report. "Shoot."

"What are you looking for?"

"A client list with names and addresses and what they've purchased. There are numbers handwritten in the margins."

"I haven't seen it." Mom gestured to the coat she'd been steaming. "I like this."

Lucie glanced at the tiny bright pink coat for the Jaspers' poodle. "Thanks. It needs something, but I'm not sure what."

Lucie pushed at more fabric. Where the heck was that spreadsheet? "Where's Joey? Maybe he moved that report."

That gave her mother a laugh.

"Honey, if I can't get him to pick up his socks, he's not going to move something that belongs to either one of us."

"True." Joey needed to move out and learn some lessons about taking care of himself. Then again, why should he? Mom did all his laundry and he came and went as he pleased. *Joey* never had to respond to questions regarding his whereabouts, or lack of marriage plans.

"Besides, he's working."

Yet another amusing statement. "Hanging out at the bar around the corner where the owner allows him to run his bookmaking business is not working. All he does is sit on a barstool and take bets."

The doorbell rang. A second later, the door flew open and Rosanne, Lucie's BFF, swung through, her long sable hair flying behind her. Her floor-length mink coat flapped open as she strode toward them in leather boots, a black miniskirt and a cashmere sweater. As usual, she wore just the right amount of makeup on her dark eyes. She didn't need it. Not with cheekbones that could carve through pavement and skin that glowed despite the offerings of a recently hard winter. Yep, Ro could be president of Beautiful People of America.

"Hellooooo," she called, strutting toward them on her mile-long legs.

"Hey." Lucie looked her up and down. "It's almost April. You should put the mink away."

"*You* should slap yourself."

Lucie laughed. Roseanne's husband had given her the coat for Christmas and it was a staple in her wardrobe. Fur coats weren't Lucie's style, but this silky deep chocolate number could make her a believer. The citizens of Franklin didn't seem to wonder how a thirty-year-old town council member could afford such an expense, but perhaps they had adjusted to politicians in this fine town shaking hands while grabbing an envelope stuffed with money.

"Hi, Mrs. R," Ro said.

Mom smiled a greeting at Ro, and, steamer in hand, gestured to the pink coat. "Do you think this coat needs something?"

Despite wearing the mink in fifty-five degree weather, Ro had a blazing sense of style.

The thing about Ro, she might be beautiful, but she'd take someone down if necessary. Which is what happened when Tiffy Nelson tried to beat up a much smaller Lucie in the third grade. Ro, being one of the cool girls, stepped in and put the fear of God into Tiffy. From that point on, nobody messed with Lucie. And Lucie never forgot what Ro had done for her. That's what Italian girls did. They protected their friends. Without question. In Lucie's crazy world, friendships like that were a gift.

Ro fingered the pink coat. "This is obviously for a small dog, yes?"

Lucie nodded.

"Rhinestones around the collar. Just a few." She zeroed in on another coat. "But, honey, this animal print is a hot mess."

Lucie scooped up the offending jacket. "What's wrong with it?"

"You cannot mix multicolor stones with an animal print. Well, you could, but your high-end people won't buy it. This is too trashy for *your* line."

*Coco Barknell.*

Lucie stared at the animal print. "I'll take the stones off and put them on the pink one."

Ro's lips parted and she gasped. "Have I taught you *nothing*? You need tiny *rhinestones* for the pink one. These blue stones will be a disaster on that coat."

*Here we go with the drama.*

"You know what?" Ro continued. "I'm going to help you out here. Nothing leaves this house until I sign off. I will not let you take anything gaudy to these uber-rich people. They'll eat you alive. I love you too much to let that happen."

No one ever said Lucie was the next Donna Karan. Besides, she hated dreaming up new designs. "Deal. I'll even pay you."

"You'll *pay* me? Slap yourself." Her gaze moved to Lucie's navy sweater and khaki pants. "Go change. You've had a rough couple of days with these dognappings. I'm taking you to dinner."

Lucie puckered.

"You are *not* wearing that. You look like a first grade teacher."

"What's wrong with first grade teachers?"

"Nothing, if you are one, which you're not. Now go." She waved her red tipped fingers. "Chop, chop."

Lucie turned to her mother. "When Joey gets back, would you please ask him if he moved that spreadsheet? It has hand written projections on it and I need it."

Not to mention, she didn't want the names and addresses of her "uber-rich" clients floating around. God only knew who Joey paraded through here and what they would do with that information.

Mom stood. "Sorry, honey, I'm going out. It's casino night at church and I told Father Hugh I'd be there."

"Does Joey know you're going? Seeing as you're not allowed to leave the stoop without him knowing where you've gone."

Joey's overprotectiveness had been getting on Mom's nerves lately, and Lucie couldn't help but tease her about it.

"He'd better not be on the porch tonight when I get home. He embarrassed me to no end with that stunt."

"He's a total nutball," Lucie said to Ro. "Mom went out to dinner with some friends one night, didn't tell Joey, and then had the nerve to forget to turn her cell phone on. Joey was stalking the front lawn when Mom's friend dropped her off. Before she even got out of the car, he started hollering about her checking in once in a while. Ugly scene. "

"That's actually kind of hot," Ro said. "All that protectiveness?"

"Ew."

"You don't see it because he's your brother. Trust me. It's hot."

Mom shook off a cringe. "I love him, but he's twisted."

No matter what kind of lunacy invaded this house, Mom always loved them. That alone earned Lucie's undying adoration. "I'll tell him you're at church. Leave your phone on."

"Yes, dear." Mom kissed her cheek, grabbed her purse from the buffet and walked out the back door.

Ro continued her inspection of coats. "This piece is a total loss." She stopped at the large rhinestone on the neckline of one of the items and let out a low whistle. "Hello, my sweet."

"What?" Lucie asked.

"You used a *real* diamond on here?"

Lucie rolled her eyes. What the hell was Ro thinking? Real diamonds. Why use real stones on dog accessories? Furthermore, where would she get the money for such an expense?

"It's not real. That coat was from the first batch. I used whatever stones I found in my attic stash."

"Luce, I'm telling you, this is a real stone."

A banging started behind Lucie's eyes. Maybe it was panic, she wasn't sure, but she flicked a glance to the stone in question.

When Ro reached across the table to inspect another coat, Lucie moved beside her. "How can that be?"

Ro tilted her head. "Are you questioning whether I can tell the difference between real and fake stones?"

Point scored there. "Well...no, but I don't understand how it could be real."

Ro motioned to the empty Notre Dame glass sitting on the table. "Give me that,"

Lucie handed it over. "Why?"

After tapping on the outside of the glass, Ro set it upside down on the table. "We'll do a scratch test. Diamonds are the hardest stones. If this stone is real, it'll scratch the glass. The harder mineral will always scratch the softer one."

Now that was impressive. At least Lucie thought so. "I can't believe you know that."

"I did research when we were shopping for my wedding ring."

If Ro was right about the diamond, they had problems. First, how did a real diamond get into the craft supplies? Were there others? And, more importantly, who did it belong to?

Had Lucie unknowingly been selling real stones? "Let's do this test."

She could go straight to hell for this. *Bless me, Father for I have sinned, I had no idea I was selling someone else's jewelry.*

Had this sparkling stone caused the chaos of the past two days?

The stone clinked upon contact with the glass, but went silent as Ro dragged it across the surface. The only sound in the room became a mixture of soft breathing and a hissing from the floor vent as the furnace kicked on.

Suddenly, Ro gasped and Lucie craned to see a smooth white line in the stone's trail.

"Oh, crap," Lucie said before everything went black.

## 4

"Wake up, sister."

Ro's voice. Time to get up. Lucie's eyelids sat like bricks over her eyes. No movement.

Something pointy dug into her hip. "Wake up."

Gentle Ro had left the building. No mistake there. Lucie squeezed her eyes shut then tried to open them again. Too heavy. Finally, she wrenched her eyelids up. Ro stood over her, eyebrows drawn together, looking...pissed off. Typical. "What happened?"

"You passed out." Ro held out her hand to help Lucie sit up.

That's right. The vision of Ro scraping the stone against the glass flashed in Lucie's mind. *Ohmygod.*

"You okay? Can you get to a chair?"

Lucie pushed off the floor and into a chair. "I don't understand."

Ro picked up the coat with the diamond. "We need to figure out what we're dealing with here. None of these other stones look real. They're also smaller than the real one. Where did this big one come from?"

Was Ro swaying? Lucie dropped her head into her hands. "All the stones I used in the beginning came from the box in the attic. I hadn't touched that box since I was in college."

Ro scratched the remaining stones against the glass and tossed them aside. Obviously nothing amiss. "So, you took them from the box and then what?"

"Nothing. I started playing with different designs. Most of the stones were separated into bags by size. One bag had different sized stones, but I didn't think much of it." She pointed at the diamond. "I took this stone from that bag."

"Where's the bag?"

"Upstairs." Lucie jumped from her chair, felt a wave of vertigo slam her and steadied herself against the table. "Ro, were those poor dogs stolen so the diamonds could be recovered? The stupid dognappers didn't know I never used the real stone on anything but the test coat."

"Don't get crazy. Let's just see what we've got here."

*Joey.*

That made no sense though. He knew she was using the supplies from the attic and never bothered to stop her. He was an ass, but he wouldn't put her in danger. Never. She charged up the stairs and retrieved the bag of odd-sized stones from her desk.

Lucie handed the bag to Ro and dialed Joey's cell.

"What is it? I'm working."

*Working.* Whatever. "Can you come home for five minutes? Ro and I need to show you something,"

"Is Roseanne running through the house naked?"

"No."

"Then I can't come home."

Lucie gripped the phone tighter because marching around the block and bludgeoning him with a barstool suddenly seemed like a good idea. "I need you to come home. *Now*."

"Seems to me it's all about what *you* need lately. I'm filled up."

Leave it to him to make this difficult. Fine. She'd play. "Okay. Ro and I will figure out how a real diamond got into my craft stuff. Thanks for your help, jackass." She hung up, punching the button so hard she split a nail. Damn him for that, too.

"I'm guessing he's not coming home," Ro cracked.

"Not unless you're naked."

She tapped her fingers against her lips. "No. I won't do that."

She'd actually considered it?

"I'll have to check the diamond chart I have, but this stone looks to be about fifteen to twenty carats."

*Holy cow*. Even as she dropped into the chair, Lucie wondered if the boulder in her chest would eventually suffocate her. She grabbed the phone again. "I'll try Frankie." She stared at Ro while waiting for the line to connect. "I don't understand how you can be so calm."

Ro began checking the remaining stones. "I may appear calm, but I am, in fact, about to birth a double-wide."

Four rings later, just before Lucie's call went to voice-mail, Frankie picked up. "How's it going over there?"

"Terrible."

The *clickety-clack* of his keyboard in the background went silent. "This should be good."

The back door opened and Lucie stepped into the doorway separating the kitchen and dining room to see who it was. Joey. "I thought you were busy cracking skulls."

Joey stomped into the dining room. "What's this crap about diamonds?"

"What diamonds?" Frankie wanted to know.

She focused on her brother. "Oh, now you're willing to help?"

"What diamonds?" Frankie yelled.

"Hang on." Lucie punched the speaker button and placed the phone on the dining room table. "I'm going to do this once and the two of you can enlighten me."

"Uh-oh," Frankie said.

"Ro just informed me that I used a real diamond on my first dog coat."

"Please." This from Frankie. "I think you'd know if you were using real jewels." A hesitation. "Wouldn't you?"

"Apparently not. Ro did a scratch test to prove it. The stone left a groove in the bottom of a glass. And she thinks it's fifteen carats."

Silence crowded the room. Even fat-mouthed Joey was struck mute.

"How the hell?" Frankie finally said.

"That's what I want to know." She turned to Joey. "Well?"

"You think I put it there? Newsflash, genius; if I wanted to hide a real diamond, I'd do a hell of a lot better than putting it in your craft crap."

"That makes sense," Ro said. "He's no dummy."

All true. Never hurt to ask though.

"Frankie?" Lucie asked. "Have you heard anything about this? Maybe from the guys at Petey's?"

"Hell no. I'd have told you."

Of course he would have, but desperation made a girl think odd things and Frankie holding out on her would be odd. Lucie sighed. "We need to figure out who this diamond belongs to."

"Could it be your dad's?" Frankie asked.

"I doubt it," Joey said. "He'd have told me in case I had to move it."

Lucie twisted her fingers together. "Neither of you has heard about a diamond? Nothing?"

"Not me," Frankie said. "But the guys don't talk about that stuff in front of me."

Joey looked pensive. "I'd have heard."

"It has to be stolen. Why else would it be hidden in my things?"

And wasn't that a screwed up scenario. Harboring stolen jewelry. They could all go to prison when they hadn't even known about the stone. The police would never believe that.

Not from the Rizzo clan.

Lucie put her hand over her mouth in case the screaming in her head broke free. How the hell would they get out of this? Joe Rizzo's family involved in stolen jewelry. Nobody would bat an eye.

Trying to contain her internal hysteria, she turned to Joey. "We can't tell Mom. Whatever this is, she can't be involved. I don't want her to worry. She's been through enough with Dad."

"Luce," Frankie said in his deep, strong voice. "Calm down."

So, apparently, containing her hysteria wasn't working. Screw it. "How can I calm down? This is a nightmare."

"No kidding there," Ro said.

Lucie pressed both palms into her forehead. "We have to figure out how that stone got into the attic."

---

THAT NIGHT, FRANKIE STOPPED BY THE RIZZO'S AFTER

finishing at the newspaper. Lucie couldn't remember a time she'd been so happy to see him. Simply put, Frankie deflated chaos.

They stood in the dining room, staring at the newly discovered diamond in his hand.

"Wow," he said.

Total understatement. She'd stepped in deep doo-doo this time. She leaned her head against his shoulder, felt the soft cotton of his dress shirt against her cheek and took sanctuary in the feel of him next to her. "This stone has to be what the dognappers are after."

Frankie held the diamond against the light. "I don't know."

The wall clock chimed midnight. She could sleep for a week. "I checked my files. The stolen dogs all have coats and collars I made."

Using his index finger, Frankie rolled the diamond in his hand. "Are we sure this is real?"

"According to Ro."

"And she became a gemologist when?"

Lucie eyeballed him. "This is Ro. She doesn't need a degree to spot a real stone."

He stared at her as if one of her eyes was hanging out. "And you guys went through all the other stones in the bag?"

"Yes. All fakes."

Frankie laughed, but the sound—that little bit of sarcasm—expressed itself as anger. "Someone's mutt could have been walking around with fifteen-carats on a collar."

If Lucie had used the real diamond, yes. She didn't want to think about what would have happened then. "I need to hunt down every item I've sold and check for real diamonds."

"That'll be a job."

"I don't have a choice. If the dognappings are related to this, I can't have my clients in danger."

At some point, with any luck, she'd find it all humorous. Lately, though, luck had been running last in the stretch. She grunted and dropped into one of the dining room chairs.

"You okay?" Frankie asked.

*Not so much. No.* "I don't think so."

Stepping behind her, he set his hands on her shoulders and drove his fingers into aching muscles. "Your shoulders are tight."

"Can you blame me? I lost my job, moved back to the nuthouse and now I'm into diamond trafficking. I can handle the job loss and the nuthouse. The stolen jewelry taxes me."

*Side note: check the penalties for unknowingly harboring stolen diamonds.*

"First off," Frankie said, "we don't know anything is stolen."

Despite the fact that his magic thumbs were plowing through the knots in her shoulders, Lucie shifted toward him. "You think this thing is a family heirloom that accidentally wound up in a box in the attic?"

"I didn't say that."

"Oh my God."

"What?"

Lucie bolted from the chair and headed for the stairs. "I didn't check the attic for more stones. I have another box up there."

"What about your mom?"

"She's in her room. I'll tell her I'm getting supplies down. She won't think anything of it."

Ten minutes later, they dumped the box on the dining room table and were sifting through each of the plastic bags. Lucie wasn't sure she'd recognize a real diamond, but at least now, she knew how to test anything suspicious.

She studied a large stone, dragged it against her trusty Notre Dame glass. Nothing. *Thank you.* "Frankie, I should be down at police headquarters telling them about the diamond. But if I do that, it'll look like someone in my family—namely my father—is into something hinky. And what if, insane as it might be, my father is innocent? The cops will never believe him."

Being a bright guy, Frankie held up his hands, obviously surrendering to the idea that, as much as the situation stunk, she was right.

"How about I talk to my father about this? He'll find out who the diamond belongs to and kick someone's ass for being stupid enough to hide it in your house."

"No. I don't want him involved. It'll just make things worse."

Nobody messed with a boss. Or his family. And if they did, they suffered. One way or another, they suffered. She didn't want to live with that. Nope. Not gonna happen. They were on their own with this one.

And she had clients to think about. What a mess. "I can't put the dogs in danger by walking them. I could be a *target*."

Frankie scratched his knuckles along the side of his face. "Hang on. Either Joey or I will walk with you. If you get dogjacked again, we'll nab the guy. I promise you, Luce, no other dogs will get boosted while you're walking them."

## 5

———

The sound of Aretha Franklin belting R-E-S-P-E-C-T pierced the darkened quiet of Lucie's bedroom. She shot to a sitting position and snatched her cell phone off the nightstand.

"Hello?" Her sleep clogged voice grumbled like a stalling tractor and she cleared her throat. "Hello?"

"Lucie, this is Elaine Bernard. They're back."

Huh? Who? Lucie jabbed two fingers into her eyes, then glanced at the clock. Six-oh-five.

*They're back.* Please. Let her be referring to the dogs. "Josie and Fannie?"

"Yes. Lenny called a few minutes ago and said he had them in the lobby. Apparently, they were scratching the door to get in."

The thumping behind Lucie's eyes gave way to waterworks. She swiped at the tears. What a wuss. Her father would be disappointed.

"They look fine," Mrs. Bernard said, "but we're taking them to the vet to be sure."

The poor things had been through an ordeal. They

could have internal injuries. Or be traumatized. Dogs could suffer horrible post-traumatic stress. She had to make it up to them. "Would you like me to do that for you? No charge of course. I feel horrible about what happened."

Mrs. Bernard got quiet. Why would this woman trust Lucie with her dogs again? Mr. Darcy hadn't. Why should anyone trust her with their dogs? She flopped on the bed and absorbed the screeching sound of her backup job careening to a halt.

"Oh, well—" Yep, here it comes, the kick to the curb. "— if you wouldn't mind, that would actually help me out. We're not blaming you for what happened. We know you love the girls."

Maybe the backup job had a chance. "Absolutely."

How the hell she'd get the other dogs walked *and* take the girls to the vet, Lucie had no idea. "Do you know what time?"

"No. The vet doesn't open until eight. I'll let you know."

Lucie disconnected and smacked the phone against her lips. Suddenly she needed an assistant dog walker. Unfortunately for her—or him, depending on how they looked at it—the only other person who knew the route, because he'd done it with her yesterday, was Joey. Asking him would require that she not only swallow her pride, but also digest it. *Ugh.*

*Coco Barknell.*

The little voice, *Frankie's* voice, tickled her thoughts and warmed her. This dog walking thing might have been a small side job, but it provided income. Plus, she had to protect her reputation. Mrs. Bernard could have easily blamed Lucie for the loss of her dogs, yet she chose to trust her.

A good businesswoman would cherish that trust. Even if it meant dealing with Joey.

An hour later, she heard the toilet flush through two closed doors and, assuming it was Joey, cornered him. At least he'd thrown a pair of shorts on his otherwise naked body. Well, she assumed he was naked beneath the shorts. All he ever talked about was how he slept naked because he turned into an inferno in pajamas. As if she wanted to know that. Ew.

"Are you out of your flippin' mind?" Joey asked from the bathroom doorway.

"You owe me."

"For what?"

"For every rotten thing you ever did to me. And, if you don't help, I'll tell Dad when I visit him this weekend."

Talk about hitting a man where he lives, but their father finding out Joey wasn't doing right by his family would give her brother loose bowel movements. Lucie shook her head. "And you know Dad. He'll hold his two fingers together and say 'this is you, this is your brother. These fingers better never come apart.'"

Total blackmail. It should have sickened her. Should have made her feel like pond scum.

Eh, she didn't mind so much. For once, *she* held the power.

Joey put her in a headlock and gave her a noogie that would scar her scalp. "You are a sneaky little witch."

"Ow. That hurts. Knock it off."

He pushed her away. "I'm not riding that butt-ugly scooter. You'll have to pay my parking."

Parking wouldn't be cheap, but she supposed that was fair. She held out her hand to seal the deal. "Agreed."

Joey clasped her hand, gave it a hard pump. "Deal."

She wanted to think the angels were singing because she and Joey had actually agreed on something—without screaming—but the only feeling was a warm blood rush. Maybe her brother *was* human.

"By the way," Lucie said. "Did you find a spreadsheet of mine? I had handwritten notes on it."

Joey twisted his mouth. "Why would I care about some spreadsheet?"

"I can't find it. And Mom hasn't seen it."

"Sorry, kid." He went back to his room and shut the door.

"You need to walk Otis at ten o'clock."

"Whatever."

"I'm serious."

No answer. Clearly, he understood. She smacked her hands together. Now all she had to do was figure out what happened to that damned spreadsheet.

---

LUCIE ARRIVED AT THE BERNARDS' JUST AFTER NINE O'CLOCK and found Mrs. B. talking with Detective O'Brien. Him again. Great. The detective wore a black suit with a crisp white shirt and Mrs. B. looked equally polished in a pair of cream slacks and a matching blazer. Lucie, in her jeans and Notre Dame sweatshirt, missed the memo about the dress code for this party.

Josie and Fannie barreled down the hallway and landed in front of Lucie, dancing by her feet and pawing at them. She dropped to her knees and gave each dog an enthusiastic rub. "Hi, girls. I'm so happy to see you."

An onslaught of licking ensued and Lucie giggled at the feel of their warm tongues against her neck.

"I guess they're happy to see you, Ms. Rizzo." Detective O'Brien smiled, and the ease of it made Lucie think he might be a dog person.

"I'm happy to see *them*."

"How's the shoulder today?"

"A little sore." Lucie set the girls back and stood. "Party is over, girls. We need to leave in a few minutes."

The girls scampered down the marbled hallway into one of the bedrooms, and Lucie turned to Detective O'Brien. Looking at those green eyes and freckles would never be hard labor, but the man wasn't her type. Besides, he always looked at her as though he wanted to figure out her angle.

No angle. Just an out-of-work banker trying to flee her father's reputation.

"Do you have any idea why anyone would take the dogs?" Lucie asked. *Talk about a fishing expedition.*

O'Brien gestured to Mrs. B. "We were just talking about that. It's fairly common among show dogs. It could also happen with rare breeds. The dog is stolen so it can be bred and the perpetrators sell the puppies."

Lucie gasped. "That's awful. Don't they know what these animals mean to their families?"

O'Brien responded with that patronizing half smile people gave her when it came to issues surrounding her father.

"Right," she said. "They don't care."

He flipped his notebook closed and slid it into his jacket pocket. "The good news is the dogs are safe."

"That's the important thing."

"Ladies, thank you. Call me if there's anything else."

Lucie sidled up behind him. "Is the case closed?"

"We'll keep a lookout for the van, but it's unlikely we'll find it. You never know though."

Basically, the case was closed. She wasn't sure if that was a good thing. At least she wouldn't have the police sniffing around as she hoarded a monster of a stolen diamond.

---

JOEY HUSTLED DOWN THE SHORT BLOCK TO THE LUTZ PLACE. Being a half-second off schedule would get him in a load of trouble with Lucie, and he didn't want to hear her yapping.

All in all, it wasn't a bad day to be helping. The sun shone at high-voltage and the temps were supposed to hit sixty. This deal could have been worse. Maybe he'd schlep the mutt down to the lakefront. Weren't dogs chick magnets?

He glanced at the house next to him, a rockin' three-story brownstone with a gated front yard. Who the hell put a gate around a four-foot lawn?

Whatever. The Lutz place was yet another sweet-looking brownstone. This one didn't have a gate so he marched up to the garage, punched in the code and the door eased open. Any other day, it would have shocked the living hell out of him that Lucie trusted him with the code. But what the hell? Did she think he'd rob the place? She *was* his sister. Even if he liked annoying the crap out of her, he wouldn't screw her over by robbing one of her clients.

The dog started howling inside the house. Otis. Good name for a bulldog.

As he was told, Joey bent low to block Otis from bolting when the door opened. Sure enough, the little bastard tried to run, but a body block took care of that and Joey edged his way into the house.

"Step back, you turd."

Otis responded by clamping his jaw around the bottom of Joey's jeans and snarling like a son of a bitch.

"These are new jeans. Back off."

The dog, still attached, showed his teeth and tried to back away.

*I should strangle this bastard.*

Instead, Joey reached down, unhooked Otis's jaw and shoved him back. "No." He put a little mean into it to show this hound who the alpha was. Otis plopped his ass down.

"You know it."

With the alpha-war settled, Joey grabbed the leash off the hook and snapped it on. He needed to get this walk done. Helping his sister would only take him so far.

"Let's hit it. You need to do your thing so I can get out of here."

Otis blasted through the door, nearly taking Joey's arm with him. The runt stopped just outside the garage and Joey punched the button. Otis shot off, forcing him to reel in the leash.

"You are not gonna drag me around, pal. Just telling ya."

Dogs needed to know who the pack leader was. Joey loved being pack leader.

He stopped a few times along the route and let the junior alpha do his thing. No problem there. The poop-scooping bags were holed up in a small dispenser attached to the leash, and Joey eyeballed them with the disdain of a man going to the electric chair. He hoped the dog would crap in an inconspicuous place so he could avoid the off chance somebody he knew would see him cleaning up the mess. This was embarrassing.

The sound of fast footsteps behind him sent a stinging warning up his neck.

He shifted the leash to his left hand before turning. Sure enough, some butthole—a big one—holding a steel choker-chain, came right for him.

*Whoa.* Now at full stride, the guy raised the chain overhead and shouted, "The dog. Give up the dog."

With a second to spare, Joey flicked his wrist and the leash jettisoned from his hand.

"Run, Otis."

Otis charged away, leash trailing behind. The butthole glanced at Joey, raised the chain overhead and swung. The loop at the end bit into Joey's left shoulder and a sweltering burst of pain blasted across his back. His legs buckled and he fell to one knee.

*Get it together, man.*

"I wanted that dog," Butthole said.

A juicy adrenaline buzz ripped through Joey and he knew he could kill this son of a bitch. If he wanted to. Right now, he needed to defend himself.

A rattling sound drew his attention. He looked up; saw the glint of steel coming at him, and the chain sliced across his forearm. He winced at the contact but caught the loop end of the chain and yanked.

Butthole toppled forward, taking the chain with him. He rolled to his back and swung at Joey's legs, but the links sailed out of his grip and dropped to the lawn.

Joey dove and straddled his attacker's chest. He was about to unleash a downward punch when Otis ran back, snarled and latched onto the attacker's pants. The guy kicked out and blasted Otis close to his ribs. The yelp shattered Joey's eardrum. He clamped his hand over the guy's throat. "You kick that dog again and you're done."

"Arghhh."

Joey eased the pressure and stuck his knee into the guy's chest. "Are you out of your friggin' mind coming at me? Do you know who I am?"

A gurgling came from Butthole's mouth. "Want...the...collar."

"I'll ask again. Do you know who the hell I am? Because if you do, you'd know there is no way I'm letting you near this dog. He's a pain in the ass, but word gets out that I got dogjacked, I'm a laughingstock. I should beat you for being stupid."

Joey leaned in and the guy groaned. "Are you the guy that boosted those dogs from my sister?"

"No."

The guy's face turned a nice tomato red. *Liar.* "Leave her alone."

"Can't."

The sound of screeching tires sent Otis into a growling fit. A white van barreled around the corner and Otis jumped for it. On instinct, Joey reached for him and, using the opportunity, Butthole bucked hard, knocked Joey off-balance and sent him to the pavement. His hip connected with the concrete and a tearing sensation shot down his leg.

The dogjacker rolled to his feet and Joey made a grab for him, but the guy slipped away.

Otis lurched forward and Joey snatched up the leash before bursting into a run.

No dice. The dogjacker reached the corner and jumped into the van before they could catch up.

Joey skidded to a stop, accidentally clotheslining Otis who was still in a dead run. He gagged once before giving Joey the what-the-hell look. "Sorry, pal."

The sharp odor of the van's wheels burning rubber sent the dog sniffing all around. Joey bent over, sucking air through his nose as the sinking edge of adrenaline disappeared. He hated the come down.

With the excitement over, Otis squatted and took the mother of all dumps right on the sidewalk.

"Oh, man. That's nasty."

Regardless, he let Otis finish and then did the deal with the poop-scooping bags. Lucie had supplied antiseptic wipes and he cleaned his hands before pulling his phone from his pocket to call Frankie, who had the day off. He'd better freaking answer.

"Hey," Frankie said.

"Some dumbass just tried to boost Otis."

"No way."

"Yes way. This guy has got to be whacked to come at me. And he wanted the collar."

"Lucie guessed right."

"Looks like."

On the other end of the phone, Frankie stayed silent. Otis gave the leash a tug. Might as well finish the damn walk.

"Joey, don't tell Luce about this. She'll freak. I'm calling my father. Maybe he can figure out where that diamond came from. Then we'll tell her. Meantime, we'll have to keep walking with her."

"*What?*"

"I can take the morning shift, but I need to be at work by two. You'll be with her in the afternoons."

"Hey, I got my own business to run."

"Please," Frankie said before hanging up.

---

CRAVING SOME ANSWERS ALONG WITH A MEATBALL SANDWICH, Frankie walked the two blocks from his house to Petey's. Maybe his father would be there and he could get with him on this dognapping thing. The only good news so far was that it was Joey who got hit this morning rather than Lucie. Joey could defend himself better.

Lucie had her own form of toughness. Precisely why Frankie was only mildly concerned over ignoring her request to keep his father out of this diamond issue. But when it came to her safety, some things were worth the risk. The way Frankie figured, he hadn't actually said he wouldn't speak to his father.

Reaching?

Probably.

Too bad.

Keeping Lucie safe was the priority, even if she didn't agree with his methods.

He turned the corner and spotted a Franklin P.D. cruiser double-parked in front of the luncheonette. Jimmy Two-Toes' Caddie was right behind it. Chances were Frankie's father would be here because wherever his father went, Jimmy was usually close by.

The bell on the door jangled when Frankie opened it, and the cop at the counter—an old high school classmate—looked over.

"Hey, Brian."

"How ya doin', Frankie?"

The chatter from the tables mixed with Sinatra and the smell of garlic and baking bread converged on Frankie. Not much beat fresh-baked Italian bread with crust so hard it could split a lip.

The place, the people, the smells, might as well be part of his DNA. That's how well he knew it. And Lucie wanted him to give it up.

"Ho!" Jimmy Two-Toes yelled. "Frankie's here."

Sitting with Jimmy at the four-top table were Slip and

Lemon. Slip got his name because the government could never get any charges to stick. Lemon; who knew? But that poor bastard had jumped off a two-story building some years back and landed with one foot in a garbage can and one out. That would teach him to run from the cops.

Frankie looked around. A few of the tables were occupied, but the people weren't locals or he would have recognized them.

"Your father is in back," Lemon said. "He'll be right out."

*Translation: he's talking business, don't go back there.* Somewhere along the line, Frankie had gotten used to this life. He couldn't say he was comfortable with his father's occupation, but had grudgingly accepted it. What else could he do?

He made his way to the counter to order. "Anybody need anything?"

"We just ate," Jimmy said.

Petey, dressed in his usual track pants and white T-shirt, handed Brian his sandwich and he took it to one of the corner tables.

"Meatball?" Petey asked, retying his grease-stained white apron. The apron tended to slide under his growing belly and he had to keep hiking it up. Between the gut and the thinning gray hair, Petey looked way beyond his fifty-five years.

"Throw some mozzarella on it," Frankie said.

"Living a little today, eh?"

Frankie considered responding with scathing sarcasm but decided to let it go. He probably deserved it since a meatball sandwich was the only thing he ever ordered. And wasn't that one of Lucie's complaints? That he liked his meatball sandwiches from Petey's? And why not? Petey made an exceptional meatball.

"Kid," his father yelled, emerging from the back room

wearing a white dress shirt with no tie and tan dress pants. His typical daytime look.

"Hey, Pop."

"Petey, feed my son." His father clapped him on the back once, put a hand on his shoulder and pushed him into a chair. "You off today?" Pop snagged an unoccupied chair from another table, hitched his pants up and sat.

"Yeah. Can I get a minute outside?"

*Away from any bugs planted in here.*

His father angled his chin toward the back door. "Sure."

Frankie opened the door leading to the alley and the pungent smell of four days' worth of garbage smacked into him. He held his breath for a minute.

"What's up?" his father asked, clearly oblivious to the smell.

"This dognapping thing with Lucie took a turn."

Pop crossed his arms, readying himself for bad news. "What happened?"

This was where his famous temper could fire. He had promised to take care of the Rizzo family while Joe was in prison, and he took that promise seriously. Someone hiding a stolen diamond in Joe's house would be a serious infraction.

*Here goes.* "Lucie found a real diamond in her craft supplies."

His father stared at him, his face full of nothing in particular, and Frankie wondered if he'd understood.

"Heh?" Pop finally said.

"Yeah. It's nuts. Roseanne found it and did a scratch test. It's real."

"Whose is it?"

"We don't know. Joey doesn't think it belongs to their father and Lucie won't ask Theresa. She doesn't want to upset her. We think someone hid it in her dog accessory crap and that's why the dogs are getting boosted. We're guessing the dognappers think one of the dogs is running around with the diamond on it. Joey just got—"

"Hang on, Frankie. You're telling me you think someone snuck into Joe's house and put that diamond there?"

"Exactly."

"No chance."

Disagreeing with his father had never gotten him anywhere, but in this instance, he needed to try. "How else would it have gotten there? If it was Joe's, he would have told Joey about it."

Pop ran his palm across his lips, curled his fingers around his mouth and blew air into his hand. "A diamond."

"Yeah. So far it's the only one. Lucie is checking her stock to make sure."

"That's good. Does Joe know about this?"

"Not about the diamond. Joey talked to him on the phone and told him about the dognappings to see what his reaction would be, but that's it. Joey is convinced Joe doesn't know about the diamond."

The screen door, one of those rickety wooden deals, flew open and smacked against the brick building. Jimmy stuck his head out. "Ho, your meatball is ready."

Frankie did a thumbs-up. "Thanks." Jimmy went inside and Frankie turned to his father. "Can you ask around? See if you can find out about this diamond? Who it belongs to?"

"It better not be one of my guys. I'll tell you that much."

---

LUCIE SAT AT HER MOTHER'S DINING ROOM TABLE SETTING A new collar for a customer Mrs. Lutz had referred. The dog's owner was a stickler for detail, and Lucie wanted to get the placement of the rhinestones in a perfect X pattern. Not so easy on a collar barely an inch wide.

The lack of sound in the house brought an odd sense of peace. Her parents' home usually equaled a fair amount of stress, but now, with Joey and her mother out, Lucie thought about family get-togethers—Christmas, Easter, birthdays— that happened here.

She smiled to herself, reminiscing about parties where loud voices barking orders mingled with the laughter of friends and extended family.

One thing about her family, they threw a great party.

Someone knocked on the front door. *Shoot.* She'd have to put the collar down and risk the stones shifting. Her go-to Notre Dame glass caught her eye. She picked it up, slammed the last of the diet pop hugging the bottom and turned the glass on its side. After stabilizing the glass between two bead containers, she draped the collar over it to dry. That might work.

The knock came again, harder this time, and Lucie ran to the door expecting Sasquatch to be on the other side. She checked the peephole. Detective O'Brien.

As uncomfortable as this guy made her, might as well be Sasquatch. Maybe there was a break in the case? Lucie tugged her faded T-shirt into place and swung the door open.

"Hello, Detective."

He offered a closed-mouthed smile. "Ms. Rizzo, sorry to disturb you. May I come in?"

"Of course."

She led him to the living room where he sat in Frankie's favorite wingback chair. Lucie took the couch. "What brings you here?"

"We had a call from the Glencoe P.D. this morning. One of their residents had a dog stolen yesterday."

*No.* It must have been one of her dogs or O'Brien wouldn't be here. But wait. Glencoe? She didn't have any clients in Glencoe.

"Do you work in Glencoe?" O'Brien asked.

"No."

A fiery punch of guilt landed square in Lucie's chest. This poor dog was missing, the owners probably heartbroken, and she was relieved because it wasn't one of her dogs. Could she be any more selfish?

Not likely.

"What's the owner's name?"

O'Brien checked his notes. "Winthrop."

*Whew.* "Sorry. I don't have a client by that name."

Still though, the name sounded familiar.

The detective nodded. "I thought I'd see if we could connect the thefts. You haven't had any more trouble have you?"

She shook her head. "No." *Aside from the possibly stolen, fifteen-carat diamond in my safe deposit box.*

O'Brien clucked his tongue in a way that screamed disappointment. Clearly, the good detective wanted to tie these dognappings back to Joe Rizzo's daughter. *Sorry, pal, I'm legit.*

Most of the time.

Diamond notwithstanding.

"That's good." O'Brien tapped his left thumb on his thigh. "Be sure to call me if anything comes up."

"I will."

He stood. "Sorry to disrupt your day."

"No problem. I hope you find the missing dog."

*I also hope it doesn't have anything to do with me.*

As soon as O'Brien left, she charged up to her micro-bedroom and opened the revenue file on her laptop. *Please don't let there be anyone from Glencoe.*

She clicked on the master spreadsheet and searched for Glencoe. Bingo. She eyeballed the row. *Oh, no. Please, no.* Sweat bubbled on her palms and Lucie rubbed her hands over her jeans. Evelyn Winthrop attended Mrs. Lutz's trunk show and bought a royal blue coat adorned with rhinestones. She also bought a collar.

She stared at the Winthrop name on the spreadsheet and a flashing panic crawled up her throat. She opened her mouth, but nothing happened. The only sound was a sucking noise. She bent at the waist, the pressure behind her eyes building, building, building, as the floor shifted beneath her.

She smacked a hand against her chest. She needed air. *Calm. Slow.* She closed her eyes, concentrated on one small breath, then another. Within seconds, the banging behind her eyes stopped and she stood straight. She spun around, but there was nowhere to go. The room was too damn small.

Good God. The dognappers knew who her clients were. And her missing spreadsheet might be the reason.

An afternoon breeze tickled her arm through the window she had cracked opened that morning. She stuck her face against the small gap. The lacy pink curtains billowed against her cheek and she shoved them back. She hated this room and the I'm-going-do-die-of-suffocation feeling that came with it.

She had to get out.

Now.

A LOUD POUNDING ON HIS FRONT DOOR BROUGHT FRANKIE OUT of a monster REM cycle. *Jeez. Where's the fire?* He tossed the sheet off, rolled out of bed and slipped on a pair of gym shorts. Couldn't even take a damned nap on his day off.

He swung through the living room, stepped into the outer hallway and saw Lucie standing on the stoop in ripped jeans and a sweatshirt. The disturbing lack of color in her face resembled one of his new white dress shirts.

He opened the door and the cool air pricked his bare chest. "You okay?"

She looked him up and down, stopped at the bedhead. "You were napping? I'm sorry I woke you."

The quiver in her voice sent Frankie's blood humming, and he suddenly wasn't cold anymore. "What's wrong?"

She pushed by him, walked through the hallway into his living room. "I just talked to Detective O'Brien."

Still groggy from sleep, Frankie jammed the heels of his hands into his eye-sockets. When pain erupted from the pressure, he pulled his hands away "What did he want?"

"A dog was stolen in Glencoe. Frankie, oh my God. It's the same family."

He didn't know what the hell she was babbling about. "Luce, take it easy."

She shook her hands in the air. "The dog that was stolen —I sold his owner a coat and collar at the Lutzes' trunk show. This is no coincidence."

The Glencoe development, coupled with Joey almost getting dogjacked, brought a hell of a mess.

Frankie couldn't keep the Joey thing from her any longer. She'd be mad, but he had to be straight with her. He rolled his lips together and scratched a sudden itch on the back of his head. "Luce, take a seat."

"I don't want to sit."

"Sit."

They stared at each other for a solid minute. She gave in and dropped into the hand-me-down black leather recliner he'd gotten from his folks. He sat on the arm of the matching sofa across from her. "Okay. You're not gonna like this."

She squeezed the arms of the chair until her knuckles bulged and her blue eyes remained fixed on him like a locked-on missile. The last time he'd seen that focused intensity her father had been found guilty of tax evasion.

"What is it?"

His girl liked things straight on, so he'd let it fly. "Joey had an incident when walking Otis this morning."

"What kind of incident?"

Sink or swim. He had to tell her. Unfortunately, his tongue turned to lead. This would not go well. "Attempted dogjacking. The guy told Joey he only wanted the collar."

She squeezed the chair tighter and the veins in her hands popped. Yep. Pissed. He reached for her, smoothed the tension from her grip. "Before you yell at me, I'm sorry I didn't tell you."

"You *should* have told me."

"Joey fought the guy off. At that point, I figured it wouldn't do you any good to know. I was going to tell you, but not yet."

She leaned forward. "Putting aside you kept this from me, my fears were dead on. The dognappings are about that diamond. I have to stop offering services. It's the right thing to do. Besides, my reputation will be ruined and I'll lose my clients anyway."

That would kill her. A reputation as a responsible, law-abiding businesswoman was what Lucie craved most. It was time to get herself focused again.

"How would the dognappers know the Winthrops are your clients?"

"The only thing I can think of is my missing spreadsheet. It had all my client info on it."

Frankie did a yes-no thing with his head. "Or someone could have followed you to the Lutzes' for the trunk show and then followed Mrs. Winthrop home."

Lucie sat back. Thought about it a second. "It's possible, but my money is on the spreadsheet."

"How are you doing on collecting everything you've sold?"

"It's slow going, but we're getting there. I told my clients I wanted to check the glue. Ro has been going through everything, but hasn't found any real stones. A good thing, I suppose."

"Yeah. We just have to make sure the dognappers know that."

Their gazes met and held for a long moment, which only confirmed she understood what he was thinking.

"No. I don't want your father involved in this."

*Too late.*

"Oh, no," she said.

Frankie didn't move. Not even a blink. "What?"

"You did it, didn't you?"

*Busted.*

"Dammit, Frankie! O'Brien probably already suspects the dognappings have something to do with my dad and you went and told *your* dad, which I asked you not to do. Are you trying to drive me crazy?"

He waved her off. "Of course not."

"Well, telling your father will only bring more attention."

She had a point there, but he was willing to risk it. "If I

75

have to choose between keeping you safe and pissing you off, you should know what I'll pick. I knew you wouldn't like it, but my father can put the word on the street that you haven't sold any real diamonds. It'll help. And maybe he can figure out who the damned thing belongs to. Or doesn't belong to."

Frankie waited for the yelling. Nothing happened. She sat, shoulders slumped.

"Luce?"

She closed her eyes and breathed in and out a couple of times. Finally she looked at him. "I'm mad at you, but you're probably right. From now on, we figure this out on our own. Got it?"

This could be trouble, but he had to say something. "Not if I think you're in danger. You'll have to live with it."

"Do I have a choice?"

He shrugged. "We're already broken-up, so that response is cooked."

That wrenched a smile out of her. "You're impossible."

"Yes, but you love me."

"And that's always been the problem."

## 6

Lucie's feet fused to the ground when Frankie held the door open at the Bruce Correctional Facility. This damned place. She despised it. A Zen moment was what she needed. Particularly after yesterday's discovery about the Winthrops' dog being stolen. She closed her eyes, let the sun warm her back and took three deep breaths of fresh air. When she entered the building, the staleness would burn through her nostrils like a California wildfire.

As far as medium security prisons went, she supposed it wasn't the worst. Although, she hadn't seen any other prisons. Either way, the idea of this being her father's home left her with deep-rooted heartache.

The only positive was the geographically desirable location just over the Wisconsin state line. On a traffic-free day, she could get here in ninety minutes.

"Are we going in or what?" Frankie asked.

She nodded, but didn't budge. "I hate this place."

"Does anyone like it?"

"Good point."

The check-in desk sat a few feet in front of them. Lucie signed her name, waited for Frankie to do the same and the guard waved them to the x-ray belt. *Another day in paradise.* She slipped off her jacket and shoes and placed them on the belt. Early on, she had learned to leave her purse in the car rather than subject herself to strangers rifling through her belongings.

She stepped through the screening machine, waited for the *go* nod and took her jacket. Apparently, she had no hidden weapons or bombs on her person. She hummed a Jimmy Buffett song. Too bad she couldn't pretend she was at the airport going through security on her way to a tropical vacation.

This was her life. No other way to slice it.

The visitor's center was a cement-walled gymnasium painted a dull gray. She stood silent as the stale air wrapped around her. The first time she came here, she had cried. Sobbed actually. No matter what age, a girl never wanted to see her daddy in a pair of orange prison scrubs.

*Hate. This. Place.*

Square and round tables of various sizes cluttered the room, and Lucie searched for her father, who sat at one of the corner tables. The good table. *Zen moment, Zen moment, Zen moment.* All she wanted was to get through this without an argument. He glanced over and held his hand up in greeting.

His peppered gray hair had been buzzed and the severity of it accentuated his cheekbones. He'd lost twenty pounds in prison and the leanness of his face made his broad nose appear wider. His body may have been fit, but the gaunt look didn't suit him.

She grabbed Frankie's sleeve and tugged. "There he is."

"And we're off," he cracked.

She should have given him a smack for being a wise guy, but he'd sat through enough of these visits to know they often went wildly askew.

"Hi, Dad," she said.

Frankie pulled a chair for her and her father stood, offered a brief smile and gestured for her to sit. Physical contact was prohibited, so the three of them stared at each other. Wasn't this fun? Lucie finally moved to her chair. The men followed.

Two armed guards stood watch. Lucie recognized one of them from her previous visits. He gave her a slight pivot of his head and she did the same. Greeting the prison guards couldn't hurt.

She turned to her father. "Mom sends her love."

"I talked to her this morning. She all right?"

*Aside from her husband being in prison?* "She's fine. She's been helping me with the dog accessories. I think it keeps her busy."

"Right." He turned his attention to Frankie. "How're you doing?"

"I'm good." That Frankie. Mr. Chatty.

"Uh-huh." Her father flipped his gaze back to her. "This poop scooping thing has to stop. Joey told me all about it and you're done. You hear? I didn't put you through four years at Notre Dame for you to shovel dog crap and get the damn animals kidnapped."

Hello? Had she missed the opening bell? Not even a warm-up before the fight? Joey had warned her he'd made the calculated decision to tell their father about the dognappings. His theory was, if the diamond belonged to their father, he'd somehow let Joey know it was hidden in her things and might be what the dognappers were after. Unfortunately, her father hadn't done that, which Joey assumed meant he didn't know diddly about the diamond.

As usual, her father's refusal to acknowledge her working her butt off to get through college and grad school irritated her. His money may have paid for it, and she still hadn't reconciled herself to the idea of being put through school with money earned illegally, but she had done the work and managed top honors. All to prove that she could be more than a criminal's daughter. "Joey shouldn't have said anything. Besides, it has nothing to do with me. The police said it's probably a dognapping ring."

If she took the diamond out of the picture, it *could* be the dognapping ring.

Frankie leaned forward and rested his arms on the table. "Joey and I are doing the walks with her. She'll be fine."

If Dad had a hair's worth of knowledge about the diamonds, he wasn't letting on. Maybe Joey was right. And wasn't that the equivalent of swallowing antifreeze?

"What's this garbage about you two breaking up again?"

"Don't start, Dad."

"You need to get your head examined. Why won't you marry him? How many times are you gonna make him ask?"

Lucie sucked in a breath. How humiliating that he should bring up the one time that Frankie asked her to marry him in front of both their families. He'd surprised her with it and, in her blindsided state, she hadn't known what to do. "Dad, I'm not talking about this now."

"He's good for you. He'll take care of you."

Frankie shifted in his seat, and she thought she would die right there. "Can we not talk about Frankie like he's not here? This is inappropriate."

That probably wasn't the right thing to say, because Dad's face turned a scary shade of red. Maybe even purple.

"Don't you tell me what's inappropriate. Did you forget who you're talking to?"

Frankie cleared his throat. "Joe, everything is good. Luce and I are on a break."

Her father poked a finger at him. "I should crack you one. You gotta control this."

"Dad, it's not your business." The hammering inside Lucie's skull set her eyeballs throbbing. She couldn't do this. Couldn't sit here and have her father, inmate number 3-5-7-9-2-4, lecture her. The man was in prison and *he* dared to lecture *her*?

She shot out of her chair and the screeching of the metal legs caused a vibrating buzz against her leg. "Visit is over."

"Sit down," her father said.

"I will not. I'm done here." She looked at Frankie. "You can stay if you'd like. I'll be outside."

He reached for her hand. "Luce—"

"I won't sit here and have him yell at me. Not when *I* can walk out of here."

———

FRANKIE WATCHED LUCIE MAKE A BEELINE TO THE DOOR. Being in a room with these two was like visiting a snake pit. He faced Joe. "That went well."

Joe held his hands wide. "I don't understand."

Did he think he was the only one? Joe Rizzo was as thick skulled as they came. Frankie had always been respectful to him but never held back when it came to offering his opinion. Joe didn't like weaklings, and Frankie always made sure to shoot straight with him. Particularly if the situation involved Lucie. "I don't understand either but with all due respect, yelling at her won't help. You know your daughter. If you push, she'll push back. I'm giving her space. She's trying to survive here, Joe. I figure if I give her time to sort out what's going on with her career, she'll be happy and then we can work on our relationship."

"Or, she could marry you and she won't have to worry about the career. My wife was pregnant at Lucie's age."

Maybe Joe was deaf in addition to being thick skulled? His solution was to get married. And what a rotten reason for someone to get married. These old-school guys were impossible.

"I don't want her to marry me because I can support her. I want her because I love her. All this other stuff will work itself out. Give her some room."

Joe slouched back in his chair. Relinquishing control had to be brutal for him. Being locked up didn't help. Not when the people in his life came and went and he had nothing to say about it. "I know you're worried, but I'll take care of her. Whether we're broken up or not, I'll take care of her."

There weren't many things Frankie knew for sure, but that was one of them. It didn't matter what it took, he'd make sure Lucie stayed safe.

Joe nodded. "I know you will, but her life would be easier if she got married."

Frankie laughed. "You're a pisser, Joe." He stood. "I gotta go."

"I put the word out. Anyone touches my daughter, there's gonna be problems. You check in with me about this dognapping business. I want to be updated. Don't screw with me on this."

As if he'd dare? "If anything happens, I'll make sure you know."

How he'd do that without upsetting Lucie, he had no idea.

He stepped into the waiting area and found her reading a copy of the prison newsletter. "Anything good?"

She slapped the paper on the side table and stood. "Family picnic next week. Can we go home now?"

"These visits are always fun."

After pushing through the door, she stopped on the outside landing. "Am I wrong?"

He shrugged. "You push his buttons, he pushes yours. When he asked about us getting married, you could have said we're talking about it. He would have been satisfied. Instead, you blew your stack."

"So, it's my fault?"

"No. It's his fault. Definitely. You need to be prepared, though, or it'll always wind up this way and everyone loses."

*And I land in the middle.*

"I won't give in."

"You don't have to. He's locked up. Just say what'll make him happy and he'll leave you alone."

"You want me to lie?"

"I want you to spin. Spinning will buy you time and save me grief."

She leaned against the steel railing and crossed her arms. When the sun lit her blue eyes and made them twinkle, Frankie sucked in a breath. He loved her. She terrorized him, but he loved her.

"Spin," she said, clearly calculating the merits.

"Yep."

"We'll try that."

"Perfect. Let's go home."

THE NEXT MORNING, LUCIE FIGURED THE DEAD-LAST THING Frankie wanted to do before work was drive her downtown for her dog duties. As always, he smiled and pressed on.

They walked the half-block to Otis's house because, with the magic of the Frankie Factor, they found a spot on the same street. Parking spaces, like women, just appeared for him.

"You don't have to walk with me. I'll be fine."

He grinned. "I *want* to walk with you. It'll force you to spend time with me."

Looking at him, that beautiful face, the dark hair, it hurt in a way that carved out a piece of her. Plus, she'd been thinking about the colossal disaster of the visit with her father and how Frankie fell into the drama. He deserved better.

"I never apologized about the visit with my dad. He shouldn't have cornered you."

Frankie shrugged. "He didn't corner me. You're the one he wanted answers from. I was collateral damage."

"Still, it's none of his business."

"What's your point?"

She laughed. "It makes me realize that no matter how old I get, he's still trying to control everything."

"He's your dad. Him trying to control you will never change."

"Unless I change it."

"Good luck."

They reached the driveway and Lucie moved to the garage, pressed in the code.

"I'll wait here," Frankie said.

Two minutes later, she came out with Otis leaping around, all too ready to start his walk. Frankie stood in the middle of the driveway, his eyes closed and his head tilted to the clear blue sky. He looked...peaceful.

"I love this time of year," he said without looking at her.

Spring meant the start of a new baseball season and she knew it brought mixed emotions for him. He loved the excitement of getting outside, playing on his rec team, watching the games, but at the same time, he mourned the loss of his dream.

"You okay?" Lucie asked while Otis sniffed around her foot. The rhinestone collar she made him twinkled in the sunlight and she wondered if she should have Ro double-check it for real diamonds. She bit down. No. That one had been checked already. All fakes.

Frankie finally looked at her, his eyes a little distant. "Are we going to make it through this break?"

After shifting the leash to the other side, she reached for his hand. "I want to."

"How do we fix it then? It seems like you want me to give up my life. I won't do that."

"I don't want you to give up your life. I want it to not interfere with our relationship. I've worked hard to get beyond being Joe Rizzo's daughter. I want more than that. You don't mind people gossiping about your family. I do. And I want you to defend me to your parents. You never say anything when they bug me about getting married. And you also told your dad about the dognappings when I specifically asked you not to."

"Hey, if he can keep you from getting hurt, I'd do it again. The other stuff? Not defending you? On the big stuff, I defend you. Arguing with them about when we're getting married is pointless. Nothing will change. I ignore them." He blew air through his teeth. "Regardless, I'm not turning my back on my family."

They'd been over this a hundred times. With the way her heart craved him, it was worth making it a hundred and one. "Don't you remember that feeling you had when you first figured out what your dad did for a living?"

"Sure. But it doesn't determine how I live my life."

Otis barked and Lucie gestured to Frankie to walk with her. "When I was ten, a kid in my class told one of my friends that my father wasn't away working, that he was in jail. That's how I found out. My mother had told me my dad was building a new restaurant in another state and would be gone a few months. When I came home and asked her, she admitted it. That was when I realized my dad wasn't who I thought he was. I never got over that."

"We don't get to choose our parents."

Otis stopped at his favorite oak and sniffed. He'd be here a minute. "But we can choose to separate ourselves."

"If we want to. I don't. I don't agree with what my dad does, but he has always supported me. I can't turn on him for that."

"Stalemate."

Frankie pulled a twig from a low hanging branch and snapped it. "No compromise?"

"Sure. We don't go to dinner with your parents every other Saturday."

"Luce—"

"Why does it have to be set in stone? Why can't we pop over on a Friday? What if we want to do something else on Saturday?"

Frankie shrugged. "Then we do something else. No big deal."

Otis zeroed in on his spot and assumed the position for one of his colossal poops. "It *is* a big deal. If we don't go your mother will flip."

"Probably, but I'll deal with it."

"I want to move back to the city. *You* like having a three-flat in Franklin so you can walk to Petey's, get a meatball sandwich and shoot the bull with your dad's friends."

"I can drive in from downtown."

*Ugh.* He didn't get it. Didn't understand how the pull of "the life" came between them, defined them. She wanted to separate herself from it and he wanted to hang on.

Otis finished pooping, and Lucie cleaned up the mess and dropped the package into the larger grocery bag she carried.

Frankie grabbed her arm to get her attention. "I'm willing to make changes, but we both need to. Otherwise, one of us will get everything and one of us will get nothing."

The flatness in his brown eyes split her in two and made her realize the hurt she'd put him through. It would be easy to give in. If only to make him happy, but this issue was too big and menacing. "I can't come up with a compromise, but if you can, I'd be ecstatic."

They wandered a few feet and Otis stopped at his second favorite tree. Frankie shifted toward her and stuck his hands in his jacket pockets. "We've had three years together, Luce."

"Three great years."

"Definitely."

"I love you, Frankie. I want to wake up with you every morning, have babies with you and watch you teach them how to play ball."

He grinned. "I'd be good at making babies."

She rolled her eyes. A flock of squawking geese flew overhead and Otis lunged forward, yanking the leash and throwing Lucie off balance. Frankie grabbed her, and she hung on to his jacket for balance.

She gave the leash a correcting tug. "Relax, Otis." Frankie laughed and she made the mistake of looking into his eyes.

At that moment they were them again; two lovers enjoying a laugh over an inconsequential thing. The moment drifted between them, suspending them in the muck between love and hurt. He leaned down and brushed a kiss over her lips. She let it happen. Let the loneliness of these last weeks and the loss of his body next to hers melt away. What could be the harm in that?

She finally pulled back and he nipped her bottom lip. "I love you."

"I love you, too." He kissed the top of her head and she snuggled into him, settled her cheek against his jacket and inhaled the clean, airy scent that came with him. Hopefully, this would always be her place. Hopefully.

---

After a lightning quick lunch, they headed to the Bernards' and Lucie pushed through the lobby doors with the dogs. "We have to make a quick stop at Sammy Spaniel."

"Say what?"

"The dog boutique around the corner. The girls are out of chews and Mrs. Bernard left a note asking if I could get them."

Frankie considered himself a reasonable guy, but running errands was taking advantage of Lucie's good nature. Lucie, probably still guilt-ridden over the dogjacking, didn't want to say no. "You're the boss."

She grinned up at him. "I like the sound of that."

"Depending on how far you wanted to take it, I could

think of a few areas we can put you in charge. One would involve you on top of me with a whip."

Lucie clamped her mouth shut.

"Just saying."

They swung a right at the corner and dodged the lunch hour rush with the dogs sniffing their way toward Sammy Spaniel. Lucie marched into the store with the girls leading the charge.

"Let's all go in," Frankie said.

The place looked like Cinderella's castle for dogs. Coats and costumes—costumes?—shared one wall, while collars and leashes hung on the adjacent wall. And didn't all this dog crap get his mind buzzing? Lucie needed to get her accessory line in here.

The back wall contained dog treats, and bags and bags of food. Frankie eyeballed the freezer and a big sign that said Raw Bar. He didn't want to know.

The saleslady, a fortyish woman, wore tight jeans, high-heeled red boots and a low cut V-neck sweater that screamed va-va-va-voom.

She glanced over at him and smiled. This woman was nice looking, but if she backed off on the makeup and stopped dressing like a twenty-year-old, she'd be a stunner. After giving him the onceover, she returned to her customer.

"I'm not sure what my supplier has," she said. "But I'll call this afternoon. We'll get your baby squared away."

Must be the owner. Even better.

A circular bakery case, smack in the middle of the room, held dog pastries and intricately decorated cookies that caught Frankie's eye. Seriously? People spent money on this stuff? For dogs?

Lucie headed for the wall with the dog chews while he perused the collars. Frankie picked up a pink one with hearts on it. Twenty-four ninety-five. A little pricey for your basic collar. He moved down the line and grabbed the black one with silver swirls. Thirty-five bucks. He set it back and, hanging on to the theory that these babies got pricier the farther down the line he went, he snatched a leather one with metal studs off the hook. Fifty-nine dollars. *Now we're talking.*

"I found the treats." Lucie came up behind him.

"Check out these collars. You need to get hooked up with this place."

She glanced at the rows of collars and leashes and bit her bottom lip. "I left the owner my number last week. I'll follow up with her in another week or so. I don't want to do anything until we settle the *issue.* If you know what I mean."

"Yeah, I get it, but they have a built-in customer base here. All you need to do is show the owner your stuff."

"Excuse me." The other customer in the store squeezed by.

"Sure," Frankie stepped aside, spotted the owner coming their way and leaned closer to Luce. "Roll with me, here."

"What are you doing?"

"How are we all today?" The woman's cherry red lips eased into a smile. She looked first to Lucie then stared at Frankie. He glanced down at her left hand and didn't see a ring. *Cougar.*

This would get him in trouble with Lucie, but he offered up one of his surefire crooked grins. "I could be better." He reached to pat the dogs. "The girls have their bling on and I'm feeling underdressed."

"Bling?" The woman squatted, giving him a nice view of her fleshy cleavage. *Yow.* He glanced at Lucie and she did the spare-me eye roll.

"Oh, aren't these fabulous," the cougar said when she

spotted the collars. "Where did you get these? They're just fabulous."

Second fabulous within seconds. He shot Lucie a look, but she stood there as if facing down a ravenous tiger. Well, maybe in the cougar's case, she was, but that was beside the point. He gritted his teeth and went back to the queen of all things fabulous.

"Coco Barknell."

The woman's eyes went wide. "Oh, I love it."

"Yep," he said. "Lucie here is the owner. She makes everything. Collars, coats, leashes. All one of a kind."

The cougar stood and faced Lucie. "Did you leave me your number last week?"

Luce slid her gaze to Frankie, then back to the other woman before holding her hand out. "Yes. I'm Lucia Rizzo. The company is new. I've been doing private trunk shows."

*Finally.* After a pat for the girls, Frankie stood to join the cougar and Lucie, who had pulled the leash closer to keep the dogs from chewing on a rack of toys. They flopped onto the floor with a whimper.

"I'm Jeanette Owens. I own the store." She turned to Frankie, held out her hand and nearly purred at him. "And you are?"

"Frank Falcone." To his credit, he tried to make the handshake quick, but Jeanette gave his fingers a squeeze. He slid his hand away and took a step closer to Lucie before he got sucked into cougar quicksand. "Luce, honey—" the honey couldn't hurt, "—why don't you bring some samples by to show Jeanette. Your products would fit right in."

Jeanette turned her attention to Luce. "Yes. I'd love to see what you have. I'm always looking for new items. Let me get you my card."

She cruised her bombshell body over to the register,

leaned over the counter and gave Frankie an unimpeded view of her rear. *Ho-kay.* Not looking. *Not* looking.

The sound of Luce rummaging through her messenger bag drew his attention and she pulled a stack of business cards.

"Are you here tomorrow?" Luce asked. "I could stop in with a few things. Maybe around this same time?"

Jeanette moved back to them, her eyes square on Frankie. He bent to pet the dogs. Mr. Innocent. That was Frankie.

"That would be fine." Jeanette handed Lucie a card. "I'm looking forward to it."

---

OUT ON THE CROWDED SIDEWALK, LUCIE COULDN'T CONTAIN her frustration a second longer. What was he doing pushing the accessory line when they had this tiny problem of a stolen diamond holding them captive? She cracked Frankie across the arm.

"Ow."

"You did it again. Completely ignored what I asked you to do." A few pedestrians sent her horrified glances, but she was beyond that. "Are you out of your mind?"

"At times, yes."

"*What*?"

"You asked a question, I answered."

Typical deflection tactic. She leaned in. "Are you forgetting about the dognappings? The hijacked accessories?"

He waved her off. "Doesn't matter. Your father put the word out to leave you alone. And *my* father told me he's on it. From now on, you're good."

Wonderful. That made her feel so much better.

"And another thing," Lucie said. "That woman was looking at you like her next meal."

An iron stab of jealousy flooded Lucie and she despised it. After all this time, she'd thought she'd accepted women being attracted to Frankie. Obviously not. Frankie might have been putting on a show, but Lucie felt like the extra in that little extravaganza. A sick feeling rumbled in her stomach.

"I *got* you in there," he said.

One of the girls stopped to sniff a fire hydrant. "By pimping yourself."

"Please. With all this drama, I should call you Roseanne. You know I was playing her."

"Yeah, but she didn't know that. She thinks you want to have sex with her."

"My goodness," an elderly woman hissed as she went by.

Frankie stopped walking. "You're pissed because I flirted with her? You had to know what I was doing."

The steam inside Lucie scalded her. No. He would not make this her fault. "I'm not pissed that you were flirting. I'm pissed because she's attractive."

There. She said it.

He burst out laughing, but it was an incensed, you're-next-on-line-for-the-psych ward laugh. "And that's *my* fault?"

"She was *sexy* and you went for that. A little voice in my head kept whispering at me that maybe if I weren't there, something *would* happen. We *are* broken up."

The crowd on the street suddenly gave them a wide berth. A tall man with dark hair and shoulders the size of a Buick walked by with a knowing, entertained grin.

Frankie, his face resembling granite, dragged her and

the dogs down the side street so they could keep the conversation semi-private.

He held her elbow and spun her to face him. "Are you serious? You think I'd do that to you?"

When he put it that way, it sounded bad. Really bad. She closed her eyes and tried to unbunch her shoulders. *Relax.* How to explain herself? "No. But everyone always silently questions why you're with me."

"That's ridiculous."

"No, it's not."

A ball of self-doubt spewed open inside her, submerged her in ways she normally had enough self-confidence to ignore. But this time, it picked at her, bullied her, made her sick with wonder because she loved this man and didn't want him with anyone else. Anyone more desirable. Combining that with losing the job she had worked so hard for, the job that made her someone other than Joe Rizzo's daughter caused a vile sickness to swell in her throat.

"What do you see when you look at me?" The words came out soft and strangled and Frankie stood there, his mouth slightly open.

*Say something.*

A truck roared around the corner and honked at them. Frankie, with the ease of a man ordering a beer, reached his hand over his head and shot the driver the bird. Then he stepped back. She needed something from him, anything, and he moved away. What did *that* say?

"Frankie." She reached for his arm. "I'm having a rough time here. Between all this craziness in my life, I'm desperately trying to hang on. Everything is an emotional trigger and sometimes, *sometimes*, when we meet new people they look at you first, then me, then back to you. I wonder if they're thinking you should be with someone else. Someone more stunning. And right now, the way I'm feeling, watching you flirt with that woman just destroyed me."

He stepped back again and continued to stare at her as if she'd shot him. "Please say something."

But he closed his eyes and slid his head side to side. His lips moved, but nothing came out. Talking to himself. He did that.

"Frankie?"

When he opened his eyes, he stepped forward, pulled her into him and squeezed. "I'm sorry. I didn't know. I swear I didn't know."

He backed away, but continued to hold her arms. "Luce, when I looked at that woman, yes, I admit it, I thought she was stacked. And, okay, she has a nice ass. I'm a guy. We're stupid that way. When I look at you I think, yeah, she's stacked and she's smart and funny and when the world kicks her to the curb she fights her way back."

"You don't have to—"

"Yeah, I do. I'm the idiot who never tells you that when light hits your eyes a certain way they twinkle, and I think, *she's mine* and I'm proud because for whatever reason, a smart girl like you, someone who can go anywhere and be anyone, chooses to be with me. At least when we're not broken-up. That's what beautiful is to me. *You* are beautiful to me. You're the whole damn package and that's nearly impossible to find. You, Luce, are the one thing I couldn't stand to lose."

She leaned back against the building, flattened her palms against the dirty bricks and concentrated on drawing air into her lungs. Breathe. She needed to breathe. He thought she was beautiful and smart and capable. He'd said it a hundred times before, but somehow, this time it meant so much more.

ADRIENNE GIORDANO

She reached up, slid her hand over his cheek because this was Frankie, *her* Frankie, the man she'd loved for years. Even before they'd gotten together, she'd had a mad desire for him. Those schoolgirl feelings had been pounded into submission because...well...what would he want with her when he had an army of girls chasing him? Such a fool.

She went up on tiptoe and kissed him. His arms came around her in a tight squeeze and she leaned in, savoring the feel of his body next to hers. "I wish I would have said something sooner."

"No kidding."

The girls woofed. They didn't want to be hanging around doing nothing. Lucie gave the leash a tug. "Let's walk."

He held a hand for her to go first and Lucie, needing the contact, slid her hand into his. Ready to offer the comfort she needed, he laced his fingers with hers.

His eyes narrowed...the thinking face. "What?" she asked.

"Do you want to go to dinner with me?"

"A date?"

"Yeah. A date. Dinner and a movie. A fresh start. *Again.*"

She thought about it a minute. Let the idea of dating roll around her brain. Had they ever really dated? She didn't think so. They went from being friends to having lunch a few times and—*bam*—they were a couple and everyone was ecstatic and talking marriage and babies.

A date meant working on their relationship. It couldn't be casual between them, not with all the baggage. Still, that feeling in the pit of her stomach, like a rose blooming couldn't be ignored. "I'd love to."

# 7

The next day, Lucie had finished the dog walks by four-thirty and was home sorting her inventory to see how many collars, coats and leashes she had ready to sell. Ro sat to her left, thumbing through fabric samples and separating them into what she considered acceptable versus unacceptable piles. The unacceptable pile had a large pool of candidates.

"Mom, forget the coffee. We need to get started."

"Coming." Her mother entered from the kitchen carrying a carafe and three mugs. "It's too bad Roseanne won't let us eat sweets. I have a nice coffee cake in there."

"No cake," Ro said.

With the coffee poured, Lucie set her mug aside. "This is the first official meeting of the Coco Barknell executive team."

"Ooohhh." Ro clapped.

Mom's eyebrows cinched. "What?"

"I met with the owner of Sammy Spaniel today. They sell dog accessories. The owner placed an order. A big one. Can I count on you two?"

"Of course," they said in unison. No thought necessary. This was love.

"We have three days to make forty coats, collars and leashes."

"Three," Mom said.

"Forty," Ro said.

Lucie nodded. "Ro will do the designing and I'll help sew. We'll have to buy extra beads and stones. And we'll need more fabric."

"You should go to that place in Pineville," her mother said. "Best fabric around. It'll cost more, but it's worth it."

Ro nodded. "She's right. You can't go cheap with these high-end people."

"Can you go there with me after we're done here? We'll hit there and the craft stores so we can start sketching right away."

"Sure. I have some ideas and none of the fabric you have will work."

Lucie perused her notes as the unintended insult hit home, "Also, the store owner wants me to be on hand the first day." She shifted her gaze to Ro. "Are you available to do the, 'I'm-beautiful-and-you'll-do-what-I-tell-you' thing? If you say buy a two-hundred dollar collar, they're going to."

"Absolutely." Again, no questions asked.

The front door opened and in came Frankie. That familiar ping flicked in Lucie's chest. She didn't know where their upcoming dinner date would take them, but for now, the idea of them coming together instead of drifting apart was enough to make her hopeful.

Frankie bent to kiss Lucie's cheek. "Did you get done early?" she asked

"I had to go in early and they owe me a couple hours anyway. Figured I'd stop in and check on you."

"We're having our first official executive team meeting," Ro said.

Frankie stared at her then turned to Lucie. Half of what Ro told Frankie was a crock and he never knew whether to believe her or not. "Luce?"

"She's not kidding. Your wannabe sex slave placed a big order today."

Mom tsked. "Lucia, what a thing to say."

"Mom, if I'm lying you can send me to confession. The woman was all over him yesterday. It's okay though, he got me the sales opportunity."

"Nice." Ro held her hand up for a high-five from Frankie. She could appreciate the finer points of him using his charm to get something accomplished.

"Your good work got you in there," he said.

"Guys," Ro interrupted, "do I care? All that matters is that she's in."

He pointed at her. "Thank you."

"Anytime, Charm Boy."

He glanced at the supplies on the table and ran a hand over his mouth. The hand over his mouth meant he had something cooking.

"You'll need more supplies," he said.

"We're going shopping as soon as we're done here."

Mom held up her hand. "How about some coffee cake, Frankie?"

"No cake," Ro said.

He crossed his eyes at her. "I want cake."

Mom jumped from her chair. "I'll get it."

With Mom out of the room, Frankie turned to Ro. "I need to talk to Luce. Go grab a smoke."

"I quit."

"Then take a whiz or something, but get out."

Ro stared at the ceiling and held her palm up. Frankie reached into his pocket for his money clip, peeled off a twenty and smacked it into Ro's hand.

"Thank you." She shoved the twenty into her cleavage. "I'll be back."

Lucie laughed. "She's been doing that to you for how long?"

"Ten years, but it beats arguing with her. The sooner I pay her, the sooner she's out of my hair."

He had a point there. "What's up?"

"How are you paying for the supplies you need?"

"Probably my credit card."

"I want to be your investor."

Just like that. No preamble, no sales pitch, just boom. "Uh."

She should have known this was coming. Four years ago, Frankie had been an investor when a friend opened a smoothie bar in one of the local health clubs. A year later, after a major juice company bought the smoothie business, Frankie's five thousand dollars turned into half a million. His share of the sale. Since then, Frankie had investor fever.

"Luce, you don't want to be jacking up your credit card. I'll be the very silent money guy that gets you started. You run the show. All I want is to watch my money grow."

The way Frankie looked at her, his eyes glued to hers so steady and sure, fired her confidence. He believed in her. But was this a good idea? Going into business together had the potential to obliterate the strongest of relationships, never mind the ones in limbo.

Then again, driving up her credit card would put her further in debt, and the more debt she carried, the longer it would take her to get out of Franklin. "You have that much faith in me?"

"No doubt."

"Are you sure?"

"Yep. Coco Barknell is going places."

Lucie held out her hand to shake on the deal. Frankie clasped her hand and held it for a second while the normal buzz shot through her. He pulled her into him and kissed the hell out of her, sliding his tongue along her bottom lip. *Mmmm.* She had missed the magic of his tongue. The familiar heat fired low in her core and she imagined them together again in his bed, making love the way they used to. Touching every spot they each knew would make the other frantic. She squeezed his hand and moaned and Frankie inched closer, wrapped his free hand around her waist and pulled.

Softly kissing, he worked his way over her jaw, up her cheek to her ear. So good. *So good.*

Finally, he reached her neck and nibbled her earlobe. "Let's slip out and go to my place."

Oh, how she missed him.

"Eh-hem!" Ro glided back into the room. "I thought you two broke up."

"Her timing always did suck." Frankie straightened and waggled his eyebrows. "We did. I'm working on her."

---

"I still can't believe you didn't tell me about Otis," Lucie said the following day when she and Joey walked up the Lutzes' driveway for Otis's afternoon visit. Only two more dogs after Otis and they were done.

The overcast day held the temperature in the fifties, and the cold from the driveway stones stabbed through the bottom of Lucie's sneakers. The whole day had been like this. Raw and damp. She wanted a hot shower and a cup of tea.

"Jeez," Joey said. "Drop it already. Frankie told me not to say anything. Take it up with your boyfriend."

Lucie halted and waited for Joey to do the same. He wore his typical tight-lipped expression that silently screamed boredom.

*Too bad.* "I've been dealing with these dognappings for a week. Until we finish examining all the accessories I've sold, if there's an issue, I need to know about it."

"Are you gonna keep busting my balls about this?"

"Pretty much, yes."

"Okay." Joey wrapped her in a headlock and gave her a noogie. "As long as I know."

*Moron.*

Two minutes later, Lucie had Otis leashed, and upon seeing Joey, the dog shot toward him nearly tearing off her arm.

"Don't jump," she yelled as the tape leash unraveled to its full eight feet. Otis did one of his gravity defying leaps into Joey's arms and knocked him back a full step.

"This dog is an animal," he said.

"He's a little high strung."

"A little?"

He plopped Otis to the ground. "Luce, I'm thinkin' Otis needs obedience training. I mean, are you walking him or is he walking you?"

On cue, Otis bounded to his favorite tree and Lucie planted her feet. With gritted teeth and a steel grip, she held the leash with both hands, waiting for the impact when the dog ran out of slack. "He's just spirited."

*Wham.* The leash jammed to a stop and so did Otis. Lucie's muscles strained and she shifted her weight back.

Joey snorted. "High-strung and spirited? Just say he's a pain in the ass."

As much as her brother tortured her, she laughed. Joey always spoke his mind. It might be verbal vomit, but he'd tell you. There were times, though, that his logic made sense.

Luckily, those times didn't come often. "Thanks for walking with me. Even if I moan about it, I am more comfortable having company."

He shrugged. "No sweat. You're my sister. I'll always take care of you. Besides, Dad would kill me if I didn't."

"Well, there you go."

"What?"

"Isn't it funny that no matter how old we are we're still afraid of him?"

"There's still a lot to be afraid of."

That wasn't the point, but she should have known better. Joey would never change. He would always allow their father's influence to guide him. Simple as that. Maybe he was happy that way. Did she have a right to question it? A soft humming noise caught in her ears while she watched Otis sniff around his favorite tree. "Go pee, Otis."

A car turned the corner, slowed, and Lucie's temples throbbed. When did a car inching along suddenly put her in a panicked state?

She watched them go by and caught a glimpse of the passenger. Didn't recognize him. Paranoid. That's what she was. "Onward ho, boys."

Otis made his way to the next tree and stopped. From behind, a car door slammed and they shifted to see a man running at them.

Joey slid in front of Lucie. "Again? These guys are starting to irritate me. Run, Luce. I got this."

The hammering at her temples should have blown a hole right through her skull. She gave the leash a tug. "Let's go, Otis."

He continued his sniffing as Joey charged the guy.

"Otis!" The dog lifted his head in question. "Let's go." Nothing. *Dammit.*

"Run, Luce," Joey hollered just before he tackled the would-be assailant. The two men rolled on the ground, punches flying, and Lucie jerked the leash.

Otis wouldn't move.

A hysterical bubble of laughter shot up her throat. The laughing could only be her sanity taking leave. She'd have to carry the dog—not an easy task. She bent low, scooped him into her arms and straightened. The tension in her back could have cracked her in two, but she focused on steadying the wiggling canine. "Stay still."

As usual, Otis wasn't listening. He was busy staring up at her and licking her chin while she half ran, half walked past her brawling brother and the attacker.

*Get to the Lutzes' garage.* Her quasi walk-run caused Otis to slip, but she hefted him against her chest. A stream of air exploded from her mouth. *Don't drop him. Get to the garage.*

She gave him another good boost to strengthen her hold and he arched his back to get loose. Then the licking started again. That big, wet tongue slapping across her cheek. She craned out of his reach.

"Otis, we have to get to the garage."

She continued the crazy gallop toward the house and, with quaking arms, set Otis down to punch in the garage code. She caught a glimpse of Joey hammering his fists into their attacker.

Once inside the garage, she smacked her fingers across

the button to close the door and ran into the house. She should call the police. Shouldn't she?

She ran to the front window and Otis, thinking it was playtime, leaped at her, his paws connecting with her butt and pushing her off balance.

"Off." She righted herself against the window frame and looked out.

The battle between Joey and the attacker wore on, the two men tearing up the perfection of the neighbor's sprouting green grass. Joey rolled to his feet and sent a kick to the guy's midsection. It looked so painful that Lucie jumped back from the window.

Then, a disheartening thought looped inside her. What if the guy Joey was beating to a pulp was some random person coming down the street? Maybe he wasn't interested in them at all. He could be a neighbor rushing home to an injured child.

The car that originally let the man off came around the corner. Two men bounded out. Okay. Not so random. She analyzed the men. One older, maybe mid-fifties. Gray hair, slicked back. Black slacks and a zip front jacket. The other, maybe around thirty, blond hair, huskier build, white track pants, red piping with the matching jacket.

"Joey!"

As if he could hear her.

She ran to the mudroom, flipped open the cabinet where Mrs. Lutz stored poop bags and seasonal items. The can of bug spray had gotten pushed to the back over the winter, but she snapped it up and sprinted to the front door. With Otis in a crazed barking frenzy, Lucie cracked the door an inch, blocked the dog from escaping and squeezed through.

Bug spray in hand, she charged the three men. "The police are on the way." A bluff, but the bad guys didn't know it. All they knew was, their friend lay at Joey's feet in la-la land.

The men tossed her a questioning glance and spun toward her. One laughed at her. *Laughed at her?*

That did it.

The sound of Otis howling from the safety of the house penetrated her mind and whipped like a live wire caught in a hurricane. Every inch of her tingled.

*I am so done with these jerks trying to take my dogs.*

She settled her finger on the nozzle of the bug repellent —one she knew caused substantial but temporary eye pain —and sent a blast into the first man's eyes. He flew backward and rubbed his eyes. *Yeah, go ahead, make it worse.* She turned left, saw guy number two reaching for her—*not a chance*—and gave him a shot to the eyes. He too became blinded and stepped backward.

From the house, Otis launched into another howling fit. "Ahhhh-wooooo!"

The men dragged their half-unconscious friend to the waiting car while Joey's mouth hurled a steady stream of curses. One thing about her brother, he never backed down. One of the men, his eyes nearly swelled shut, flipped them the bird.

"What?" Lucie waved the can of bug spray. "You want more of this?"

Apparently not. Their attackers jumped into the car, a white Chrysler 300, and Lucie craned her neck to see the license plate. No chance. The car peeled off, its tires squealing as it stormed the car-lined street.

Hopefully, they'd hit one of the city's world famous

potholes and blow a tire. She lost sight of the car and brought her attention to her brother, who dragged her by the elbow toward the house.

She pushed through the door, locked it behind them and, with the sudden crash of adrenaline, took note that Joey's eye and lip were streaming blood. "You're hurt."

"No, I'm not."

"You're bleeding."

"That's not hurt."

She gave him a once-over. His gray windbreaker was torn at the shoulder and his jeans, in addition to splattered mud stains, were blown out at the knees. What a mess. His battered eye was already turning purple.

Joey pulled his phone from the pocket of his jeans.

"Who're you calling?"

"Frankie."

"Why?"

"Because, now I'm mad." He held the phone to his ear while Lucie ran to the kitchen for paper towels.

"Come in the kitchen. There's no carpet there."

Having this whole crisis unfold where half the neighbors on the block could see was bad enough. She didn't need to get blood on Mrs. Lutz's carpet. That would require explaining.

*You see, Mrs. Lutz, dognappers are stealing my clients. Yes, as a matter of fact, one of them did try to get Otis. Twice. Why didn't I warn you that your beloved pet could be in danger? Well, I'm hoarding a stolen diamond, but have no idea where it came from.*

She waved Joey into the kitchen.

"Yeah, it's me," he said into his phone. "Call me ASAP. Got a problem."

"Sit." Lucie grabbed paper towels and ran them under

the faucet. Water splashed off her hands onto the black granite counter. She'd worry about cleaning up when they were done. She turned to Joey, who for some unknown reason remained standing. She waved her arms toward the nightmare of a kitchen chair.

The white upholstered chair was lovely, but fresh blood wouldn't mix well with this particular style.

How did she get to this place? All she ever wanted was to be an investment banker, and here she sat in her old boss's home while her brother fought off dognappers and bled on the pristine furniture.

"We need to clean you up. I have a first-aid kit in the car."

"First-aid kit. That's funny."

"Why?"

He shrugged. "You always have a plan."

And what was that supposed to mean? At least *one* of the Rizzo children should be a responsible adult. "There is nothing wrong with being prepared."

Joey threw his head down on the table and started snoring.

"Watch the blood. Mrs. Lutz will freak if we stain something."

She grabbed him by the hair and pulled his head up to find him grinning in a way that reminded her of every moment of torment he'd inflicted upon her.

She didn't have time to smack him around right now. Her schedule was so completely screwed. Plus, Otis still hadn't had his afternoon poop. That window only stayed open so long, and Lucie didn't want to risk him doing it in the house. She'd have to walk him until he pooped. That could take an hour.

An hour she didn't have.

"I need to clean that lip." She scrunched her nose and dabbed at Joey's lip while he sent a text.

He finally held up his hand. "Enough, Luce. The hovering is weird. If you weren't my sister, maybe it would be nice. Now it's...blech."

"I was trying to help."

"Don't be mad."

"I'm not mad." She stopped. "No. That's a lie. I am mad. I wanted to help you and you got nasty. To hell with you."

He laughed. "That's more like it."

"Ugh."

But he gave her a small grin and his eyes held a softness she wasn't accustomed to seeing. "Sorry."

Wow. Joey apologizing. A monumental occurrence. Maybe there was a human inside him after all. His phone rang and he glanced at the screen before punching the button.

"Here's the deal," he said without bothering to say hello. "Some guy—different guy this time—tried to grab Otis... Yeah, hold up."

He put the phone on speaker. "You there?"

"Luce," Frankie said, "are you okay?"

The sound of his voice gave her that instant sense of relief she'd known for years now and a gush of air escaped. Frankie brought sanity when insanity loomed. "I'm okay. Joey is bleeding though."

"He'll live."

"I shot bug spray in their eyes."

"You did?"

"I had to do something. There were three of them."

"Holy hell," Frankie said. "Luce, you have to vary your pattern. Please."

He knew her well enough to know she liked routine.

"These dogs have a schedule, Frankie. I can't just change it. It'll confuse them. Poor Otis is probably freaking out right now because I came running back in here with him and he hasn't pooped yet. Do you know what that can do to a dog?"

"He'll live, too."

Clearly, Frankie didn't give a lick about Otis's mental health.

"You don't understand."

"No. I understand. I *understand* that you are going to get hurt. I *understand* that we need to do something to throw these people a curve. I *understand* that you want to do your job."

"Hey," she said.

"Sorry," Frankie said. "But, please, change your pattern. Each day, change it up again."

Joey tilted his head. "He's right."

"Of course he's right. There's just nothing I can do about it. I have a schedule to keep. I have the routes mapped out to maximize my time. If I start messing with it, I won't get all the walks in."

"I don't know what to tell you," Frankie said in his holier-than-thou voice. She wanted to wallop him. Just smack him one.

Joey looked down at his phone and spoke directly to Frankie. "What if we get a couple of the guys from my father's crew to help out?"

No wonder he wouldn't look at her. "Are you insane?"

"Knew she'd say that," Frankie said.

"How could they possibly help?"

Joey made a huffing noise like she was a complete idiot. "A show of manpower. If they see five guys around you, they'll go away."

Lunacy. Apparently, her brother had missed the last ten years of her hating their father's lifestyle. That would be the only explanation for him to suggest such a ludicrous plan. She held up a finger. "Even if I liked that idea, there is no way I'd do it, because one of them is bound to tell Dad, and I don't need him hassling me. He's already on me because my Notre Dame education is supposedly being *wasted* on the dogs."

"Plus," Frankie began, "I promised him she wouldn't get hurt. Enlisting his guys would make him wonder. I don't want your father pissed at me."

Joey nodded. "How about *your* dad's crew? Will they keep their mouths shut?"

"No," she said. "I don't like this plan."

Particularly because she wasn't convinced this didn't have something to do with her father's business and the people that worked for him. She knew her father would never put her in direct danger. He had always tried to shield her from the life by not discussing it in front of her. No, if this had something to do with her father, he didn't know about it. The men that worked for him, though? She had no idea.

"I can't count on them keeping quiet," Frankie said. "They're a bunch of old ladies."

"We are not enlisting anyone's help," Lucie said.

Frankie stayed quiet. Too quiet. When he went dark like that, it meant he wanted her to think he was agreeing by not disagreeing.

"Whatever you're thinking, Frankie, forget it."

"Yes, dear."

Joey laughed.

She smacked his arm. "Shut up."

"I gotta go," Frankie said. "Luce, I'll call you later and we'll talk about it."

She rubbed her fingers across her forehead hoping to make the pounding stop. "All right. We have to finish Otis's walk anyway."

"*What?*" Frankie said.

"Don't start. I'm being paid to walk these dogs. Poor Otis's back teeth are floating he has to pee so badly. He needs to be walked."

"Joey, don't you let her walk that dog."

This was it. Joey would side with Frankie. He always did. She bit down on her bottom lip.

"I'll take care of it." Joey hung up.

The best course of action was to start talking first. "I have to get Otis walked. I'll do it with you or without you. I don't care. This is my job and the Lutz's have helped me. I owe them."

Joey held up his big hand, and she noticed blood staining his palm. "Chill. You'll get Princess Puff-Puff walked."

Hold on. Did he just say what she thought he said? "Huh?"

"Can we get through the yard to the other block?"

Seriously? He'd break ranks with Frankie and walk the dog with her? A roar of affection for her degenerate gambler brother swarmed. He was siding with *her.*

"The backyard isn't fenced. We can cut through there. Do you think it's safe?"

"I have no idea, but your threat of calling the cops probably chased them off for now. If we take a different route, you can get Puff-Puff's walk in and finish the other dogs."

"You need to get that lip looked at."

"Nag, nag," Joey said. "Can we get this damn dog

walked? I got my own business to run and these dogs are costing me."

Lucie nodded. Suddenly, she and Joey were a team. No matter how odd it seemed, she'd get her job done. And right now, that's all she wanted.

## 8

---

Lucie made Joey load the merchandise for the Sammy Spaniel trunk show into Ro's Escalade and winced when he threw the last box of collars.

"For God's sake, Joey. The rhinestones will be all over the bottom of the box."

He shrugged. "Then load it yourself."

Ro stepped off the front porch in a murderous red sheath and matching coat. "Stifle it. Let's get moving. The traffic on the Kennedy is filthy."

"By the way," Lucie said. "You look fabulous. A real professional."

After stalking by, Joey turned to check out Ro's backside. He stared for a second, looked up at the sky and blew out a breath. Typical. Lucie peeked at her black slacks and gray cardigan. An hour ago, she thought she looked darn good. Next to Ro? Might as well be homeless.

"Ro, I need your help."

"Anything for you, sister. You know I've got your back."

"Frankie and I are going on a date tomorrow—"

"I thought you broke up."

"We did. We're starting over."

"Again?"

"Har-har. I need a change. Will you make me beautiful?"

Ro clucked her tongue. "You're already beautiful."

"I'm not a man-killer. I don't want people wondering why Frankie is with me."

Ro linked her arm with Lucie's and walked toward the car. "Anyone that wonders is an idiot and doesn't deserve your time."

Good response. *Excellent* response. "Blah, blah. I still want to feel beautiful next to him. Help me step out of banker mode into something sexy."

Ro rolled her bottom lip out. "You've got the tits for it."

Lucie couldn't control the laugh. Ro, like Joey, simply said what was on her mind. "You'll help me?"

"Of course. Even if you've only given me a day, this is my specialty. I'm great under pressure."

Yes, indeed. "Am I crazy, Ro?"

"Not in the least. You're in a rut. Why shouldn't you want a change?"

"Not that. Dating Frankie. We've broken up and gotten back together so many times, I'm not sure what we're doing anymore."

Ro stopped next to the driver's side door of the Escalade and turned to Lucie. "You love him. You got lucky because the sex is hot *and* he's dependable."

That was certainly all true. "Well, sure."

"Love like that is all-consuming. The extra benefit with Frankie is you never have to worry about him screwing around, or walking out when you need him. Finding both at once is special."

Lucie didn't understand. There hadn't been any men in her life that came close to what Frankie meant to her. Wasn't it always this way when two people loved each other? "So, I'm crazy if I let it go?"

Ro tilted her head. "Didn't say that. I'm saying you need to be aware of what you're risking. Most people don't get an inferno of passion *and* the security."

A snaking feeling curled inside and whispered that she and Ro were about to discuss something they, unbelievably, had never explored. "Did you?"

*Please say yes. Let me believe in happily ever after.*

Ro smiled and it was one of those smiles that carried the edge of regret. "Not at the same time."

Lucie took a tiny step back.

"Don't get me wrong," Ro said. "Tommy is the guy I want to spend my life with. He's a man I know I can come home to and he'll take care of me. He'll be kind and respectful and that's what I need. At some point, the security became more important than the constant adrenaline rush. The adrenaline guy tore me to shreds, and I'd had enough of that."

Lucie must have been brain-fried, because for the life of her, she couldn't think of a damn thing to say. There had been a lot of men in Ro's life, and Lucie flipped through her mental file trying to determine who the shredder was.

"You chose security?"

"Yep. And I don't regret it. Not for one second. I'm happy with good sex and stability. It beats off-the-charts sex and no stability."

The damn mental file in Lucie's head was empty. Not even a hint. "Who shredded you?"

Ro glanced toward the house. Probably checking on Joey Big Ears. "I never told you."

No. And Lucie couldn't believe it. Weren't they best friends? She thought so, and the ache in her chest couldn't be ignored. Why the secrets?

"I had good reason."

"What was it?"

Ro shifted her gaze before blowing out a breath.

*God, please don't let it be Frankie.* If it was Frankie, Lucie would...she'd...she'd...hell, she didn't know what she'd do, but vomiting could be at the top of the list. Right below that would be pulling a Lorena Bobbitt on Frankie and tearing out Ro's hair. Brutal punishment. For both of them.

"Joey," the soon-to-be-hairless one said.

Tension left Lucie like a blown tire. *Thank you.* "My brother Joey?" Lucie's gaze shot to the front door. No sign of her brother. Good. She might have to kill him.

Ro stared up at the sky, ran her gloved hand down the long column of her neck and breathed deep. Ro looking wistful. Over Joey. Go figure.

"Yep. You were in graduate school. We were together for all of two months. It was two months of exquisite torture."

"What happened?"

"Insanity is what happened. We got together one night. Every night after that became a mad rush to get into bed. He'd show up, we'd find a place to go, have crazy hot sex and do it all over again the next day. After eight weeks, I needed more. I wanted to go to the movies or to dinner, and all he wanted was to hang out with his friends."

"That shithead." Lucie's voice was louder than she'd anticipated and she slapped her hand over her mouth.

Ro laughed. "Nah. He cared about me. I saw it in how affectionate he was. Even when the sex was a little adventurous, there was always trust. But that can't sustain a relationship. I needed more. I needed him to grow up. Not right then, but eventually, and I was smart enough to know that Joey would always be a wildcard." She stared back at the house.

Joey and Ro? Adventurous sex? Definite *ick* factor. And yet, her obnoxious brother kept this from her. From everyone, really, otherwise Lucie would have heard about it.

"And I was right. Can you picture me married to your brother? One of us would be dead."

Igniting Lucie's temper had become a favorite pastime for Joey, but he had never once made a crude remark about her best friend. "Wow."

"Don't be mad, Luce. Joey and I were okay with it, and when you came home, we didn't want anything to change. It nearly killed me for a while because every time I came over, all I wanted was to curl into that big body of his. My heart was gutted."

Gutted.

Joey? *Ick.*

"And then you met Tommy?"

Ro smiled at the mention of her husband. "Yep. He saved me. He's everything I wanted Joey to be, but without the drama. I wouldn't change anything. That's me though. You have to know what you want. If Frankie is the hot sex guy *and* the stability guy, then you've hit the mother of all jackpots."

Doubting that was a waste of time. Frankie affected her in ways she'd never experienced. She thought about the implosion inside when his hands slid over her skin, or when he talked dirty in her ear. The idea of that happening with anyone else seemed impossible. She didn't want it with anyone else.

But they needed different things.

Lucie glanced at the row of houses packed into the block and the cars parked bumper-to-bumper on the street. Two houses down, Mrs. Frasier had put her garbage can in the vacant spot to save it for her son, who worked odd hours, and nobody had moved it. This neighborhood had a flow to it, an unspoken set of rules no one dared to break.

Frankie wanted this neighborhood. She didn't.

"I can't let go of him," Lucie said.

"If it's because you love him, then it's a start. But don't hang on to him because it's comfortable. You both deserve better."

"It's more than comfort. When I think about my life in five years, I'm with him. I just don't know how to get there."

"Maybe you should stop thinking and just let it be."

Could she do that? Not chart out her life? All she'd done for the past ten years was set a course and follow it. She had wanted a respectable job—got that—and to get out of Franklin—got that. And yet, years later, all that planning had simply returned her to the place she'd started.

She closed her eyes and absorbed the fact that planning wouldn't guarantee her what she wanted.

"Luce," Ro finally said. "Give yourself a break and stop analyzing. Let's get you some smoking hot clothes and drive Frankie crazy."

An already shaky budget flashed into Lucie's mind. "I can't spend a lot."

"We'll go see a friend of mine. He'll give us a good price."

"His stuff didn't fall off the truck, did it?" All she needed was a stolen dress to go with the diamond.

Ro shrugged. "I don't think so, but you never know."

Dealing with anything stolen would put Lucie over the edge and she didn't want to risk it. "After the trunk show, let's go to Macy's. We'll find something there."

———

THE RIDE DOWNTOWN TO SAMMY SPANIEL TOOK LONGER THAN

they had hoped and a steady drip of sweat wormed along Lucie's spine. Damned Kennedy construction. Would it ever stop? Being late on the first day would hardly be a good start to a business relationship. It was so not Lucie's style.

They arrived at the store with only fifteen minutes to spare before opening. Thankfully, Jeanette had cleared a corner for them and had already set up a long, rectangular table.

Ro whipped out a white tablecloth and spread it on the table. The banner with the newly made Coco Barknell logo came next, and she hung it over the front of the table. They had a logo. A cute one with a winking poodle wearing a diamond collar. How incredibly sassy.

*Coco Barknell.*

"You like?" Ro asked.

Lucie's throat swelled. "You did great, Ro."

"Thanks. I think I'm pretty good at this doggie thing. We're a good team."

"I guess we'll know after today if we can make this a side business or not."

Ro waved her off. "Forget side business. I'm thinking Fortune 500."

"That'll be the day."

Ro handed her an empty box. "You'll see."

But Lucie wasn't sure she wanted to see. As a banker, she wanted to see mergers and acquisitions, initial public offerings and credit facilities. *That's* what she wanted to see.

The two of them worked in tandem with Lucie unloading and Ro artfully arranging the coats, collars and leashes on the table. Ro had even picked up steel necklace stands to display some of the collars. A nice touch.

By the time they were done, an inviting array of collars and coats had been arranged on the table. Lucie smiled at

Ro and their eyes met for a few seconds. They might actually pull this off.

"What do you think?" Lucie asked.

"I think it's amazing."

Lucie leaned closer and whispered. "You checked all these stones, right? None of them are real?"

"All checked. We're good."

That was positive news. So far, they'd checked all the stones in Lucie's stash, plus the items she had collected from her clients. No diamonds.

Jeanette, in what Lucie had come to realize were trademark second-skin jeans, chose that moment to wander by. Ro gave her a long once-over. Jeanette returned the favor.

"How are we doing, ladies?" Jeanette asked after she and Ro finished mentally dissecting each other.

"We're ready," Lucie said.

After a quick perusal of the table, Jeanette picked up a coat to study the stitching. "I must say, these are exceptional. You're an excellent seamstress."

"My mother did that one. And yes, she is an excellent seamstress."

The bells on the entry door jangled, and a woman with a droopy-lidded dog came in. The dog had a few—more like ten—extra pounds on him, and Lucie felt sure they had nothing that would fit him. *Shoot.* Mental note: plus-sized dog coats.

The woman stopped at the table and Ro dove in, letting her know they custom made all the pieces and, yes, of course, they could make something for Muffy. Muffy? Frankie would have a heart attack over the injustice of naming that dog Muffy.

The bells jangled again and Lucie, letting Ro handle

Muffy the fluffy, turned to see the Falcones and Jimmy Two-Toes entering the store. *Good God.*

She planted a big-butt smile on her face and wandered over. "Hi, Mr. and Mrs. Falcone." She never called them by their first names like Frankie did with her parents. She didn't have that comfort level and wasn't sure she minded. "Hi, Jimmy."

"Hello, Lucie," Mrs. Falcone said. "Frankie told us about your trunk show and we thought we would offer our support."

Mr. Falcone waved toward the table. "Giovanna, look at this stuff. Unbelievable."

"Ho!" Jimmy said. "You got talent, kid."

Frankie's mom nodded. "These collars are wonderful. The craftsmanship is lovely."

"Welcome," Jeanette said, making a beeline for her potential customers. Frankie's father turned, and his eyes went straight for Jeanette's chest. *The apple didn't fall far from this tree.*

Mrs. Falcone's instincts must have roared to the front of her brain because she pressed her lips together and turned her attention to a zebra print coat. Mr. Falcone though, he wasn't going *anywhere*. Neither was Jimmy. Jimmy looked as if he wanted to plow head first into Jeanette's cleavage.

"This emerald collar is lovely." Mrs. Falcone pretended to ignore her husband and his sudden interest in Jeanette, but Lucie knew better.

"Thank you. Roseanne helped me with that one. She has a flair for this."

"I'll take it."

Lucie gasped. "You don't have a dog."

Mrs. Falcone's eyes zeroed in on her husband, who reluctantly released his gaze from Jeanette's chest when she went toward the back of the store with Jimmy. "I'll take the emerald *and* the sapphire one. I'll give them to my girl-friends for their dogs."

Hell's bells. That was two hundred and fifty dollars' worth of collars for a woman who didn't own a dog. This was about pissing off Mr. Falcone. He'd humiliated his wife by becoming enamored with Jeanette's boobs. Now he would pay. Literally.

"Thank you, Mrs. Falcone. This is most generous of you."

"We're practically family." She grabbed a few business cards. "I'll take a couple of your cards to put with the collars. My friends may want more and I'd rather they work directly with you."

Meaning Jeanette wouldn't get one red cent. "Certainly. I'd be happy to design something for them."

Frankie's father stepped up and his wife shoved the collars into his chest. "Pay for these."

With that, she left the store.

Rather than send Mr. Falcone back into Jeanette's vortex, Lucie took the collars from him. "I'll get these rung up for you. Cash or credit?"

"How much are they?"

"A hundred twenty-five each."

His jaw flopped open. Served him right. He pulled a money clip from his pocket and peeled off three hundred-dollar bills.

After ringing up the merchandise, Lucie returned to Mr. Falcone and found him eyeing a couple of coats.

"These are something else, Lucie."

He set the coats down and took the bag from her. "Thank you. I appreciate the purchase."

"Happy to do it." He took a final long look at the table.

"Is there something else I can show you?"

He laughed. "Nah. If I didn't see my wife buy this stuff, I wouldn't have believed people spend this much on dogs. Good for you." Turning toward the back of the store, he yelled, "Jimmy, we're going."

Jimmy shot from behind a shelf loaded with dog food and scurried by her.

"Take care, Lucie."

Ro stepped behind the table and adjusted the coats Mr. Falcone had moved. "That was interesting,"

"No kidding."

"I snuck back to where Jimmy and Jeanette were. They're having dinner together Sunday night."

"You snooped?"

"Sure. Did you know she lives above the store?"

"Really?"

"I heard her tell him. You get to her apartment from the back of the building."

"Makes for a short commute, I guess."

"Plus, she could always run down here and get Jimmy a snack, dog that he is."

Lucie laughed. Why not? Jimmy *was* a dog. A dirty, rotten one. Putting aside what he did for a living, he had a wife.

Some women could put up with it. Not Lucie. She would make her own way in the world.

# 9

---

Lucie questioned her own sanity when Ro came to the Rizzos' house to do her magic with Lucie's hair and makeup for the big date. Within minutes of Ro's arrival, using the force of a bludgeoning, she manipulated Lucie's shoulder-length hair around barrel-sized plastic rollers. Ah, the suffering of a woman trying to "fluff" her hair.

Thanks to the ancient portable radio on the shelf above her head, Lucie tapped her foot to Madonna as Ro applied layer upon layer of brown eye shadow in a multitude of hues. Espresso liquid liner came next, along with gobs of jet-black mascara. Lucie tried not to blink as Ro perfected what she called the smokey look.

Lucie called it a lot of stinking work and hoped it didn't leave her looking like a crack whore.

"Let's get you into the dress and I'll do your hair. You're almost there, kiddo."

"Glory be. I'm not made for all this primping. Who has this kind of time?"

"You make the time, babycakes. You think I roll out of bed looking like this?" Ro marched across the hall to Lucie's bedroom, her head high and her long hair flying behind her.

Footsteps, or perhaps they were bombs dropping, came from the end of the hallway. Joey emerging from his lair.

"I need the john."

"We'll be done in ten minutes. If you can't wait, use the yard."

Lucie laughed. Good old Ro knew just how to deal with men.

A second later, Ro reentered the bathroom. "Here's the bra. This baby will keep the girls in place."

Lucie held the contraption in front of her. "If I can figure out how to put it on."

Ro pointed to the straps hanging from the bottom of the bra. "These wrap around your waist. Then this top strap buckles around your neck."

Lucie focused hard.

"Forget it. Strip and I'll put it on you."

"Ew. No." Lucie snatched the bra. "I have an MBA. I can figure it out. Just turn around while I do it."

Jeez, this was a lot of work. Frankie had better appreciate it. And if he even thought he was getting her out of this bra once she got it on, he'd better think again.

Joey's iron fist smacked against the door, and Lucie and Ro both jumped.

Ro smacked her open palm against the door. "Don't make me open this."

"Yeah," Lucie yelled.

"Five more minutes and I'm busting this door down to take a piss. You can watch if you want."

"Won't that be exciting," Ro shot back.

"Five minutes."

Lucie, with the contraption of a bra in place, slipped on her robe. "Keep your drawers on. We're done."

She swung the door open and Joey stepped back to let them pass.

"Finally," he said.

Ro blew him a kiss when they marched by.

"He's such an idiot," Lucie said, closing her bedroom door behind them. "But there are times, like when he helps me with the dogs, that he's so nice. That's the brother I want. The dog walking one."

"And I want to be Angelina Jolie. Let's not count on either. Time to get you dressed."

Ten minutes later, after a toxic level of hairspray had been applied to Lucie's coif, Ro waved toward the mirror. "Take a look."

Lucie rose from the bed, took a second to balance on the high-heeled silver sandals. If she tumbled down the stairs in these stilts, at least she'd have a hairspray crash helmet to absorb the impact.

She stepped over to the closed door where the full body mirror hung, but didn't look into it. A sudden fear gripped her. What if after all the shopping and primping, she hated the image? What if Frankie hated it? It would be her luck that her one attempt to be more than plain old Lucie would be a disaster.

No. This would be good. She reached deep into herself and thought about all the years she and Ro had been friends, and realized Ro wouldn't let her down.

"Luce, just look. It's good. I promise."

Lucie glanced up and saw a woman in a red halter dress.

A woman whose body she barely recognized and whose hair curled wildly around her face. She grinned at herself, at the woman who had become a man-killer.

The sound of the doorbell carried from the first floor. Frankie.

Lucie grinned. "He rang the bell. Like a real date. How sweet is that?"

"Charm boy is working it." Ro held the door open for her. "This is your night. Enjoy it. Think about all the reasons you love him. Not the ones that tear you apart."

---

AFTER DINNER, WHILE WAITING FOR ONE OF THE TWO VALETS to chase down the car, Frankie wandered to the garbage can on the corner to toss something and Lucie admired the modern minimalism of his navy suit. He wore a pressed white dress shirt, sans tie and she realized, no matter what he wore, his clothing choices added to his no-nonsense persona.

She closed her eyes, tilted her head back and breathed in the cool air. The sounds of cars speeding through the intersection, pedestrians chatting and the *click-click-click* of a woman's high-heels surrounded her. She loved this city.

Feeling something tickle up her spine, she opened her eyes and caught the second valet staring at her. Really staring. Then the guy gave her the once over and nodded.

She had just scored the coveted double take and the feeling became something bright and warm and so incredibly luscious.

This deserved something special. What the hell, she offered up a little finger wave.

Frankie returned wearing a landslide of a grin. "I turn my back for one second and you're flirting?"

"I couldn't help it. Did you see the way he looked at me... like he wanted to lick something off me? How incredibly exciting."

But Frankie didn't look too excited. Not with the whole teeth-gritting thing going on. "You think?"

She laughed. "I *know*. This is a proud moment."

Frankie nuzzled her neck. "I could make that licking thing happen. The Hyatt is right around the corner."

*Oh, my.* With a tiny shift of her head, his warm breath crossed her cheek and she moved closer to feel the heat and softness of his lips against her. She reached up, glided her fingers over his perfect cheekbone.

Her Frankie.

Enjoying the familiarity of his arm sliding around her, she kissed him, lingered there, loving the feel of him, and then slowly backed away. "You can lick something off me later. I don't want to mess up the dress before we go dancing."

"Oh, I won't mess up the dress. That I can promise. And I'd still take you dancing." He moved closer, right up to her ear. "Come on, Luce, we'll get a room and stay downtown tonight."

They had no clothes or toothbrushes and he wanted to do a sleepover? "We aren't prepared for an overnighter."

"So what? I'll buy us a couple of toothbrushes—maybe some chocolate syrup for that licking thing—and we'll do the walk of shame in the morning. Only, I won't be feeling shameful."

She thought about it; let the idea take shape. The bad girl. The dirty stay-out.

"Yes," she said, and he smiled like a gold medalist. "You're still taking me dancing though."

"Anywhere you want to go."

"Frankie?"

"What?"

She had to ask. "Do you like me better dressed like this?"

"No."

All this work and he didn't like it? Yikes. "You're not even going to think about it?"

He shook his head. "Don't need to."

Hiding her disappointment didn't come easy, but she plastered a smile on her face and held it until it set.

"Luce, I want you any way I can get you. I *love* this look on you. It's sexy and outrageous and a huge turn-on. So, if you want to do this, great, but I don't like it better. I love you being you. If this is a side of you, then I'm all over it."

She could simply be her and it didn't matter to him. What a gift. What a catch. "Thank you."

And yet, for all the happiness he gave her, she wanted more. She wanted him to leave his home so they wouldn't always be known as mob kids. That's all Franklin, Illinois saw in them. She wanted more.

Frankie ran the pad of his thumb across her bottom lip then kissed the same spot. "You know what I'm thinking?"

"What?" Not that she cared at the moment.

"I'm thinking we should do this date thing again next Saturday night."

Lucie did the math. "That's the fourth Saturday of the month."

"Do you need to check your calendar?" He kissed her again. "Maybe you have another date?"

This was unbelievable. Shocked cold, she pushed back

and waited for the moment he would realize what he'd just done. One, two, three...nothing.

"What?" he asked.

"You go to your parents' on the fourth Saturday of the month."

He nodded. "Normally. Next Saturday though, I think I'd like to take a hot brunette on a date. Of course, if you don't want to go, I'll just go to my parents' and tell them you blew me off."

Telling his Frankie-can-do-no-wrong parents something like that would make them furious. "You wouldn't dare."

The Frankie Factor grin rocketed across his face. "You know I would."

Lucie laughed her horror. "That's blackmail."

"Persuasion."

"Blackmail!"

He shrugged.

Were they truly joking about this? After it had been such an issue between them? Or was he simply trying to please her. "You're just doing this because you think it'll make me happy."

Finally, the grin faded and he blew out a breath. "Luce, I'm trying here. You're always on me about taking your side. Now I'm doing it and you're still on me. You wanted me to compromise. I'm doing it."

Yes, he was. And she sounded like a woman who was never happy. She grabbed the edge of his suit jacket and pulled him tight against her. "You're right. I'm sorry. I'd love a Saturday date."

He pulled back from the hug. "Maybe this dating thing is what we need. We've never done it before."

"I think I'll like it. We'll start over. Take day trips and

talk. Not worry about our families. They won't be the tie that binds us."

Frankie did a clipping action with his two fingers.

"What's that?"

"The cutting of the ties that bind."

Within fifteen minutes, Frankie shoved her through the hotel room door. A fierce, buzzing energy blazed low in her belly and she realized she loved sneaking around like a couple of high school kids. Every flipping second of it.

Having never been the bad girl, this little romp *screamed* sinner. Particularly when Frankie flattened her against the door and hiked her dress up, his long fingers frying her skin. She drew a hissing breath and closed her eyes. How long she'd been without him.

*Don't stop.* Please don't stop.

He bent low, slipped his fingers under the edge of her underwear and...yanked.

Holy moly.

The damned things only made it as far as her thighs, though.

Frankie laughed. "Damn. Thought I had that."

"Try again, fella."

On the second try, they hit her knees and he slid them off her. Were they really going to have sex against the back of a hotel room door? Where millions of strangers did the same thing?

God, she hoped so.

Frankie slid his hands up her thighs and over her boney hips, and the inferno in her stomach spread to her legs. Totally crazy—the lust she still had for him.

He trailed frantic kisses over her neck. "Are you okay with this?"

Locking one leg around him, she pulled him tighter.

"I guess that was a yes."

He unzipped his fly, boosted her against the door and she wrapped her other leg around him, ready for that moment, that first press of him against her that she'd memorized from the thousands of times they'd made love.

He entered her with the quick self-assuredness that Lucie adored about him. Frankie knew his talents, and pleasing a woman ranked high. Her breath hitched and she let out a long moan. It had been too long since she felt this need for him. This want for more. This passion.

When he pulled back, she breathed in, waiting for the next slow slide when her backside would bump against the door. How had she ever believed she could live without him? Yes, she could be anything with Frankie. He'd never judge her. Pity her. Patronize her.

"I love you," she said, invading his mouth, nipping at his lips. The ferocious hunger tore into her and she pumped her hips, needing him deeper and deeper still, while her world spun in a glorious whirl and she shook her head, fighting off the explosion, wanting it to last. But he knew her. Knew the rhythm of her body. Knew the magic spot that would undo her. He hitched her a little higher and—*boom*—sent her over the edge, tumbling, tumbling, tumbling until the cry trapped in her body broke free.

His body stiffened and he grunted before collapsing against her. "Love...you...too."

"Easy in there," someone cracked from the hallway.

She popped her eyes open, stared at Frankie and burst out laughing. They stood there, her back plastered to the door with him still inside her and breathing heavy.

"You're destroying me tonight," he said.

The words caught in her brain. She wanted to destroy him. "Good."

"I might die, but I'll go with a smile on my face."

He stepped back and an instant chill slammed against her. Nothing unusual. Every time he left her, the cold came. He pulled up his pants, grabbed her panties off the floor and handed them over before reaching around the bathroom wall to flip on the light. "It's all yours."

"Thanks," she said. "And lucky me, I didn't have to take my bra off."

## 10

——————

Late Monday afternoon, Lucie finished with Fannie and Josie and dropped them at home before heading to Sammy Spaniel's to retrieve her share of the trunk show sales.

Of course, to celebrate a day without dognappings, she and Frankie ducked into the alley next to the Bernard's for a make-out session before he left for work.

That Frankie.

That tongue.

At certain times, that was all she needed to smooth her edges. They argued a bit over his leaving her alone, but she reasoned the dogs were the targets. As long as she didn't have a dog with her, she'd be safe. Besides, her ongoing investigation of the items she had sold hadn't produced any other diamonds. She'd have to keep looking.

Lucie made quick work of getting to Sammy's to pick up her check. From there, she'd take a cab to the Lutzes' to retrieve her car. Frankie had been reduced to taking the train home from work every night so she wouldn't drive into the city alone in the morning. It seemed like overkill to her, but spending time with him would never be a bother.

She pushed through the door at Sammy's and the doggie bells on the door jangled.

Jeanette stood along the sidewall restocking coats and collars. An open box sat on the floor next to her. She wore her typical dark jeans paired with a wrap sweater that showed off her chest. No shock there. Her hair was pulled away from her face and when she looked up, her eyes carried extra luggage under them.

"Hi, Lucie." Jeanette's voice didn't have its usual bubbly excitement and her questioning stare forced Lucie to check her mental calendar.

Yep. Monday. "You told me to stop by and we'd settle up from the trunk show." Jeanette pressed her fingers to her forehead. *Uh-oh.* "Are you okay?"

Jeanette nudged the box on the floor and stepped toward Lucie. "The store was robbed last night."

Robbed. Oh, no. "I'm so sorry. Were you here when it happened?"

"No. I was out with Jimmy. After he dropped me off, I came down to do my orders and the place was a mess."

"What about your alarm?"

Jeanette shook her head. "They cut a hole through the second floor window and unlocked it. I only have glass-break sensors up there. They must have carried everything through the window."

Lucie glanced around the store, but every collar, leash and shelf item seemed to be in its rightful place. Jeanette must have been up all night. "Well, it looks like you have everything organized."

"Yes. I had back stock and got right to it after the police finished. If the store isn't open, I don't make money."

"What was missing?"

"Mostly cash. I usually do my deposit on Mondays after the busy weekend."

"Ah, Jeanette. That stinks. Do the police have any leads?"

"Who knows? They fingerprinted all over, but so many people come through here, they didn't seem too hopeful. Maybe they'll get a print from the register."

Lucie nodded. There would be no way she could take a check from her today. Not after being robbed. "Forget about the check. We'll settle up at the end of the week."

"Are you sure?"

Lucie nodded. "Absolutely. Can I help you? I'm done with the walks so I could help if you need to do orders or something."

"I appreciate that, but I have it under control. Besides, you may not want to stay here when I tell you the rest."

Good God. "What?"

"I lost mostly cash, but a lot of my high-end stuff was stolen. They took all the wooden dog feeders, the oversized beds..." Jeanette held her hand to her forehead again. "Some of the coats and collars are gone. I'm sorry, Lucie. They took everything left from your trunk show."

Suddenly, this random robbery didn't seem so random. "Everything?"

"I'm so sorry. I'll pay you for them. My insurance should cover it. I feel horrible."

Insurance. Right. Lucie would still earn money, but that wasn't the damned point. What a nightmare. Could the diamond thief have robbed Jeanette's store to get to Lucie's items?

A screeching sound in her brain made her a little woozy. She propped a steadying hand against the wall.

"Lucie?"

It was her fault. Should she tell Jeanette? She wanted to, but what did she really know? Nothing. And trying to explain something she herself didn't understand would be impossible.

She needed to get out of here. Get her thoughts together. She should have followed her instincts and not put any merchandise in this store. Instead, she let Frankie, with all his Fortune 500 Coco Barknell crap convince her. She *should* have done it her way.

Lucie said goodbye to Jeanette and ran to the corner for a cab. No luck. *Dammit.*

She tore down the street and cut over one block to Sanford's, a local hot spot, where she easily found a cab. She pulled her phone and dialed Frankie's cell.

"Hey," he said. "I just got to the office. What's up?"

"Can you meet me in the lobby in ten minutes?"

"Here?"

The pounding in Lucie's head traveled to her eyes. "Yes."

"What's wrong?"

"Jeanette's store was robbed. My accessories are gone."

"Son of a bitch."

Eight minutes later, Lucie stormed through the revolving door into the cavernous lobby of the *Herald* and found Frankie standing next to the security desk where a guard checked in a visitor. Frankie waved her toward the windows and a modicum of privacy. Her sneakers squeaked against the marble floors and the guard and lone visitor tossed her a look.

"I feel like I'm getting nowhere. Ro has gone through every stone in my stock and hasn't found any other diamonds, which means the thief still thinks the diamond we found is on one of my coats. Clearly, the warnings our fathers put out are not helping. We have to figure out who is doing this. Waiting for another dognapping so we can capture the thief has failed."

Frankie pulled her into him and squeezed. He was as lost as she was.

"I've had it, Frankie."

He pushed back and eyed her with that focus he reserved for split-finger fastballs. "Have you finished collecting the stuff you've sold?"

"I'm working on it. It's not easy getting all that stuff back."

"I know."

"Jeanette being robbed just days after my stuff landed in her store was not a coincidence. You have to know that. I'm responsible for what happened to that woman. And don't give me any of your can-do attitude crap. I need to do something. Fast."

"I know. We'll figure this out."

There it was. The can-do attitude. He simply couldn't help it. She let the sound of his voice settle her quaking nerves. He always provided the calm in her storm.

"It's crazy, Frankie. The dogs being dognapped, Jeanette's store being robbed. It has to stop."

"Yeah, it does." He glanced at his watch. "I gotta get back upstairs, but I'll get a couple of the guys from my father's crew to help out."

"Are you insane?"

"Knew you'd say that."

"How could they possibly help?"

"If the dognappers see five guys around you, they'll go away."

She held up a finger. "Even if I liked that idea, there is no way I'd do it. One of them is bound to tell my father, and I don't need him hassling me."

Obviously fed up, Frankie squeezed his fingers over his forehead, his nails turning red from the pressure. Lucie filled the gap of silence. "And I'm not convinced this doesn't have something to do with my father's business or the people who work for him."

"Your father wouldn't put you in direct danger."

Yes, she believed that, but she didn't trust the people working for him. "We are not enlisting anyone's help."

Frankie stayed quiet. Too quiet.

"Whatever you're thinking, forget it."

He grinned. "Yes, dear." His phone rang and he checked the screen. "It's my editor. I gotta go. I'll call you later and we'll talk about it. For now, please, go straight home and stay put."

After dropping a quick kiss on her lips, he took off toward the elevator.

Lucie turned toward the revolving door. She'd stay put, but she wouldn't be idle. Time to show these dognappers what she was made of.

———

THAT EVENING, TIRED OF FEELING HELPLESS OVER THE dognappings and non-random robbery at Sammy Spaniel, Lucie devised a plan. That plan included pepper spray and a stun gun. She had a vision of herself dressed as Wonder Woman—God help her giant boobs in that outfit—zapping the you-know-what out of any man trying to steal one of her dogs.

"Wonder Womaaannnnnn!" Lucie sang as she planted herself at her makeshift desk and booted up her laptop. The whirring subsided and she quickly went to her search engine and typed in 'stun gun'. She would work on the pepper spray next.

Taking this step was bold and who knew if she had the nerve to actually use either of these devices; but she'd carry them just in case.

Once the purchase was made with overnight delivery, Lucie checked pepper spray and stun gun off her to-do list. Next up, she'd have to start varying walks. No sense making it easy for the bad guys to find her. For this project, she would need the expanse of the dining room table. She scooped up her laptop, grabbed her Chicago street map and headed downstairs.

She'd make this work. How she would do it in a car, she had no idea. The guys had been rotating driving her from client to client, but the traffic and parking issues were murdering her schedule. Precious time had been wasted battling traffic and searching for parking spaces.

Time for a scooter resurgence.

Lucie reached the dining room and found her mother at the table stitching buttons on a new pea coat for Otis. "That coat looks great, Mom. Otis will love it."

"I want to meet this Otis. Maybe I'll walk with you one day."

*Oh, boy. Not gonna happen.* "Mmm-hmmm." *Safest answer*.

Mom set the coat aside and flexed her fingers while reading the production list Lucie had prepared. "The pea coat is finished. Now on to the leopard print with the velvet collar."

"Mom?"

She looked up and stared at Lucie over the top of her reading glasses. "Yes?"

"Thank you. I couldn't do this without you."

She smiled her perfect smile that made Lucie think of hot chocolate and marshmallows. "Sweetie, I'm enjoying it. I'm part of the executive team for Coco Barknell. It's exciting. I think I needed something. This might be it."

"And don't forget you'll get paid."

"And won't your father love that?"

Lucie shrugged. "Don't tell him. At least not now. It can go on the what-he-doesn't-know list."

Lucie unfolded her map and started checking cross streets and side streets. Internet mapping searches would need to be performed to see if she could get a visual on where the alleys ran.

She could do this. No problem.

At some point later, her phone rang and she glanced at the screen. Frankie. Off of work already? What time was it? She checked the wall clock. Ten-thirty. Wow, she and her mother had been sitting here for over two hours.

"Hi."

"Hey. You still up?"

"I'm talking to you aren't I?"

"Duh," he said in his teasing voice. "Are you up for a visit? I got done early."

"Sure. Mom's working on a coat and I'm rotating between paperwork and collars."

"See you in five." He hung up. No goodbye. Nothing. She was so going to break him of that.

"Frankie is coming by. Is that okay?"

"Of course. You know I adore him."

She knew all right. At least her mother didn't nag her about marrying him.

Mom stood and arched her back into a long stretch. "I'm turning in. There's an old Cary Grant movie on. It's a good night for Cary."

After finishing her stretch, Mom stepped around the table and kissed Lucie on the cheek. "Goodnight, honey. If Joey comes home, tell him there's a plate in the fridge."

Lucie smiled. "I will. You're too good to him."

"He's my boy."

Frankie knocked lightly on the front door just as her mother hit the lower landing. She turned, checked the peep and opened the door. "Hi, Frankie. Goodnight, Frankie." She pecked him on the cheek and headed upstairs.

He walked toward the dining room. "Did I break up the party?"

"No. She's tired. I hope I'm not working her too hard."

"She'll tell you if you are." He stared at the street map. "What's this?"

"I'm varying my route."

His face lit up. "Really? Is that what all the highlights and dots are?"

"Yes." She pointed to yellow dots. "These are alleys we can cut through to avoid traffic lights."

He scanned all the arrows pointing different directions. "Ouch."

"Yep."

"You can do all this in one day?"

"Yes."

He eyed her. "You sure?"

"Pretty sure."

"In a car?"

Here's the sticky part. "Scooter."

He gave her the psych ward look. "Well, you need to do it by car if Joey and I are going to be with you. Non-negotiable."

Non-negotiable. *Pfft. That's what he thinks.* "I'll never get it done by car. It has to be done by scooter."

Frankie held out his hands. "How's that gonna work?"

*And now the fun really begins.* Lucie handed him print-outs of the scooters. "What color do you like?"

He tossed the pages on the table. "No."

"It's the only way. In order for me to keep my business running, I need to make adjustments. Those adjustments include riding scooters. You and Joey are rotating days so you ride it one day, he rides it the next."

"Luce, I can deal with the scooter. It'll be tough, but I'll suck it up. Joey? Forget it. He'll look like a gorilla on a tricycle. You won't get him on it."

This, she expected. Had even prepared for it. "Oh, I'll get him on it."

"I'd like to have a ringside seat for that conversation."

The back door opened and in came Joey. Lucie glanced at Frankie. How the hell did he do that? "I guess your request has been granted."

Joey entered the dining room wearing jeans and a Bulls slicker. "What?"

She swore he had inherited their father's hearing. She could be screaming and if they didn't want to hear it, they wouldn't. Start whispering and they had bionic ears.

"Mom left you a plate in the fridge."

"I ate at the bar." Joey shifted to Frankie for a fist bump. "What's up?"

Preparing for the show, Frankie pulled a chair and sat. "Ask your sister."

They both turned to Lucie and she shoved the printouts at Joey. "What color do you like?"

Joey glanced at the picture. "My ass."

"Your ass will be sitting on that scooter. Pick a color."

He looked at Frankie, who wore the smile of a man quite

comfortable with the direction of the proceedings. "Is she *stunade* or what?"

*Stunade.* Stupid in Italian. He knew better.

Frankie leaned back and wrapped his hands behind his head. "She charted a new route. It's so damn complicated we'll have to ride scooters."

With narrowed eyes, Joey stared at Frankie, and then turned to Lucie. It would be a miracle if he agreed to this. He still hadn't gotten over scooping poop.

"I'm not doing it." He pointed a beefy finger at the picture of the scooters. "My six-foot-four body won't fit on that."

She waved him off. "Of course it will."

He planted his hands on his hips. "No."

Lucie turned to Frankie. "I don't really care if he rides the scooter. I'm still walking the dogs. These dognappers will not dictate how I live my life. I'll find a way to protect the dogs with or without bodyguards."

"Now she's being a brat," Joey said.

Were they kidding themselves? These men had been around her long enough to know she wouldn't back down. The truth was, after the incident with Otis, she was terrified to do the walks alone, but she knew Frankie wouldn't let that happen. That was the joy of being together so long. They had fallen into a rhythm of understanding. Where her thoughts left off, his picked up and, at the moment, she could sense him calculating a compromise.

Frankie finally pulled his hands from his head and leaned forward on the chair. "You're not doing it yourself."

Then he turned to Joey. "We can't let her walk those dogs alone."

"Frankie promised Dad you two would walk with me."

"Oh, son of a bitch." Joey dug his fingers through his hair. "You have got to be kidding me with that tactic."

"Is it working?"

"Well, yeah. We wouldn't have to worry about my ass fitting on that thing because Dad would rip it to pieces."

Sometimes Joey's fear of their father worked to her advantage.

Frankie high-fived her. Lucie grinned at them and picked up the picture of the scooter. "I like the midnight blue for you boys."

FRANKIE STEPPED INTO PETEY'S FOR LUNCH THE NEXT DAY TO find the walls of the place busting with locals. He took a second to enjoy the familiar scent of garlic and baking bread before a few neighborhood people stopped to say hello. As usual, his father's crew sat in the four-top table in the center of the room and their voices carried over his conversation with Kimmie, the little girl from down the street who was now seventeen and looking all of twenty-eight.

Kimmie didn't hide from Frankie, but he hid from her. Last thing he wanted was the neighborhood thinking he had an interest in getting busy with a minor. She was a nice enough kid, but she got around, and made no secret of wanting to get around him. Literally.

"Ho!" Jimmy said and Frankie thought back on all the years of *ho*. When had those two letters become the all-purpose word? When someone pissed Jimmy off, they got a big *ho!* An off-color joke also received a *ho!* It worked for him. It fit.

"Hey." Frankie shook Jimmy's hand, gave Lemon a slap on the back and looked for his father.

"Taking a piss." Lemon didn't bother looking up from the newspaper spread in front of him.

"Could have done without that info, but thanks. Who's buying lunch?"

Jimmy scraped his chair back. "I got this one. Meatball?"

"Yeah, thanks."

Lemon gestured to Frankie's dress pants and shirt. "You're gonna mess up your big boy clothes."

"Ho!" Frankie did a spot-on imitation of Jimmy. "I'm on my way to work."

"Frankie," his father yelled from the hallway leading to the single restroom.

"Hey, Pop. Jimmy's buying lunch, jump in there."

"Give me a chicken parm."

"On it," Petey said from behind the counter.

Frankie hung his jacket on the back of the empty chair next to Lemon and sat. Being in Petey's sometimes felt like revisiting his childhood. As a kid, he'd come in here on his way home from school and the guys would slip him money and tell him to fill his gas tank or, his personal favorite, go play in traffic.

At ten, it made him feel like a man that his father's friends joked with him. At the time, he never questioned why most fathers worked in an office while his father considered a luncheonette his workplace.

Pop copped a squat in the seat across from him. "Can you get me tickets for the Bulls tomorrow night?"

The newspaper, in an effort to schmooze advertisers, kept season tickets for all the sports teams in Chicago and employees were permitted to request unused tickets. Since Frankie's editor liked him—it didn't hurt that his family provided a constant flow of breaking news—he never found it difficult to scoop up leftovers. "How many do you need?"

Pop turned to Lemon. "I'm in."

Then he spun to the counter where Jimmy hammered Petey about not using too much vinegar on his sandwich. "Jimmy, Bulls game tomorrow night?"

"Ho!"

That would be a yes. "Three tickets?"

"Yeah."

"Let me check if advertising has anything left."

Jimmy finished harassing Petey and joined them at the table. "Ho. I took that Jeanette out." He held his hands palm up in front of his chest. "What a coupla melons on that one."

A cringe snaked up Frankie's back. He didn't have a problem with commenting on a woman's brick houseness, but hell, in a room packed with females, he liked to keep it light.

The young woman at a nearby table gave a hard stare and looked away. *Yep, sorry.*

"I heard," Frankie said.

"About the melons?" This from Lemon.

After a valiant attempt to stay straight-faced, Frankie laughed. He couldn't help it. "That Jimmy went out with her. Her store got robbed while they were out on Sunday."

"No foolin'?" Jimmy asked.

Frankie nodded. "A bunch of Lucie's stuff is gone."

"She can't catch a break," his father said.

"It's like a black cloud is hanging over her." Frankie checked his watch to make sure he was doing okay on time.

"The cops have anything?" Lemon asked.

"Not yet. They took some prints, but who knows."

"Hey, Jimmy," Lemon said, "maybe you need to call that Jeanette. Make her feel better."

"Ho!"

Frankie blew out a breath. He needed his sandwich.

Possibly to go. The stress over the dognappings must be getting to him because the joke about Jeanette's chest, combined with the *ho*ing, were pounding his nerves. Call it a bad freakin' mood, but he couldn't deal today.

"Any more dog problems with Lucie?" his father asked, just as Petey yelled that their order was up.

Jimmy and Lemon stood to retrieve the plates. Frankie seized the opportunity to grill his father about the dognappings. Pop already had his head tilted back to tuck a napkin into the collar of his shirt. The chicken parms made a mess.

"Someone tried to jump Joey and Lucie."

Pop poked his bottom lip out. "What happened?"

"Nothing. Joey beat the crap out of the guy." *And Lucie paralyzed him with bug spray.*

"Poor schmuck. What kind of idiot gets into a street fight with that animal?"

"Have you heard anything?"

His father glanced over his shoulder to see where Jimmy and Lemon were. "Nah. I'm still checking around."

"Thanks. This diamond is freaking Lucie out. Plus, she can't understand how people can steal animals. It's tearing her up."

His father shrugged. "When you hit someone, you make it hurt."

A wicked hiss filled Frankie's head. Hearing his father talk like this created too much reality. A reality he had no interest in.

A meatball sandwich, via Jimmy, landed in front of him and he stared down at it until the hissing subsided. Had he just run ten miles? Sure felt like it. Time to go. He did an obvious check of his watch. "I gotta head out. I'll see you guys later."

His father pointed to the sandwich. "You haven't even cracked it."

"I'll take it with." No sense wasting a good sandwich. He'd eat it at his desk. Frankie slid his jacket on and took his plate to the counter. "Petey, I need a box."

"Ho," Jimmy said as a farewell.

Lemon raised a hand. "Take it easy, Frankie."

His father stood and, as he'd done thousands of times, laid a hand on Frankie's shoulder. This time though, the weight of it pressed into him, confined him. He pushed his shoulders back.

What the hell was wrong with him today?

"Let me know about the tickets," Pop said.

"I'll call you this afternoon."

"You need anything?" His father always asked.

"Nah. I'm good. But if you talk to Joe, Lucie is trying to keep this dognapping thing quiet."

"I'm on the list for the weekend. I won't bring it up, but if he asks me, I gotta tell him. I'm not gonna lie."

His father wouldn't lie. Didn't that beat all? He'd steal, he'd run numbers, he'd bribe officials, but he wouldn't lie to Joe Rizzo.

Before he said something he'd regret, Frankie walked out the door and suppressed the jolt of seriously pissed off taunting him. He was too damned close to this situation. He wanted Lucie happy, and maybe expecting his father to cooperate was asking too much. Didn't seem so.

Not in his father's world anyway.

## 11

_____

As screwed up as it was, Frankie didn't so much mind spending his day off riding a scooter. On a sunny morning two days after the discussion about buying another scooter, he and Lucie tore down West Fullerton on the way to Buddy, a three-month-old Wheaten Terrier.

The wind whipped at Frankie's face, and he decided he needed a helmet with a face shield. He'd already swallowed a few errant bugs of dubious distinction.

The face shield wouldn't matter because psycho scooter girl might get him killed storming these alleys. All in all, he found it fun to chase her around town.

They made a quick right, hauled tail down an empty alley. Lucie pulled into a driveway and jumped off the scooter, her petite body moving fast as she ditched the helmet and unzipped her jacket. By the time Frankie had gotten his helmet off, Lucie had reached the back door.

"Where's the damn fire?" he asked. "That garbage truck nearly flattened me."

"You're the one who said to change the route. We're

already eleven minutes behind schedule." Lucie shoved the key into the lock and turned it.

Eleven minutes. Big deal.

"And don't say big deal, either. We have to stay on schedule. My future depends on it."

A round of applause for Lucia Rizzo, drama girl.

Thirty seconds later, Buddy bounded out the back door, his light brown hair flying in the breeze.

Frankie took a step back. "Pee on me you little bastard and I'll kill you."

Luce laughed. "Leave him alone. He's just a baby. He can't control his bladder yet."

The baby lunged at Frankie's feet and he reached to push him away, but the monster chomped on his hand, those baby teeth like daggers digging into his flesh. "Ow! Off." He shoved Buddy away, but the pup barreled back, latched to Frankie's jeans and tugged. "Off!"

Luce stood back. "Stop engaging him."

What the hell was she talking about? "I was standing here. How is that engaging him?"

"He thinks it's a game. Stand still and ignore him. Pretend you're a tree."

"Ow!" The dog's teeth plunged into his ankle and he lifted his foot. Stand still? The dog was making sushi out of his leg. The terrorist switched to the other leg. "Luce! Get him off."

"Be a tree."

"Screw the tree."

Finally, Lucie tugged on the leash. "Sit, Buddy."

The dog's furry butt hit the ground. *You little S.O.B.*

She bent low, patted Attila the Hun on the head. "Good boy, Buddy. You're a sweet boy." She made kissing noises at Attila, and Frankie suddenly wanted those lips pointed at him. These were the times he realized how much he loved her. The simple times when she didn't feel self-conscious about being silly or showing unabashed affection to an animal.

Buddy stuck his snout in the air and licked her face. She giggled at the bath, and craned out of his reach, but Buddy kept at her until he pushed her off balance and she fell over. The dog jumped on her stomach and went into a licking frenzy. The more she pushed at him, the more he licked, and Frankie knew he and Buddy were of the same mind.

She looked so damn cute trying to wrestle the puppy.

And then her belly laugh broke free. "Frankie, how about a little help?"

"Be a tree," he mimicked. "Stop *engaging* him."

That cracked her up even more and he couldn't stand it. He stepped up, pushed the dog off, straddled Lucie and kissed the hell out of her. Right there on the ground. What did he care? Of course, the woody he sported would have to be patient because doing Lucie on the street with Attila the Hun watching could get them arrested.

His girl didn't seem to mind. She kissed him back and even offered him a little tongue. His Lucie. He loved her, but he could do without the puppy nipping his ear. Little bastard.

When she pulled back he said, "How about when we get done, I put a smile on your face?" He grinned. "I could lick something off you."

She shoved him away. "*If* we ever get done. I'm way more than eleven minutes behind schedule."

"Let's get moving then."

AFTER FINALLY COMPLETING THE WALKS, LUCIE AND FRANKIE zoomed into the Lutzes' driveway to store the scooters for the night. Thank goodness, Mr. Lutz had built extra storage space in the garage. There wasn't an inch of property left to spare, but the man had managed to get a building permit so he could extend the garage.

She'd already given Otis his afternoon walk, but maybe since she was here, she'd give him another one.

Mr. Lutz parked his Mercedes in the driveway and got out just as they parked the scooters. "Hi, Lucie. I never get to see you anymore."

For a man not yet fifty, Mr. Lutz rocked a full head of gray hair—he could thank the stressful job for that—but even with the gray hair, the man had a way about him. Sort of a fifty-year-old Frankie Factor.

"You're home early today," Lucie said.

"The missus has us scheduled for some charity thing tonight."

Lucie introduced Frankie to Mr. Lutz and they chatted about a story Frankie had done on the new Cubs' manager while Lucie stowed the scooters.

"Lucie," Mr. Lutz called, "I saw that leather jacket my wife ordered for Otis. The dog is better dressed than I am."

"Wait until you see the chaps that go with it."

He shook his head. "Moving on from that, a friend of mine called today. He has an opening at his bank and asked me if I knew anyone. I could set up an interview for you."

Lucie's heart thumped. A job. *Yes.* "Absolutely."

But then her mind wandered back to Buddy licking her and Frankie doing the follow-up work. An office job didn't offer those perks.

No. She needed to be an investment banker. Her education couldn't go to waste.

"Good," Mr. Lutz said. "I'll give him your credentials and have him call you."

"That sounds great." She jerked a thumb toward the door leading into the house. "Otis had two walks already today, but I thought I'd treat him to another."

Mr. Lutz smiled. "I won't argue. It'll save me from walking him."

"I'll come in and grab him." She turned to Frankie. "Be right back."

"I'll be here," he said.

The two men exchanged the normal nice-to-meet you pleasantries, and Lucie followed Mr. Lutz into the house with her mind absorbed in the possibility of another banking job. Somehow, she wasn't as relieved as she should be. She shouldn't get her hopes up anyway.

"So," Frankie said when Otis dragged her through the door. "A job interview. You can get back to what you do."

She nodded. Three times. *What's up with the bobblehead bit*? "That would be good. It could get me out of Franklin."

"Yep."

Otis fired off to the big oak tree in front of the house and Lucie glanced back at Frankie. "I know what you're thinking."

"What?"

"You're thinking if I get a job, I'll be happy and everything will be peachy with us."

"I don't think that. Your job isn't our only problem. Granted, I'd like to knock that problem off." He caught up to her and reached for her free hand. "Luce, I want you to be happy. Whether it's in banking or dogs. That's all I want for you."

How did she wind up with this man? He had always been the steady one who never needed much. *She* always seemed to need more, but lately, despite the horrifying dognappings, she felt...well...settled. "I'll go on the interview, but there are a lot of out-of-work finance people floating around."

"Right. And the good news is, you have Coco Barknell as a backup. You're not desperate."

"Right," Lucie agreed. "Coco Barknell."

---

"This is it." Lucie pointed to the assortment of coats, collars and leashes on the dining room table. Mom had just left for her weekly dinner with her friend, and God only knew where Joey was.

Ro slipped off her jacket and set it over the back of one of the chairs. "The last of everything you've sold?"

"Yes. Frankie and I collected it today. Let's go through it all and see if there are any diamonds."

From her oversized tote, Ro pulled a headband with a monster-sized magnifying glass attached—no one could accuse her of not taking the situation seriously—and slipped it on her head. She looked like a mad scientist. Lucie snorted a laugh.

"Laugh all you want. You'll thank me one day."

"Wrong," Lucie said. "I'll thank you now. You still look like a nut, though."

Ro picked up a coat and started her inspection.

"Mr. Lutz thinks he can get me a job interview with a bank."

Ro stopped, and, funky headband glasses and all, looked at Lucie. "Is that good news?"

Lucie shrugged. "Of course."

"Except you just shrugged. What's the real answer?" Ro went back to work.

"That might be the problem. I'm not sure what the real answer is."

"Which means what?"

"I like dog walking. The winter stinks, but the dogs are fun. If I combine that with the accessories—minus the stolen diamond mess—I can make a good living. Maybe better than good."

"You're confused then?"

She nodded. "Totally. I mean, what is going on with me that all of a sudden I'm not sure I want a banking job? That's all I've ever wanted. The banking job gives me credibility. Shows people that I'm more than Joe Rizzo's kid. That corporations trust me with millions of dollars."

"Well," Ro said. "Ponzi schemers aside, right? Because banking has crooks. How do you know the world isn't looking at you and wondering if you're sucking money out of accounts?"

"Hey!"

Ro flipped the magnifying glasses up. "How do we know? Even the most straight-laced people get sucked into doing dumb things. The world could be thinking that about anyone."

True.

Ro put the glasses back into place and started on the leopard print coat. "Luce, be an investment banker because you want to, not because you think it validates you. The people that matter know you're a good person."

Lucie twisted her lips. "Now you sound like Frankie."

"Frankie is a smart guy. Most of the time."

"Doesn't it seem crazy though? To leave banking for dog walking?"

"No. You're an entrepreneur. You're walking the dogs while getting an accessory line off the ground. I'm telling you, think Fortune 500. It'll be bigger than investment banking." Ro dropped the coat and pulled the headband off. "These are all fakes. Are you sure you've collected everything?"

"Yes. I cross-checked all the items against my spreadsheet and marked them as finished."

"Well, sorry honey, this exercise was a bust. Now what?"

Lucie fiddled with the leopard print coat, but dropped it. "I have no idea."

---

FRANKIE TURNED IN HIS STORY ON THE BASKETBALL GAME AND swung by the Rizzos'. He sat in the kitchen with a freshly showered Lucie smelling like lemons—probably her shampoo—and wearing her beat up Levi's and an old Notre Dame sweatshirt. Her damp, shoulder-length hair had been pulled into a ponytail and combined with the sweatshirt, she looked like a college coed. His Luce. He liked hot Luce too, but this Luce was where he belonged. This was the girl he wanted to wake up with every day. In a kitchen just like this one.

The Rizzo kitchen hadn't changed much over the years. They had added a fresh coat of beige paint a couple of years ago, but the few feet of laminate counters and the thirty-year-old maple cabinets remained. Those cabinets were thick enough to crack Joey's fat head.

All in all, the place reminded him of family and bunches of people packed tight when Theresa Rizzo prepared food.

"Hey," Joey said, shuffling into the kitchen with his hair all crazy. He wore a wrinkled sleeveless T-shirt and a pair of basketball shorts. He pulled a sandwich from the fridge and unwrapped the foil. Late feeding.

"Eggplant parm. Sweet." He bit into the cold sandwich. "Good stuff."

Lucie rolled her eyes. Frankie would have preferred the sandwich to be hot, but maybe next time he went to Petey's he'd try the eggplant. Change things up a bit.

"What are you doing here?" Joey wanted to know.

"Let's talk dognappings."

"Perfect," Luce said.

Joey shrugged.

"We can't keep mixing up the routes this way," Lucie said. "We need to shift to attack mode. We've been waiting for them to come after me and I'm sick of it. *I* want to go after *them*."

"Exactly." Frankie said. "I think we should find a way to tell your dad about the diamond. He'll smoke out whoever hid it."

"No." This from Lucie. "He already knows about the dognappings. He'll freak on me. Besides, there's no way to tell him. Not with every conversation recorded."

"He and my father talk in code all the time. It's worth a shot."

Lucie shook her head. "Too dangerous."

Joey raised both hands. "I'll rattle some cages and let everyone know if they want that diamond, they'll have to see me about it."

Luce shot him a look that could have left him bloody. "Seriously? That's your plan?"

"It's pretty simple."

When she started with the snoring noises, Frankie reached over and pinched her cheek. Too damn cute.

"You got a better idea?" Joey asked.

"For starters, I bought pepper spray and a stun gun."

That statement dropped like an eighteen-wheeler from the top of a building. Frankie stared at her, trying to wrap his mind around the idea of Lucie and a stun gun. Nuh-uh. This nonsense had to stop.

The pepper spray he could live with. The stun gun? No way.

With her luck, she'd cook herself.

"Honey, that stun gun is a bad idea. You could get hurt."

"How am *I* going to get hurt? I'm not using it on myself. It's for the bad guys. Anyone comes near me or the dogs, *zzzzpppp*, he gets juiced."

Frankie laughed. Unfortunately, the laugh died fast when she narrowed her eyes at him. "You think this is funny? God knows what could happen to one of those dogs."

"I don't think this is funny at all. Suppose the dognapper wrestles the stun gun out of your hands. He could use it on you."

"That won't happen if you and Joey are with me."

"You don't know that."

Lucie leaned forward and jammed her index finger into the table. "Maybe not, but I refuse to let a lowlife dognapper dictate how I live. I will not be afraid to walk the streets of the city I love. I'm working my butt off trying to stay ahead of this situation and I'm tired. T-I-R-E-D."

Frankie dragged his hand over his face. The complications continued to grow. "Of course you're T-I-R-E-D. After two weeks of this garbage, we don't have jack on these guys and you get pissed every time I talk to my father. How long are we going to let this go on?"

She stared at him for a full thirty seconds. Finally, her snappy eyes settled back to that calm ocean blue. "I was hoping we'd be able to catch them ourselves and figure out who they are. I'm not bringing your dad into it though. You know how I feel about that. Let's just figure it out ourselves."

"How?"

"Well, Ro just checked the last batch of accessories we collected from my clients. So far, all the stones are fake. If there are any real ones, they're not on anything I've sold or in my stock."

"Good."

"Not really," Joey said.

Frankie clutched the edge of the table and prayed for patience. "What the hell does that mean?"

"You told your dad about Lucie hiding the diamond, right?"

"Yeah. He put the word out that she hadn't used it on any of her accessories."

"And what happened?"

For the life of him, Frankie didn't know where Joey was leading him.

"Oh, no," Lucie said.

"What?"

"Jeanette's store got robbed."

"Ding, ding, ding." Joey said.

But Frankie didn't get it. "And?"

Luce turned to him, gripped his forearm. "There are definitely more diamonds, but they're not on my dog accessories. They must be somewhere else."

———

Frankie stared at her as if she'd just shredded one of his designer suits. "Somewhere *else*?"

"It has to be. Why else would the dognappers still be

coming after me? If there was only one diamond and they know I have it, why would they keep stealing the dogs? They don't believe I only have one diamond."

She shoved her chair back and stood. She needed to move. Needed to feel something happening. Needed to find those diamonds.

Joey spun to face her. "You're sure the ones in your craft stuff are all fake?"

"Yes. Ro checked them."

"Then we need to search the house."

"The attic," Lucie said. "That's where I kept my craft supplies." She'd have to search when her mother wasn't around. That attic had thirty years' worth of stuff in it. It would take days to search all that junk.

"Mom can't know about this. When she goes out, I'll start searching. Maybe the dognappers scattered the diamonds in different boxes."

"Or maybe they came and got them already," Frankie suggested.

"Then why are they still stealing my stuff?"

"Good point."

"Joey, can you get Mom out of the house? I need time to search up there and she pops in and out all day."

Joey slouched in his seat, stared up at the ceiling. "She wants to see that new exhibit at the art museum. Been talking about it for two weeks. I'll buy her the tickets. Send her with one of her friends."

"You take her. That way you can warn me when you're coming home."

He swung his head back and forth, back and forth, back and forth. "I draw the line at moping around a museum. What do I care about some queen's clothes?"

Lucie spun to Frankie, held her hands out and dropped them. Her brother couldn't suck this up? Unbelievable.

"I can't blame him for that one, Luce. That's beyond the call."

Double unbelievable. "You boys need to focus on the big picture here."

Joey gathered up the sandwich wrapper and stood. "As long as that picture isn't of some queen's clothes, I'm on it."

"Fine. Get the tickets ASAP so we can get her out of here. At least take her to dinner tomorrow night. That'll give me an hour to start searching the attic."

"Not to be a downer, Luce," Frankie said, "but don't get too bent on this idea. There may not be anything up there."

Always a possibility. Lucie couldn't get sidetracked though. There were more diamonds. She was sure of it. "If they're not in the attic, they're somewhere else. We just need to find them."

"If it was me," Joey said, glancing at the wall between the counter and back door. "I'd go for the walls."

With that, he left the room.

"The walls," Lucie said. "That would be a little hard to explain."

"I'd say." Frankie squeezed her hand. "One thing at a time. Let's work on the attic. I'll help you search."

## 12

———

Lucie and Frankie arrived at the Lutzes' and, ready to fight another day, she hopped on her scooter to fire it up. "My mother went to an early yoga class, so I started searching the attic this morning."

Frankie swung his leg over the scooter. "Anything?"

"No, but I only got through three boxes."

"I'll help you."

Lucie smiled. "I know. Thank you."

He winked. "It'll cost you."

"Yay, me. And just so you know, I'm packing."

Frankie, in the middle of securing his helmet, drew his eyebrows together. "Boxes?"

What was he talking about? "Boxes?"

"You said you're packing. What are you packing?"

*Idiot.* She smacked her hand against her messenger bag. "I'm packing. As in *heat.*"

Frankie pursed his lips in that way that told her he was either about to argue, or worse, laugh. He must have decided against both because, after angling his head the way Otis did when contemplating a good poop,

Frankie shook it off and pushed his scooter from the garage.

"You're like a cross between Mary Poppins and Rambo."

Once again, she patted the bag slung across her body. "Nobody is messing with Mary *or* Rambo today. *Nobody.*"

"Do you even know how to use that stun gun?"

She tilted her chin skyward while she secured her helmet strap. "I practiced on an eggplant."

"Perfect. Now that you fried the eggplant, your mom won't have to cook it."

Wasn't he just the comedian today? "Hardy-har. Make fun all you want. I'm done with these dognappers. I'm taking control. Anyone tries to steal my dogs, they're getting zapped. *Zzzzzpppp!*"

"Luce, those stun guns are dangerous."

The sun poured over his black dress pants and grey zip-up jacket as he sat on the scooter with his feet planted on the driveway. Damn, he somehow managed to make a scooter sexy. Even when he irritated her. "Relax. It doesn't even generate an amp. I can't kill anyone with it."

"How comforting."

"Darn tootin'." Lucie hit the throttle on the scooter and zoomed by him.

After walking the girls, they headed to Lincoln Park and Mamie, the ever-regal Labradoodle that in a truly bizarre way reminded Lucie of her mother. Mamie was one of those animals that never got flustered. The world could be collapsing around her, but she'd trot without a care.

"Buddy is next," Lucie said. "Joey will meet us at the downtown Rizzo's after that for lunch. Then you can head to your office and Joey will take over."

"You're keeping on schedule. Maybe you need to make your own how-to video. We'll call it *Poop on Demand.*"

Again with the humor? A regular funny man today. "All the dogs—well, Otis is a challenge—but the rest know I'm serious. When I say poop, they do it. I learned that from the guy on Discovery Channel."

Frankie snorted. Obviously, he found it amusing that she watched Discovery Channel.

The sound of scooters pulling into the driveway sent Buddy, the Wheaton Terrorist—er Terrier—into a barking frenzy. His little head bobbed up and down in the back window, and Lucie cracked up. She took a moment to breathe in and enjoy the moment of peace. The dogs were always happy to see her. That alone made this job worth doing.

She parked her scooter and held a hand to Frankie. "Let me take care of this. After your last encounter with Buddy, I don't want him getting agitated."

Frankie dragged his helmet off. "All that howling he's doing is calm?"

"He's a puppy. He's energized."

"These pants are Calvin Klein. I'll kill the little bastard if he goes after them."

Poor, poor Frankie with his designer pants. "Just stay out of his reach and you'll be fine."

Lucie entered the house through the back door and took the immediate right to the laundry room, where a gate kept Buddy contained. The over-anxious puppy greeted her by diving at her feet and licking her shoes. She bent low and patted his rump. "Good boy. Yes. I know you're hungry."

Then he peed on her foot.

Urine seeped through her canvas sneakers and soaked her socks. *Ew.* "Outside," she said in a loud voice. The dog flopped onto his back. Clearly, the potty training hadn't kicked in yet. "Okay, Buddy. You just tinkled on me and that's not a good thing."

With the urinating out of the way, she might as well feed him before his walk. She dumped his food into the bowl and, while he ate, she wiped up the errant pee, and pulled off her shoe and wet sock. Poop baggies sat on the dryer by his leash, so she grabbed one and stuck her wet sock in it before sliding her shoe back on. The wet shoe abraded the top of her foot and she curled her toes under to relieve her mind of puppy pee against her skin. Just, ew. She would have to stop somewhere and buy another pair, because the idea of walking around with pee on her all day gave her a rash. Literally.

Buddy finished his lunch, planted his butt and barked.

"I guess we're ready."

When Lucie bent low to secure his harness, Buddy, thinking it was playtime, shot to the corner of the oversized laundry room hoping for a chase.

Lucie sighed. "Buddy, we have work to do."

"*Erf! Erf!*"

Time to call in the big guns. She sat on the floor, stared at the ceiling and waited. Dogs hated to be ignored. The eventual *tap-tap-tap* of nails on tile alerted her to movement and—*voila*—he was at her side. Slowly, she moved her hand over his back and rubbed. "Good boy, Buddy." She wrapped her arm around him, while continuing to tickle his belly. *Gotcha.*

"You little stinker." She slipped the harness on and secured it. "Good boy!"

Assuming they were done, Buddy jumped on top of her and the frantic slapping of his warm tongue against her cheek made her giggle. "Off, Buddy."

To his credit, he planted himself on the floor and let her attach the leash.

A minute later, he took one look at Frankie through the open door and charged. Unfortunately, he ran out of running room on the nylon leash and it snapped him to a halt.

Wussie boy Frankie stepped back. "What took so long?"

"He peed on my foot. I cleaned it up while he ate."

Frankie made an ick face. *Yeah, with you on that one, pal.* Just part of the job, Lucie mused as Buddy fired down the steps snarling at Frankie. He backed up another inch.

She laughed. "You're afraid of a three-month-old puppy?"

"His teeth are ice picks."

Screeching tires from the street lurched Lucie's heart and she spun to peer down the alley. Nothing. Too jumpy. Buddy, sensing the tension, barked and she bent low to pet him.

"Let's hit it," Frankie said.

He took two steps into the alley and a man the size of Cleveland flew from behind a tree. What the—"Watch out," Lucie yelled, but the man landed on Frankie's back and Buddy went insane tugging the leash to join the mêlée.

In one fluid move, Frankie flipped the guy off him and the dog leaped and barked and growled.

The assailant scrambled to his feet, rammed his shoulder into Frankie's belly and tackled him. Frankie's body moved through the air, crashed to the ground and his head—*no*—bounced off the pavement, the cracking sound carrying like a splitting coconut.

Panic flicked at Lucie. She opened her mouth, but her chest froze and she stood there, gagging on trapped air. She loved this man and someone dared—*dared*—to put their hands on him. *Bastard*. She had to fight. Had to help Frankie.

The redheaded attacker looked no older than thirty. He was big, not fat big, but his frame carried extra weight in every available spot.

He could crush her.

A howling inside her head hammered. The bad guy stepped toward her just as Buddy lunged for the leg of his pants. Oh, no. Not the dog.

"No, Buddy." The puppy clamped onto the guy's calf.

"Argh! Get this dog off me." He reached down and sent his beefy hand across the dog's back. Buddy yelped. An immediate spewing of hate consumed Lucie. How could he hurt a defenseless puppy?

Buddy came surging back. The idiot attacker didn't realize Buddy thought this was some sort of twisted game.

Frankie rolled to his side and levered himself up. Still on all fours, he kept his head low.

*Stun gun.*

Lucie reached into her bag for the device and flipped the juice switch.

The attacker hollered when Buddy clamped onto his hand.

That had to hurt. The feisty puppy wasn't giving up. She only had a few seconds before the attacker struck Buddy again. But if she shot from this distance, the probes from the gun might hit the dog. She moved closer. *God, please don't let me miss.*

She glanced at Frankie, about to stand tall. The attacker could have killed him. Anger swelled inside her and a guttural roar flew from her throat.

She jammed the device into the attacker's back and pressed the trigger. The probes flew, but her hand stayed still. No recoil or kick. Amazing. A *rat-a-tat-tat* clacking noise filled the air and she flinched from the shock of it, but held tight to the gun.

The attacker arched back, his face a mass of agony. "AGGGHHHHHH!"

The shattering wail resembled a bad Chewbacca audition and he collapsed to the ground. Buddy, clearly wanting to join the fun, clamped onto his leg again.

Lucie slammed her eyes shut as the screaming inside her head raged on. No. She couldn't waste time. The probe only lasted thirty seconds. She needed to move.

She opened her eyes. "Off, Buddy." The dog backed away, tilting his adorable little head at her and she scooped him up. She swiveled to Frankie, now moving toward her with the steel-edged look of a warrior on the hunt. "In the house," she yelled.

But Frankie beelined for the Chewie wannabe.

Lucie jumped between Frankie and Chewie. "Forget him. You're hurt. Get in the house."

Chewie grabbed her ankle, and Frankie gave him a solid kick to the ribs. "Hit him with the stun gun again."

She still had the gun in hand, but she hadn't reloaded the cartridge and didn't want to take the time. "No. In the house."

Frankie, being Frankie, gave the guy another kick. "Stay away from her. Got it?"

Grabbing his shirtsleeve, Lucie pulled him toward the house before Chewie got his second wind. Buddy yelped with glee over the excitement and nipped at her chin. "Stop, Buddy. No biting."

With her heart banging around inside her, Lucie slammed the door behind them, threw the bolt and sent

Frankie through the laundry room so she could barricade the dog.

Frankie rubbed the back of his head. "Call 9-1-1."

She glanced out the door and saw the man get to his feet and take off down the alley. "Forget it. He's already down the street."

"Dammit."

Lucie held up two fingers. "How many?"

He focused on her fingers, but said nothing.

"Wrong answer. You're going to the hospital."

"I'll be fine. It'll be another concussion."

"Yeah, and what about all those people that don't go to the hospital and wind up dead from one of those hematoma things?"

"It's an epidural hematoma. Bleeding between the brain and the inside of the skull. Trust me. I know."

"Yeah, well. You're going to the hospital."

---

"She blasted him?" Joey stood next to Frankie's hospital bed doing his damndest to hide a smile. But when he looked over at her, Lucie saw the mischief in his eyes. Maybe, Lucie thought, she wasn't a goodie-two-shoes after all.

Frankie nodded. Very slowly. "Fried him good."

Despite her best efforts, she grinned. Why not? She'd done well today. Gave that dognapper something to think about. "I zapped him once. Knocked him on his butt."

Anticipating the ER doc's return with Frankie's CAT scan results, Lucie checked her watch. "You sure the dogs had a long enough walk?" she asked Joey.

"Everyone took a dump. Even Otis."

"Really?"

"I've got the touch with him."

Frankie scoffed.

"It's true," Lucie said. "I can spend an hour trying to get him to poop and Joey steps up and—*boom*—he just goes. It's crazy. Even Mrs. Lutz is surprised."

Joey shrugged. "It's a dominance thing."

Frankie laughed, but immediately brought his hand to his head. She kissed his forehead. "Just rest."

The neckline of his hospital gown slipped and she gave it a light tug into place. She flattened her palm against his chest, felt the heat of his body through the gown and suddenly wanted to curl into bed with him, nurse him to health in her own way.

What was wrong with her? The poor man was injured and her mind was sliding into the gutter. But having him back in her life affected her, made her realize how much she'd missed him during their break-up and how much she didn't want to lose him again. Somehow, they had to make it work.

She cleared her throat.

"Was Buddy wearing one of your collars?" Frankie asked.

He just wouldn't give up. "Don't worry about it now. You need rest."

"I'm fine."

Dug in. She knew it. Might as well not aggravate him. "No. He has one, but he didn't have it on."

"And yet, they still tried to boost him."

Joey shrugged. "Seems to me these guys know who your accessory clients are. They're picking them off one by one."

How very comforting. "I think the dognappers took that spreadsheet that's missing. That's how they know my clients. They're four for four with picking the right targets."

She turned to Joey, her movements halted.

Equipped with excellent instincts, her brother drew his eyebrows together. "What?"

God, how to do this. He might tear the place apart, but she had to ask. "Remember I asked you about the spreadsheet?"

"So?"

"Did you have any friends over that would have taken it?"

Frankie blew out a breath and eased his head against the bed. He knew what was coming. He just didn't have the strength to get into the middle of a Lucie-Joey smackdown.

"No."

Joey's big body filled the room with an energy that became cold and hateful and made her feel small, so small.

Frankie lifted his head. "She's only asking."

"Yeah, because *my* friends are the losers who would steal a dog to get a collar."

"Knock it off," Frankie said, getting a little loud.

"Why don't you ask your boyfriend if he took the spreadsheet? He's my friend. You trust him, but not your own brother? After I've busted my butt to help you? Well, find someone else to clean up your messes."

"I was only asking. Anyone could have walked into the house and picked up that spreadsheet. Mom never turns the alarm on during the day."

"That's a thought," Frankie added. "With your dad locked up, people are bound to cross the line. Nobody would have the balls to do this if your dad was out, but since he's not, what's gonna happen?"

Joey scoffed. "He could still fix this."

"Yeah, but some of these lower level guys aren't geniuses. They're cocky and don't give the respect the older guys do."

Joey's shoulder shrug indicated it wasn't completely out of the question. "I'll poke around. Maybe I'll run up to see Dad one day, see if I can get anything out of him."

"Don't tell him about all this. He only knows about the first incident." Lucie turned to Frankie. "You didn't tell your father anything else, did you?"

"I told him about the Sammy Spaniel theft. That was the last thing. "

"Okay. So we know he wouldn't have told my dad about the diamond, right?"

"It wouldn't do him any good. He promised your father he'd take care of you. You having a stolen diamond doesn't exactly leave a good impression."

Joey immediately raised his hands. "I won't let on. I'm not stupid."

"I think my missing spreadsheet is part of the answer. Someone had to have taken it from the house. If we find that someone, we find the dognappers. I'm sure of it."

## 13

A loud scrape jolted Frankie from sleep and his breath came in one shuddering gasp. *What the hell?* He opened his eyes. Moonlight squeezed through the closed blinds and threw an angular shadow against the far wall. The ceiling fan spun in slow circles while the screech against his bedroom window blasted through his already battered head. He needed to trim that pain-in-the-ass tree before the wind sent one of the branches into his bed.

He inhaled and ever so slowly turned toward the bedside clock. Four-thirty. Way too early for any normal person to be awake. At least in his opinion.

The throbbing in his head went ballistic and his vision blurred. He needed a few more hours of sleep and then he'd get with his father about the dognapping problem. Lucie would skin him, but he'd live with it. His father had all sorts of connections and, even if someone close to Joey were behind swiping that spreadsheet, his father or Jimmy would have heard about it.

Wait.

Could his father have mentioned to Jimmy that Lucie found the diamond? What about Lemon? If Jimmy knew, so did Lemon. A sickness unrelated to Frankie's pounding head whirled in his stomach.

If Jimmy and Lemon knew about the diamond, could they be trusted to keep it quiet? Hell, they could have told any number of lowlifes.

Frankie shifted sideways and dry heaved into the bucket by his bed. *Dammit.* He could be the cause of all this.

He rolled out of bed, made his way to the bathroom, raised his forearm over his eyes and flipped the light. After a second, he lowered his arm and pried one eye open to locate his painkillers.

Two hours. That's what he needed to kill. By then his father would be up and reading the morning paper, perusing the sports section and checking out Frankie's column, as he always did. Frankie swallowed two pills, looked in the mirror and scared the crap out of himself. His eyes held that shiny, unfocused look that came with concussions.

Rest. That's what he needed now. Maybe the meds would kick in and by six, he'd be moving enough to get the four blocks to his folks' house.

A sleepy Lucie stumbled into the bathroom. She'd insisted on sleeping on the couch. "Are you okay?"

"Needed the painkillers. Go back to sleep." He eyed her in his beat up Cubs shirt. "In my bed."

She rolled her eyes. "Even with a concussion? Unbelievable."

"Still a guy, Luce. And that part of my brain is intact."

"Thanks for the offer, but I'll stick with the couch, for now. Do you need anything?"

"You just shot down the only thing I need." This said as

he crawled into his bed alone. He'd be no good to her now anyway. She'd have to do all the work. He pulled the sheet up and prayed for the peace of mind he needed to sleep. At least then he would stop thinking he'd put Lucie in danger.

Two hours later, after a raging battle for sleep, Frankie used his key to unlock his parents' front door and slipped in.

"Pop?" His voice was somewhere between a whisper and his regular tone. No sense giving anyone cardiac arrest by sneaking up on them.

An eerie darkness enveloped the newly painted room. His mother had finally gotten rid of the fuzzy wallpaper. A shaft of light filtered from the kitchen as Pop swung around the corner, still wearing his navy pinstripe pajamas.

"Frankie?"

"Morning."

"What are you doing here so early? You okay?"

"I gotta talk to you."

Dad put a hand on his back. "How's your head?"

Lucie's mother must have called his mother. Luce had warned him about that. He wasn't the only one flapping gums with a parent.

"Could be worse," Frankie said. "The meds help."

"Jeez, Frankie, with your history, you gotta be more careful."

Getting knocked to the ground by a would-be dognapper wasn't exactly his fault, but his father didn't know that. Not wanting to terrify her mother, Lucie had told her Frankie slipped and hit his head. Not exactly heroic, but it worked for their purposes. "Yeah. I know."

"Come in. Your mother isn't up yet. In a little while, she'll make you a good breakfast. You hungry?"

"Not so much."

Frankie wasn't a breakfast guy, especially with a swollen

brain, but his mother's ham and eggs might relieve the ache a bit. If he could keep the food in place.

His father led him into the kitchen and poured a second cup of coffee. *The Herald* sat open on the table. Pop read every article, every day, no exceptions.

"Sugar, right?" his father asked.

"Right." He handed him the sugar bowl and Frankie hoped the burn of coffee wouldn't send his tender stomach into a boycott.

"What's up, kid? Why aren't you in bed?"

Asking questions without them sounding like accusations wouldn't be the easiest thing Frankie had ever experienced. He ran his middle finger and thumb across his forehead, felt the pressure drive through his skull.

*Say it.*

"I don't know how to ask you this, so I'm gonna lay it out."

His father sat across from him, took off his reading glasses and dropped them on the table. His dark eyes held intensity, but Frankie recognized the look as being more concern than anything.

"You can ask me anything."

Yeah, well, they'd see about that. "You know all this crap with Lucie and the dognappings?"

"She get hit again?"

"Almost. She zapped the guy with her stun gun."

His father cracked a smile. "Is that a fact?"

Frankie couldn't resist smiling. Nobody would ever expect Lucie to use a stun gun. He held up a hand. "Swear."

"Maybe she's got a little of her father in her after all."

There was a scary freakin' thought. "Anyway, we think someone swiped one of her reports from the house and that's how they know who her accessory clients are."

"Someone broke into the house?"

"We think so. She had a spreadsheet go missing. It never turned up."

His father's bottom lip poked out for a second. "Reasonable, I guess."

"Pop?"

"What?"

"I told you about the diamond. Could Jimmy have overheard and told someone else. Maybe they're going rogue?"

His father sat back, thought about it for a split second. If that.

"No. Some of these young guys, they're a little..." Dad held his hand to his head and motioned like he was turning a screw, "...whacked. But Jimmy? No. Not with Joe's daughter."

Frankie slugged a gulp of coffee, set the mug down and waited for the impact. Nothing. So far, so good. "It sounds nuts, but it's the only thing I can come up with."

His father leaned forward, smacked a hand on Frankie's arm. "I'll ask around. If it's one of our guys, I'll find out and take care of it."

Frankie nodded. "Keep it low profile. Lucie doesn't want Joe finding out. He climbed all over her when we saw him last. We've got enough problems without her being pissed at me. We need to figure out where this diamond came from so we can all get back to normal."

His father held up two hands. "I'll keep it quiet, but you can bet I'll take care of it."

---

"How's it going?" Frankie asked Lucie when she came through his door carrying a white paper bag.

Grateful to see her, he rested his head back on the couch, and hoped there was a meatball sandwich in that sack. "Is that from Petey's?"

"You bet. Thought you'd like some lunch." She knelt beside him, ran her fingers through his hair and he enjoyed the comfort of the gesture. They were together again and he intended to enjoy it. "Do you need anything?"

"I need a lot of things, but they all require you naked."

She rolled her eyes. "So, your brain still isn't the only thing swelled?"

He laughed. "Come on, Luce, I'd want sex if my arms we're hanging off and I was bleeding out."

The sandwich came flying at him and he tore into the bag. "I guess I'll settle for this. Hunger set in about an hour ago, but I was too lazy to move. I can't believe you went to Petey's for me. You hate Petey's."

"Which is why I had Ro go in."

Frankie snorted. "Atta-girl. Always searching for the workaround."

"You deserve a meatball sandwich."

"Yes, I do. What are you up to the rest of the day?"

"Today is the interview for the bank job, so I need to go home and change. After the interview, I'll finish the run with Joey and tonight I'm meeting with a web-designer. I might want a website for Coco Barknell. I could put the dog walking services on one page and the accessories on the other."

"Sounds like you have a plan."

"Yep. It's the safety net if I don't get a job."

He unwrapped the foil and a bit of sauce dripped onto his T-shirt. Nice. It'd probably get a lot worse before he was done so he ignored the stain and bit into the sandwich. The sharpness of the garlic and cheese caused a riot with his taste buds and he closed his eyes. *Heaven.*

"Watching you eat one of those is always exciting. It's almost a turn-on."

He swallowed. "They're so damn good. What are you thinking about the banking job?"

"I'm not holding my breath. There are a lot of people with more experience than me out of work."

"Yeah, but you're good. And Lutz recommended you. That's gotta carry some weight. Be prepared if they offer you the job."

She switched to a sitting position next to the sofa. "That would be nice."

"Would you take the job?"

"I think I'd have to. I need health insurance. My benefits from the old job will expire soon and it's expensive to buy my own. Plus, I need to get out of my parents' house."

After three bites, Frankie set the sandwich on the cushion next to him. Might as well take a break and see how it settles in. "Is it that bad?"

"Well, Joey is Joey, but he's been laying off. I think he feels bad about the dognappings. And my mom is a dream. She's saving my butt helping with the sewing."

"What's the problem then?"

Lucie hesitated. "The old neighborhood is too stifling. And when my father calls, we have to practically line up to talk to him and all he does is lecture me about wasting my education."

"That's because you haven't told him Coco Barknell could be huge. You could open shops all over the country. Then will your education be wasted?"

"Frankie?"

"Yeah?"

"I have a business plan. I did production estimates and salary and benefit options. I've got it all figured out."

*Good girl.* A pulsing nailed him right in the gut. Might have been the sandwich, but he wanted to think it was the business plan. "You could open a store downtown."

"Not right away. It's too expensive. Unless I get another investor."

"I can give you more money."

She shook her head. "I don't want you risking any more of your money. I was thinking I should ask Mr. Lutz. He may want to do it. If he doesn't, he'd be able to hook me up with the right people."

"Luce?"

"What?"

"Are you sure about taking the bank job if they offer it? You've got all this Coco Barknell stuff figured out. Might be worth the risk."

Seemed like a no-brainer to him, but Lucie didn't have that warrior instinct. She liked to play it safe. Analyze the figures, the market conditions, the *possibilities*.

"It's the medical benefits. With a banking job, I have a safety net. All the money I'd spend on benefits could go into my savings. Once I'm working again, I can do Coco Barknell part-time until I have enough money saved to go full-time."

Frankie understood her thinking, but being unemployed seemed like the perfect opportunity for her to get Coco off the ground. All she needed was the capital. And a good dose of self-confidence.

But Lucie didn't like taking risks with her personal life. Over the years, her father's lifestyle meant living on the edge and she had never gotten comfortable with that. If only Frankie could get her to take a chance. "Then I guess you'll take the job if they offer it to you?"

"I guess I will."

Something about that seemed like a damn shame.

---

AFTER THE INTERVIEW, LUCIE JUMPED INTO A CAB TO MEET Joey at the Bernards' so they could finish the dog walks.

"Thanks for handling the morning run for me," Lucie said when Joey came off the elevator with the dogs who, as usual, greeted her by pawing at her feet in a play bow. She bent low and rubbed each of them under the chin. "Good girls. I missed you too."

"On a schedule here."

Lucie laughed. For a change, someone else worried about time. "I have jeans in my bag. Let me change and we'll finish up."

"How'd it go?"

She shrugged. "I don't know. Sounds like a good place to work."

"Yeah, but did you get a vibe?"

"No, Joey. I'll know when I know."

He waved her off. "It's all bull anyway. This is why I like my job. I don't have to deal with this crap."

Now he was comparing being a bookie to banking? Priceless. "You also don't have a 401K."

And there was nothing he could do about it because bank accounts could be seized by the government, and he wasn't about to leave a money trail.

"Hey, I got some cash saved."

Probably in a box in the attic. Which she'd find by the time she was finished searching for the diamonds. "Doesn't it bug you that you can't have a normal bank account?"

"Nope. It's safer."

"Oh, please."

"When you got your last investment statement, how much was it down?"

Oh, no. She wasn't buying into this.

Joey grinned at her. "Guess how much my *retirement* account was down?"

Nope. Not biting.

He made a zero with his thumb and index finger.

"But when the market comes back, my money has the potential to grow where yours doesn't."

"It also has the potential to tank."

She shook her head. "Forget it. You're like a brick wall."

"Yeah, but I know what I see when I look in the mirror."

Lucie hefted her tote bag on her shoulder and squeezed the strap. "What is *that* supposed to mean?"

"What do you see, Luce?"

What *did* she see? Some days she thought she knew. But those were the days where all this rising above smothered her like an extra thirty pounds. Those thirty pounds made taking an extra step a struggle.

In some ways, she wanted to be more like Joey. He never worried about what the world thought or where his life would lead. He lived in the moment, day to day and that suited him fine.

"Joey, don't you ever want more?"

He lifted a shoulder. "I'm okay with my life. I don't dream about being some corporate schmo. I can have everything I want doing what I'm doing. Hell, if I moved to Vegas I could work in a sportsbook and I'd have a legal job."

"So, there you go. Why not move to Vegas and be legitimate?"

"Too hot there. And everything I want is here."

She slid her tote off her shoulder, stared down at it while

the girls sniffed around the bottom. "We are so different. All I want is to get away from Franklin and all you want is to stay."

"Pretty much."

She lifted the bag with her clothes. "I need to change."

"Yeah, you do."

## 14

Frankie walked into Petey's a little after seven o'clock with his head still pounding like a mother. A big one.

"Ho," Jimmy yelled when Frankie pushed through the door.

"Ho," Frankie yelled back in his Jimmy voice.

Didn't this crew ever go home?

Frankie went to the counter to order. "Did you guys eat?"

"Yeah," Jimmy said. "Petey! Get Frankie his sandwich."

"Doing it already," Petey said.

Normally, Frankie liked the familiarity in Petey starting his sandwich before he'd even ordered. Tonight though, it felt ordinary. Typical. *Boring*. "Petey, did you start it yet?"

Petey turned to him, bread knife in hand. "I just cut the bread."

"Make it an eggplant parm."

"What?"

"Ho."

"I think that fall scrambled his brain," Lemon added.

Part of this scenario scraped against Frankie's nerves.

Had he become that predictable? Looked like it, because the guys were getting a hell of a ride out of it. "Yeah. Eggplant parm today. I'm living large."

A big, hulking guy with a head the size of a movie marquee came out of the back room. He spotted Frankie, swung around and went back the way he came.

What was that about?

Something about the guy tapped at Frankie's memory. Where had he seen that big square head?

He straddled the vacant chair between Jimmy and Lemon. "Who was that guy?"

Jimmy waved. "He's some mope on one of the other crews. He don't come around too much."

"Good thing too," Lemon added.

"Why is that?"

Lemon shrugged. "Thinks he's a smart guy. I'd like to show him how smart he is."

"I've seen him before," Frankie said.

"He's been around a while. Maybe you saw him somewhere."

"Maybe."

Petey slid a tray onto the counter. "Eggplant parm."

From his seat, Frankie stared at the tray, but his eyes wandered to the back room. He knew that guy. Or at least he'd seen him somewhere before. And it was recent.

Leaving the sandwich, Frankie headed to the back room. "Be right back."

"Ho," Jimmy called. "You're food is up. Don't let it get cold."

But Frankie ignored him. He needed to put eyes on this guy. He strode down the short hallway with the banged up steel gray walls and the cracking linoleum floor, halting when he got to the door where the sound of muffled voices came through. One of those voices belonged to his father. He raised his fist to knock and stopped.

*Walk in. Surprise them.*

Frankie's temples throbbed—damned concussion—but he set the pain aside and wrapped his fingers around the ancient crystal doorknob.

He pushed the door open. "Pop?"

His father sat behind Petey's desk with the square-headed guy standing on the opposite side. Dude angled back, saw Frankie and whipped front again.

"Frankie!" His father shot out of his chair, came around the desk and put a hand on his arm to usher him out. "I'll be right out."

But Frankie's eyes were on the tall dude with the square head who wouldn't make eye contact. How the hell did he know this guy?

He pulled his arm from his father's grasp, stepped toward tall dude and extended his hand. "I'm Frank Falcone."

Tall dude nodded once. "How are ya?"

"Not bad." He burned the image of this guy's face—brown eyes, scar next to his right eye, thick nose that had to have been broken a time or two—into his head.

"Frankie," his father said, "order me a sandwich. I'll meet you outside."

His father wanted him gone. Frankie usually didn't come back here when his father conducted business. Not that his father ever told him to stay out, but he never wanted to know what went on behind this closed door.

Today, his father wanted him out. Why?

"Sure, Pop." He turned to the tall dude. "What did you say your name was?"

"I didn't."

*Okay, then.* Flaming moron.

Frankie went back to the table, inhaled his sandwich and bolted. He walked the few blocks back to his house and called Joey on the way.

"I can't talk," Joey said. "The Bulls are down by three. I could lose my ass."

Frankie blew that off. With a seven o'clock start, it was way too early to be worrying about the ending. "There was a guy at Petey's before. I need to know who he is."

"Why?"

"I don't know. I've seen him. Can't figure out where. Jimmy said he's on one of the other crews. I went to the back office and he was in there with my father. He wouldn't give me his name."

"What'd he look like?"

"Tall, dark hair, square head. Big guy."

"Square head?"

"Yeah."

"Had to be Neil. He's on Mickey's crew."

"How would I know him?"

"Couldn't tell ya. He doesn't come around Petey's much. They have their own place on the west side."

Frankie reached his house, stopped in front and grazed his sneaker over the patch of lawn. Why was Neil talking to his father? The crews generally stayed within ranks. "Why would he be meeting with my dad?"

"Couldn't tell ya," Joey repeated.

Could Lucie's father have something to do with it? Frankie knew his father typically discussed business with Joe during his visits. They had been forced to work out their own coding system due to the constant recording of conversations, but they still managed to do business. "When are you seeing your dad?"

Joey sighed. "Well, Princess Puff-Puff, if you can get out of bed and play bodyguard to my sister, I'll go tomorrow."

Princess Puff Puff? Frankie should kick his ass. "I'll be ready to roll tomorrow. Ask your dad about Neil. Don't make him suspicious."

"What is it with you and Neil?"

"I don't know. He kept turning away from me like he didn't want me to see his face."

"Dude, he's probably in a jackpot and wants to keep it quiet."

"No. It's me he's got a problem with. Everyone in Petey's saw him, but he avoided me."

"Maybe he doesn't like your pretty boy looks?"

"Or maybe he doesn't like my connection to these dognappings?"

---

THE FOLLOWING EVENING, FRANKIE, JOEY AND LUCIE SAT huddled around the dining room table anticipating Mom's return from her poker game. Yes, her mother had a weekly poker game. No real money exchanged hands. Bingo chips only and Mom had a knack for raking those babies in.

"We don't have a lot of time," Joey said. "What's up?"

Mom usually got home between nine-thirty and ten and the clock hovered at nine-forty-five.

Of course, Lucie and Frankie had to wait for Joey to join them at the house and now he was moaning about being short on time. Typical.

"How'd you do you with your dad today?" Frankie asked.

"Good and not so good. He's not pissed at Lucie anymore." Joey turned to her. "You need to get up there this weekend. He's done lecturing you about finding a job, but if you don't get your skinny butt up to see him, he's gonna blow."

She hated visiting her father in prison. No one wanted to think of their parent as a caged animal. "Fine. I'll get on the list." She looked at Frankie.

He backed away. "Me?"

"Yeah."

"I'll go if you want me to, but that'll lead to him asking if we're back together."

"*Are* you back together?"

"We're dating," Lucie said. Frankie nodded.

Joey scrunched his face. "Dating? Is that like a friends-with-benefits thing?"

Imbecile. "Don't be a jerk," she said. "Tell us about dad."

"Right." Joey flicked his eyes to Frankie. "He doesn't know about any deals Neil and your dad might be involved in. Neil is a good earner though."

"Didn't he want to know why you were asking?"

"No. I told him I saw him having lunch at Petey's with a couple of guys."

Holy cow, Lucie thought. "You lied to Dad?"

Joey looked at her with a bored expression that telepathed he thought she was cow dung. "I didn't lie. The guy *was* at Petey's. He *could* have had lunch there."

"And he wasn't surprised by that?" Frankie wanted to know.

Joey stuck out his bottom lip. "Not really. Mickey likes the pepper-and-egg sandwiches at Petey's and sometimes makes Neil the delivery boy."

"Crap. I got all stoked thinking he was involved in the dognapping thing, and I've probably just seen him at Petey's buying a sandwich."

Lucie reached for Frankie's hand. "You're thinking too much."

"Dammit."

She understood though, because she'd lost plenty of sleep worrying about the dogs and the diamond and the ongoing search of the attic that had turned up nothing. For Frankie, it was worse. He'd promised her father she'd be safe. If he broke that promise, he'd hear about it for the rest of her father's life. And her father was a healthy guy.

"Who is this Neil? Do I know him?"

"I don't think so. He's not from the neighborhood. He's part of Mickey's crew and doesn't come around much."

"He's a big, tall dude." Frankie held his hands next to his head. "Square head."

She didn't know anyone with a square head. "I should get a look at him. See if I recognize him."

Joey sat back and blew his cheeks out. "Here we go with the conspiracy theories."

"It couldn't hurt," Frankie said. "Where does he hang out?"

"For Christ sakes. Let it go."

When Joey swung his gaze to Lucie, she said, "We should at least check this Neil guy out. If Frankie is this worried, there might be something to it."

Joey snorted. "You two have fun schlepping around Jasper to find this guy."

"No. It'll look suspicious if Frankie goes. You'll have to take me."

"Hell no. I'm not following Neil."

Frankie flung a hand out. "She's right. If he sees me with Lucie, it'll look strange. All you need to do is ask around, see where he hangs out and take Lucie there. In fact, you may not even have to get out of the car. Do a role reversal and pretend you're the feds. For a change, you'll be the one sitting in the car."

Joey grinned. "Nice."

Frankie leaned forward on his elbows, made eye contact with Joey. "I'll take your shift with the dogs next week."

"Now we're talking."

"*Both* shifts."

That lit up Joey's face. "Ding, ding, ding. We have a winner. You walk the mutts with Luce and I'll find Neil. Piece of cake."

"Well, I'm glad you boys figured that out." Nothing like feeling completely useless.

Frankie didn't miss the implied comment and grabbed Lucie's hand. "Your turn comes when he finds Neil. Something about that guy rubs me wrong. I feel like I've seen him recently. Maybe you'll recognize him."

Lucie shifted toward Frankie. "Do you think he's involved with stealing the accessories?"

He ran a finger over her cheek and the heat shot right to her lower core. God, she loved him.

"I don't know, but we've pretty much run out of ideas."

Joey shook his head. "This guy would have to be plain stupid to dogjack Lucie. My father would put his head on a stick."

Lucie sucked in a breath, felt the burn all the way to her lungs. On rare occasions, she heard about her father's business, but it never sat well with her.

"Oh, relax." Joey shook his head at her. "It was a figure of speech."

Right. Figure of speech.

Sure it was.

## 15

————

L ate Tuesday afternoon, a sunny day that made Lucie anticipate warmer weather and ice cream cones by the lake, she and Joey sat in his SUV across the street from the Hubbard Bar & Grill. They had completed the dog walks for the day and, despite her exhaustion, she'd pushed herself and Joey to track down this Neil character.

Supposedly Neil frequented this place, but they'd been here an hour already with no sightings of a blockhead. She pulled a nail file from her purse and began sawing.

The waning sun shined through the windshield, the meager heat radiating off the dashboard. Such a nice day.

Joey focused on Hubbard's and Lucie followed his gaze. Nothing. "What is it? Did you see him go in?"

"No. I'm hungry. Let's go eat."

*Eat.* Was he insane? They were on a stakeout and he wanted to march right into the place so he could feed his insatiable stomach. "We can't leave the car. What if he shows up while we're eating?"

Joey pointed at Hubbard's. "We'll eat there."

"*What?*"

"Why not? They serve food. We can eat and spy at the same time."

"What if someone recognizes us?"

He shrugged. "I'll tell them we were in the neighborhood and got hungry. I ate here with Dad a couple of times. Everyone knows I know the place. If Neil comes in, you'll get an up close look at him. Think about it, Luce. This is a great plan."

Before she could protest, he stepped out of the car and waved at her to hurry up. Nothing came between Joey and a meal.

"Jiminy Crickets. Give me a second."

She hesitated a minute longer, ran the plan through her mental strategizer. It could work. Finally, she scooted out of the car and followed him.

If the place wasn't a throwback, she didn't know what was. The lack of windows made it impossible to know whether it was day or night outside. Minimal can lights didn't help. An L-shaped bar sat to the right and a handful of unoccupied captain's tables and wooden swivel chairs filled the remaining space. The only sound came from a wall-mounted television tuned to SportsCenter.

The four men at the bar turned toward them then quickly looked away. Apparently, not anyone Joey knew, because he pointed to an empty table with vinyl upholstered chairs that reminded Lucie of ones her mother had back in the seventies. Still though, the place was clean and the scent of grilling meat hung in the air. Maybe she was a tad famished herself.

Upon finishing their meal, Joey lingered over a beer. His second. "I'm driving home," Lucie said.

"You think I'm loaded on two beers?"

"I don't care. I'm not taking a chance on you getting pulled over. That's all we need. The cop would take one look at the name on your license and he'd throw you in lockup."

Joey didn't argue. It could happen.

The door opened and two male voices boomed. "I banged the hell out of Gonzo's sister last night," one guy said.

Ignoring her better judgment, Lucie turned to look at the two men. If her father were here, he'd be up and beating the heck out of the guy who dared to talk that way with women present.

"Turn around," Joey said, his voice sharp, biting even. "That's Neil."

A gush of excitement left a metallic taste in her mouth and she spun back. This was it. Finally.

"Take a casual look," Joey said.

She pretended the voices drew her attention and glanced toward the door. Well, Frankie was right about one thing. The guy had a square head. Truly fascinating.

Unfortunately, she didn't recognize said squareness. That wouldn't make Frankie very happy. If she'd seen that head before, she'd remember it.

An older man followed Neil and the other guy through the door. Lucie turned back to Joey. "Mickey just walked in."

"Got it." Joey smiled big, maybe a little too big, and held his hand up in greeting. Mickey walked to the table, shook Joey's hand and kissed Lucie on the cheek. *Ick.*

"Good to see you, Joe. What're you doing here?"

*Joe.* Nobody that mattered called him that.

"We were doing errands for my ma and I got hungry."

Mickey nodded. "How's your father?"

"He's good."

"Glad to hear it. Give him my best."

*Gag.*

Mickey turned to Lucie, stared at her a minute and hit her with a slow moving, grease drip of a smile. "Lucia, I heard you got laid off. You let me know if you need anything."

That'd be the day. But because she was on a mission here, she smiled. Not too big, not too small. "Thank you. I appreciate that."

No sense being rude to a serial killer. At least that's what Ro called him.

Neil took a seat at the bar and turned to see where Mickey had gone. Lucie made eye contact and Neil, with the speed of a man running from a grizzly, turned front again. No wonder Frankie was obsessed. Neil's behavior didn't lend itself to innocence.

Still though, he wasn't anyone she recognized. Too bad. The glimmer of we're-gonna-fix-this-mess hope went bye-bye.

Lucie checked her watch. "Joey, we should go."

"Right." He stood and held his hand to Mickey. "Take it easy, Mick. I'll tell my father you were asking for him."

"Thanks, Joe. And Lucia, remember what I said. Anything you need."

*Don't hold your breath.* But Lucie nodded her thanks and they left the bar.

When they reached the sidewalk, Joey halted. "Well?"

The fading sunlight, in contrast to the darkened bar, seemed an instant relief and Lucie tilted her head skyward. "Nada. I've never seen that guy before. And with the shape of that head, I'd remember."

"Say goodbye to your boyfriend then, because we're gonna have to commit him."

Lucie snorted, but she wasn't sure Joey was kidding.

Frankie *was* becoming a bit compulsive about this. "Back to searching the house, I guess."

"Did you finish in the attic?"

"No. I have another seven boxes. No diamonds so far, but I did find grandma's coffee grinder. The wooden one we used to play with when we were kids?"

"Holy crap. Mom still has that?"

"You should see some of the stuff up there."

They reached the car and Joey turned to her. "Maybe you should think about not selling any accessories for a while. Let this blow over."

Fat chance. "Believe me, I've thought about shutting down, but I don't want to give in to these people. I don't get it, Joey. I can't find any more diamonds. We know none of the dogs are wearing them and we've been through my entire inventory, including what I've sold. There are no other diamonds. It's just the one in my safe deposit box and, according to Frankie, his father already spread the word that we hid that one. Why, if these people are so bent on getting that one back, aren't they coming straight to me?"

Joey, clearly remembering she expected to drive home, held his keys to her. "Whoever is doing this doesn't want Dad to find out who they are. Even with him behind bars, nobody will screw with him."

She took the keys, flipped to the thick black fob and pointed it at Joey. "Unless they had a darn good reason."

---

LUCIE SLIPPED IN THE BACK DOOR JUST AFTER DAWN THE NEXT morning, wearing last night's clothes. It wasn't her fault. She'd been conned into going to Frankie's to report on Neil and had been seduced by the master. For a good long time.

She gently closed the door behind her and winced when the lock snicked. *Please don't let anyone be up.*

"No sense sneaking." Her mother's voice severed the quiet air and Lucie shot upright.

Mom wasn't naïve enough to think Lucie was a virgin—not after three years with Frankie—but she didn't want her daughter sneaking around like a ho either.

The aroma of freshly ground coffee melted into Lucie making her mouth water, and she turned to find her mother dressed in her yoga gear, sitting at the kitchen table, having her morning wake-me-up. A magazine sat open in front of her.

"I'm sorry," Lucie said. "I was at Frankie's and fell asleep. He didn't want to wake me."

Not a lie. Totally. She *did* fall asleep. After a few rounds of marathon sex. Hot, slick sex that made her skin come alive and left her body limp.

Mom watched her with those expressive hazel eyes, and Lucie, expecting to see disappointment, saw nothing. No anger, no disappointment, no judgment. She curled her toes. How humiliating.

"You're a grown-up," Mom said. "Do you want breakfast?"

Not in last night's clothes. "No. Thanks. I need to get ready for work."

Mom closed her magazine and ran her hand over the cover, her movements slow and intentional. A prickle cruised up Lucie's neck.

"Are you happy?" Mom asked.

"What do you mean?"

"I feel like I'm being selfish with Coco Barknell."

Only her mother could think that. The woman had been

literally working her fingers until they bled and *she* feared she was being selfish.

Lucie slid into the chair next to Mom and linked fingers with her. "How could you think that? I owe you so much."

A moment, maybe two, fell away with Mom gazing at their entwined hands. Finally, she brought her damp gaze to Lucie's. *What's going on?*

Lucie scooted a bit closer. "Why are you upset?"

"Because I'm enjoying being part of something. With your father gone, I've been on my own and, well, bored. The sewing gives me something to look forward to. But I want you to be happy."

"Even if it means you being *un*happy?"

"Of course." Her mother smiled at her. "Welcome to the world of parenting, honey."

"You don't have to sacrifice for me anymore."

"When you're a parent, you'll understand. It doesn't matter how old you and Joey are, you're still my babies. I'll do whatever necessary to protect you."

Lucie shook her head. "You're amazing. After all these years, putting up with Dad and his antics—not to mention Joey—and you still have the energy to take care of us."

How the heck did Lucie get lucky enough to have a mother like this? One who put her life on hold for her family. Particularly when her father was...well...who he was. It seemed unfair, yet, her mother carried the weight of all their burdens on her sturdy shoulders, never allowing outsiders to see her falter. "I love you, Mom."

"I love *you*, and you never answered my question about being happy."

*Caught that, did ya?* Lucie shrugged. "I'm happy about certain things. I hate that I lost my job, but the dog walking has its advantages. I'm not cooped up in an office all day and

Coco Barknell lets me use my creative energy. My old job was all numbers and proofreading."

Mom looked toward the back door. "And what about Frankie? I take it you've reunited."

Sticky business here. She couldn't say they were dating. Her mother wouldn't understand that after she'd just busted her doing the ultimate walk of shame. Or would she?

"We're trying to start over. We never dated and didn't get to know each other like two people who met at a super-market would."

Mom laughed, but it was more of a "huh" sort of laugh. "I could see where that would be a challenge, considering you've known each other all your lives."

"Exactly. I didn't *really* know him. I knew that he liked baseball, but I didn't know that he thrived on it. That his dream made him feel whole. And that when he lost it, he had to figure out another way to be whole. Those sorts of things."

Her mother tilted her head. "I understand."

"I have to say, it's fun. We got all dressed up the other night and went out for dinner and dancing. I enjoy doing those things with him. We had gotten into a rut where we would just sit home and watch a movie. It's a nice change. We're taking things a day at a time."

"He loves you, Lucie."

That, Lucie knew without a doubt. In every touch, in every smile, in every word. "He does. What I need is for us to want the same things."

Her mother scoffed. "How incredibly boring."

"Mom!"

"Oh, please." she stood to freshen her coffee. "Why would you want that? Wouldn't it be fun to explore different wants? That's part of the journey. He wants things and you want things. As long as you both agree to be a team, you don't have to want the same things."

In Lucie's mind, this wasn't an option. Not with the one big want that she needed. The one Frankie couldn't compromise on. And then it hit her. Her mother could never have wanted a lifetime of gossip and trials and a husband in prison.

"Like you and Dad?" *Ouch.* She smacked her lips together. Of all the rotten, hurtful things to say. "I didn't mean that."

Her mother waved her off. "It's true. I've always let your father do things his way. I spoiled him. Now he expects me to always go along. It's not fair, but I helped create the monster he's become."

"He took advantage of your good nature."

Mom returned to the table; cup in hand, steam rising from its contents. After the crack Lucie made, the steam should have been coming off her mother. "I allowed him to take advantage. It's as much my fault as it is his."

"Still."

"With him gone, I've had plenty of time to think about it and decided to make some changes. I'm done doing things his way. When he comes home, he'll have to learn to compromise. I've been alone for two years now, and I've learned it's okay to want what I want instead of what he wants. He won't be happy about it, but he'll have to adjust."

*Yay, Mom.* The steely determination in her mother's eyes let Lucie know her father was in for a rough time when he got out. Good for him. Prison would seem like a cakewalk compared to the changes around here. They were his family, not his servants.

This was the difference between her parents' relationship and her and Frankie's. Frankie never insisted things be his way. He didn't scream or demand or manipulate. No, he always tried to find the compromise. Even if they fought, he would eventually agree to a compromise.

"I like that plan, Mom. He needs to appreciate you more. He's going to hate it that you've become a career girl with Coco Barknell."

She grunted. "Yes, he will, but there's not much he can do about it from a cell."

And there it was. The emotion her mother never showed. Anger over the humiliation of a husband in prison and for expecting her to keep their life in order without him.

"Mom?"

"Yes?"

"I don't know if I'm happy." Mom opened her mouth to say something and Lucie raised her finger. "I'm not unhappy though. I'm somewhere in between."

Given what was going on with the dognapping's, this was something to be thrilled about. Her mother, thank God, didn't know about all that drama.

"I raised a strong girl in you, Lucie. Don't ever settle."

"I won't. There's too much life out there to settle."

"Amen to that. If you love Frankie and he's the one, tell him. If not, let him find someone who loves him as much as he loves you."

A sudden hole opened in Lucie's chest. Let him find someone else? What did that mean? Another woman? Frankie with someone else would be beyond her pain tolerance. "Did you hear something? About him and someone else?"

Her mother pulled a face. "Frankie? Heavens no. He's a good boy. He'd end it with you before he went with someone else. I just think it's unfair to both of you, all this back and forth. If you love him, love him well. He deserves that. And so do you. That's all I'm saying."

Love him well. Had she done that? Did constantly asking him to make changes in his life represent loving him?

Could she get beyond the fact that he was happy living in Franklin surrounded by his family and the life? Maybe she was the one who needed to make changes?

Like her mother did regarding her father. It took her mother thirty years to make those changes, and Lucie wasn't about to wait that long.

She leaned over and kissed Mom's cheek. "Thanks."

"For what?"

"For being you. You're the best. You always help me. Even when I don't know I need it."

Mom smiled big. "Well, thank you. It's nice to hear."

"I'll tell you more often. I promise." She straightened. "I need to get showered. Frankie is helping me with the dogs today and I want to be on time. I have a few things to say to him."

Thirty minutes later, with her mother out for yoga, Lucie headed up to the attic to continue the diamond search.

"You up there?" Frankie hollered from the base of the pull-down stairs in the hallway.

"I'm here. Come on up."

A minute later, his head poked through the opening.

"Hey." He took a long look at her V-neck T-shirt. "You look hot today. Maybe we'll stop at my place on the way to the dogs."

She rolled her eyes. The man was insatiable. "No. The schedule is tight enough."

"I can be quick."

She burst out laughing. "Somehow a five-second lay doesn't sound like fun for me." Still, she was grinning because she found comfort in Frankie's sexual appetite. Everything came back to sex with him. Sometimes it was like a buzzing bee around her, but there could be worse things than a man constantly wanting to love her.

He boosted himself into the attic, shoved a box aside and crawled over to her. "I'll make it fun."

"I know. I also know it's important to you that I'm happy. I love you for that. I love you for not giving up on me when I constantly ask you to change the things you don't want to. I love you because you're you and I don't ever want to be without you."

Frankie settled his gaze on her as he considered her words.

Was he going to say something? Anything? Dust particles floated on the air and Lucie waved a hand at them. It was easier than thinking about how she'd just let her most intimate feelings fly.

He leaned closer and focused on her lips. "I'm definitely getting laid today."

This would be one of the times when his one-track mind irritated her, and she bit down hard to keep from spewing. Damn him. She turned and flipped the lid on the box closest to her. Had she even gone through this box? Never mind that, how could he not say something more appropriate? *Idiot.*

"Stop it," he said. With swift moves, he shoved the box away and mashed her with a lip lock that sent the familiar fire to her core. But no, he would not distract her from being mad, except his hand moved up her waist, his fingers gentle and soothing. His thumb settled at the curve of her breast and stroked and—yow—good stuff there. She inched closer, allowing a chip to form in that wall of anger between them. When he kissed her like this, he knew the power of it, how it affected her and every feminine inch of her adored that.

Still, he was an idiot. Her idiot. But she wanted him. She also wanted this feeling of floating away. No dognappings, no job loss, no crazy family. Just Frankie bringing calm and lightness to her life.

He pulled back and looked her in the eyes. "I love you. I want you all the time. Don't be pissed at me for it. It's my way of telling you what you mean to me."

"But that was a big moment for me and you reduced it to something sexual."

"I'm sorry."

He meant it. The way he refused to look away, his eyes searching hers, told her so. She nodded. "No more talk about sex. We don't have time. I have to get these last few boxes done, walk the dogs and get home so I can work on collars."

"Yes, boss." He glanced around. "How many boxes are left?"

Lucie smacked her hand over three boxes. "Just these."

"Got it."

And just like that, he settled in to go through dusty old boxes with her.

"By the way, I talked to my sister about helping with collars. She's in if you need extra help."

"Perfect. Another set of hands will help with the orders coming in. She can help with gluing the rhinestones. She'll have to do it here though. She can bring Paulie with her if her husband isn't around."

"Count on that."

His sister was another one Lucie didn't understand. "Why does she stay married to him? He's never home. What's the point?"

Frankie focused on the newsprint wrapped item in his hand. "No idea. It's her life. If she wants to spend it married to that knucklehead, I'm not going to argue with her."

"She could have so much more."

"Yep."

And yet she chose to be married to someone in the life. A real leg-breaker. Such a waste.

Lucie watched Frankie carefully unwrap the item that had probably been in this attic for thirty years. "Maybe that's what your sister knows. Everyone around her is in the life or married to someone in it. You and I are the freaks. We went legitimate."

Frankie laughed. "You're right. It's you and me, babe. We're stuck with each other."

"Pretty much. Who else could understand this craziness?"

All this time she'd been fighting, wanting to get away from here, blaming Frankie for not wanting to move. She never once tried to understand his loyalty. Truth was, she'd probably never understand, but as her mother had said, as long as they were a team, maybe she didn't need to. Tears bubbled behind her eyes and she turned to the box awaiting her attention.

"Luce?"

The softness in his rich voice, like liquid butter gliding over her, brought up a sob. She could never live without hearing that voice. At night, in the morning, when they made love and when he talked dirty. She had to have it.

The sob broke free and she bent over the box and let the tears fall because she'd been such a fool. A fool that almost lost the one thing she'd always wanted.

Fear and relief melded inside her and she hiccupped.

Frankie set the small bowl he'd just unwrapped on the

floor and pulled her from her bent position into a hug. "What is it?"

The smell of his soap, some fancy stuff he bought at Neiman's, drifted into her and she slipped her arms around him and squeezed. She had to tell him. He deserved it. "I've been asking you to move away. Moving wouldn't solve it. We'd still be part of this. We can't run from our families."

"Luce, it's okay. *We're* okay. You want things and you're trying to figure out how to get them. I want things, too. There's nothing wrong with that."

Finally, she pushed back, gripped his arms. "I'm not going to ask you to move anymore. If this is where you want to be, I'll deal with it, but we need to set boundaries. I don't want everyone up our butts all the time."

"I hear you."

"I don't know where my life is going, but I know I don't want to spend the rest of it being Lucie Rizzo, Mob Princess."

He shook his head. "You don't have to."

"And I want us to be a team. I'm tired of fighting with you about making changes and not defending me to your parents. If you're willing to set those boundaries and take my side once in a while, then I'm willing to stop bugging you about it."

"I don't want to sell my house. I want to stay in Franklin. Are you good with that?"

"Yes. As long as we separate ourselves from the chaos. That's why I liked living downtown. I was able to be me and didn't have to think about being Joe Rizzo's daughter."

"Luce, you don't have to live far away to do that. Build your own life and people will see you for what you are. You can be Lucie Rizzo, CEO, whose father happens to be Joe Rizzo."

She never thought of it that way. Again, he was right. She hated that.

"Good point."

"Damn straight. And the way things are looking for Coco Barknell, maybe you'll make me some big-time money."

Lucie grinned. "Now you're talking."

"See. You don't need to be an investment banker to become a billionaire. You can build a corporation. And I can be a kept man who travels from state to state watching baseball games."

She laughed. "You're an idiot."

"You wouldn't support me?"

"Oh, I'd support you. As long as you do all the cooking, cleaning and laundry."

Frankie made a *pffing* noise and went back to his box. "I'm not doing that."

"Then you'd better get back to work." She checked her watch. "We need to hurry with these last two boxes. I made us late with my emotional upheaval."

He shrugged. "We'll get it done."

Yes. They would. That she knew for sure.

***

WHILE WALKING OTIS, ARETHA FRANKLIN'S LOVELY PIPES sounded and Lucie snatched her phone from her jacket pocket. A 312 number. Downtown.

Who could this be? Cranky. That's what she was. Really, she should have been happy because they'd finished the search of the attic and found nothing. Nada. Not one errant diamond.

It should have been a good thing. Except it left them with another dead end.

She picked up the call. "Hello?"

"Lucie?" A man's voice asked.

"Yes."

"This is Noel Ferguson at Westerner Bank."

The guy she had interviewed with. Holy smokes. She glanced at Frankie and shoved the leash at him. Probably a courtesy call to let her know they'd hired someone else. "Hello, Mr. Ferguson."

Frankie's mouth slid into an O. He continued walking Otis while Lucie lagged behind.

"I wanted to let you know we've been through the candidates and we've come to a decision."

Here it comes, the big kiss-off. "I see."

"If you're still available, we'd like to offer you the job."

A job. She could move out of Franklin and get her life back.

A choir of angels should have been singing. Unfortunately, all Lucie heard was the sound of Otis barking at a car and Frankie telling him to shut the hell up.

She got the job. Just what she'd wanted. Back to being Lucia Rizzo, associate investment banker. Even if it meant seventy-five-hour workweeks.

Something caught in her throat. She swallowed to relieve the pressure. After the last couple of weeks, a banking job sounded pretty darn good. A relief even.

She stared down the block at Otis sniffing his favorite tree. He'd be there for at least five minutes. She knew this, because she and Otis had come to an agreement. She'd give him time at his favorite tree and then, somewhere in the next block, he'd poop for her.

If she took a job, she'd have to give up Otis and Coco Barknell. Abandon her mother and Ro. Lucie's chest seized. How could she do that to Mom and Ro?

But a banking job? This is what she wanted.

"Lucie?"

She cleared her throat, tightened her grip on the phone. "Mr. Ferguson, thank you for the opportunity. Unfortunately—" *Unfortunately*? What was she doing? "I've had another opportunity come up and I'd like to pursue it."

"Oh." His voice displayed shock. Or was it irritation?

"I appreciate your offer," she said. "I don't want to accept the job if I'm not sure it's what I want. That wouldn't be fair to you."

"I see. I'm disappointed, but your honesty is admirable."

Honesty. Wasn't that what she'd been craving all this time? For someone to recognize that in her? For someone to admire her rather than pass judgment?

After exchanging goodbyes, Lucie shoved the phone in her pocket and slapped her hands over her face. Did she really decline a job that offered security, a steady paycheck and the opportunity to move out of Franklin?

Yep. Sure did. God help her. Three weeks ago, she would never have done that. A bird flapped by her head and she straightened, took a breath of crisp morning air and settled herself. It was done now. No turning back.

"Luce?" Frankie called from three houses down. "What's up?"

She trotted up to him. "I just turned down the banking job."

His head snapped back. "Seriously?"

"Yep."

"Are you okay?"

"Yep."

He laughed. "Really? Because, I don't believe you."

She knelt in front of Otis, stuck her cheek in front of his snout and gratefully accepted a wet lick. After a second of the Otis love, she stood to face Frankie. "Here's the thing, I don't have that sick what-did-I-do feeling in my stomach. That tells me I wasn't ready to give up on Coco Barknell."

"Good for you, Luce."

"I guess we'll see."

Frankie handed her the leash. "Truthfully, I don't think you even like banking. You set a goal and getting a job was more about reaching the goal. Did you ever think about that? About actually liking banking?"

No, she hadn't. Banking gave her credibility, at least she thought so. It had never occurred to her to waver from the plan. "I know I'm not terrified that I just turned down a job. That has to mean something, right?"

He slid his arm around her. "I believe it does."

# 16

---

After getting off work early, Frankie wandered over to Lucie's having no idea what to expect. Lately, the Rizzo nuthouse had gotten nuttier. And it was impossible to ignore their kind of crazy.

Lucie sat in her usual spot at the dining room table, her laptop open in front of her and various reports, fabric samples and other Coco-related items scattered about.

"Hey," he said.

She stared at him with eyes as blank as a sheet of unused paper. *Okay, then.*

"Oh. My. *God.*" She squeezed her head between her hands. "I am completely freaking out."

He laughed. He couldn't help it. She looked...deranged, and somehow...cute as hell. "Why?"

"They ordered five *hundred* coats."

"Who?"

"Ro took it upon herself to meet with a buyer from Frampton's. I should kill her for that alone, but five hundred coats? How are we supposed to do that?"

This information, just as Frankie was about to launch

into one of his talk-her-off-the-ledge speeches, knocked him daffy. A major department store wanted Lucie's products. "Luce, that's fantastic." He grabbed her hand, smothered it with kisses. "Damn, I'm proud of you."

She snatched her hand away. "Did you hear me? Five. *Hundred*. Coats. Not to mention the two hundred collars."

Even better. Coco Barknell had arrived. Frankie could understand Lucie's turmoil, but this was awesome.

"Stop smiling," Lucie screamed.

He rolled his lips under and she jabbed a stiff hand at her laptop. "I've been working on a production schedule and it's impossible. We'll never make it. What was I thinking, agreeing to this order?"

"You were thinking it's a great opportunity and you should jump on it." He grabbed the spreadsheet she'd left on the table and perused it. "What have we got here?"

Lucie flicked her finger at the underside of the page. "Cost estimates, production schedules, man hours. The whole works."

His girl, as usual, had everything organized. The numbers looked good. Totally doable. "You've got a start on what you need. Let's work it out. You need more money? I can give you a bridge loan until Frampton's pays you."

She shook that off. "What I really need is more time. I called the buyer after the meeting and talked her into delivery spread out over four weeks, but it's still tight. We need to get them two hundred items in two weeks, then the remaining order over the following two weeks."

Frankie perused the report in his hand. "You have five seamstresses here."

"I figure we can get it done with five. They'll have to work their butts off though."

He set the spreadsheet down, looked at poor Lucie and

her tight-lipped God-save-me expression. "Your mom knows people, right?"

"Yes. We're hoping they'll jump in."

Sounded like a plan. "And my sister said she'd help."

"I don't know what to do about the dogs. I'll have to get someone to cover for me; and how am I supposed to explain this whole dognapping thing?"

Frankie shrugged. "Joey will do it."

*And won't he be stoked about that?* Frankie picked up the spreadsheet again and pretended to read.

Lucie gasped. "For a minimum of three weeks? He'll kill me. And if he doesn't, I'll have to listen to him moaning and I'll *wish* he had killed me."

He looked up from the spreadsheet and gave her his no-fail smile. "You're cute."

That earned him a big, honking eye roll. So much for his no-fail smile.

"Frankie, this Frampton's thing adds pressure. We need to figure out who that diamond belongs to so we can all get on with our lives."

"I know. With the search of the attic being a bust, we're hitting dead ends everywhere."

"Yeah. And Joey keeps telling me to check the walls for the diamonds, so I've been walking around banging on them. Next he'll have us taking a hammer to my mother's house."

"You're not doing that. This house hasn't been painted in a couple years. How in the hell would someone hide something in the walls without your mother noticing? And Joey will walk the dogs for you."

Lucie shook her head. "He won't do it."

"All he cares about is someone seeing him picking up

poop. Outside of that, he doesn't care. Plus, I have a little something that'll convince him."

Lucie leaned forward, a wicked gleam in her eye, which was a nice change from the psycho panic look.

"What is it?" she asked.

Frankie tossed the spreadsheet aside. "Nothing you need to know about. You'll owe me big, though. I've been saving this chip a long time and I'm giving it up. For you."

Where Lucie was concerned, owing him always meant sex, a lot of it, in experimental positions. In his opinion, hardly anything to cringe about.

She offered him a half grin. "If that's what it takes. I'll sacrifice my body."

He grabbed her, nuzzled her neck and hoped for different ways to distract her. He backed away, stared into her eyes and saw the spark of heat there. That spark crackled between them as she ran her hand up his forearm and his skin did that funky pulsing that always happened when she touched him. He'd kill himself if it ever went away.

"You always come through for me," she said.

And that was saying something with the crew they ran with. Never mind. This moment was too good to let it slip into drama-filled crapola. "Just make sure you do a lot of stretching. If Joey agrees to this, you'll need to be limber."

Her cheeks fired to the color of cherries. Probably thinking he was bad. But he was *her* bad. And the weeks they had spent apart before this dating thing happened had been torture.

Together, their unbalanced world evened out. He understood her life and the chaos of her family. They were a team. A damn good one.

FRANKIE PARKED THE CAR A BLOCK FROM THE LUTZES'. ONCE again, Lucie thought, he got a great parking spot. Good news considering it was already ten o'clock and they needed to pick up the scooters and get moving. She might as well walk Otis while they were here. It would blow her schedule even more out of whack because Otis wasn't supposed to be walked until eleven-thirty, but she needed to cut time. Another night with Frankie forced her to work on collars early this morning rather than last night, which of course threw off her morning.

"Who's first today?" Frankie asked.

"Walking Otis now will save us a trip."

"Hopefully, we weren't followed."

Lucie flapped her arms. "Thanks for putting that idea into my head."

"I'm just saying."

Arguing made no sense, considering he was right, but still, she didn't need the reality check. She grunted.

"Whatever, Luce. I'm not fighting with you."

"I'm not fighting with you either."

She opened the entry door, and Otis leapt at her with his tongue flying. He hit her hard enough to knock her off balance and she clutched the doorframe to keep from going over.

The dog shot out the door. "No, Otis! Frankie, catch him."

He spun around, saw Otis on the move and grabbed his collar. "Got him."

*Whew.* The Frankie Factor struck again. Even dogs weren't immune. *Damn rambunctious dog.* Lucie grabbed the leash and ran to clip it on her not-so-little client.

"Bad boy, Otis." He licked her hand. "Don't try sucking up either. It won't work."

A car came around the corner and Frankie turned toward it. Lucie glanced at the black Cadillac cruising at a slow speed.

A niggling feeling zipped up her spine. Frankie watched the car amble down the street and turn at the next block.

"Did you get a look at the driver?" he asked.

"No. You?"

"No. He turned his head when they got close. I didn't recognize the guy in the passenger seat either."

Insanity. With the million cars in this city, they couldn't get sidetracked worrying about which ones held dognappers. "I think we're being paranoid. Lots of people drive Cadillacs in this neighborhood."

"It's not paranoia. It's caution."

"Fine." Lucie planted her feet until Otis realized he wasn't going anywhere and stopped tugging. "Let's be cautious while we're walking then. This is our chance to make up the time we lost earlier."

"You have your stun gun?"

She patted her shoulder bag. "Yep."

"Keep it handy. I'll be right back."

"Where are you going? We're late."

But he was already running toward the back of the house. "Start walking if you have to. I'll catch up. Fry anyone who comes near you."

––––––––

FRANKIE HAULED ASS IN A WAY THAT REMINDED HIM OF TRYING to beat the throw to home plate. His heart pounded, his breath hitched and the euphoria pushed him to move faster.

If only he didn't have dress shoes on. He cut through the Lutzes' backyard to the other block. With any luck, the Caddie would hook another right onto this street and he could get a look at the driver.

Bursting through the neighbor's yard, he cruised by the house and hit the sidewalk. The Caddie came around the corner. *Yes!* He ducked in front of a parked car and listened for the Caddie drawing closer.

When he heard it a few feet away, wanting the element of surprise, he jumped up, drew the attention of the driver and stared right into the face of Neil the blockhead.

Son of a bitch. He knew something was off about that car.

Neil turned his head and pressed the gas, barreling down the one-way street.

Lucie.

*Damn.*

Frankie charged back through the Lutzes' yard, his muscles straining for more speed. He hit the driveway at a dead run and instinctively made a left. Lucie, being a creature of habit was halfway up the block.

"Luce!"

She spun toward him. Otis, seeing him in a full sprint, started howling and leaped. Lucie tugged on the leash with both hands to keep the dog from tearing her arm off. "What is it?"

"Watch for the Caddie. It's the blockhead."

Frankie caught up to her and ripped the leash from her hands. "Get your stun gun ready." He looked at Otis. "Did you pee?"

As if the dog would answer. He turned to Luce. "What's his status?"

"Peed. Didn't poop, but he's about to."

Frankie glanced down the street. No Caddie yet. It should have been there by now. Must have veered off. "Neil was driving the Caddie. He circled around to the other block and I saw him." He pulled his cell phone from his jacket pocket. "I knew it."

"Who are you calling?"

"Joey. He needs to get down here and help you while I ask my father what's up with this guy."

They finished Otis's walk, keeping close watch for Block-head until they jumped on scooters and headed to Buddy's house. Joey met them there and Frankie headed back to Franklin. He had two-and-a-half hours before work, so he made a quick call to his father.

"I need to talk to you. In person. It's important."

"Now?"

"Yes."

"Meet me at the house in an hour."

An hour. That left plenty of time for him to grab a cab to the Lutzes' and head back home.

Finally, a break in this dognapping mess. He would lay odds that Neil was behind this whole thing and the son of a bitch was going to fry. He'd make sure of it.

How stupid could this guy be? Messing with Joe Rizzo's daughter. He had to be a world-class schmuck.

*Well, schmucko, you are toast.* Worse than toast. A crouton.

Feeling smug, Frankie arrived at his parents' house a few minutes early and used his key to let himself in. "Ma?"

No answer. Must be out. He marched into the kitchen, threw his keys on the table and spotted the morning's left-over coffee sitting in the pot. After touching a finger to the pot—still warm—he helped himself to the brew. Last thing he needed was caffeine in his already buzzing body, but it was there, and why should he waste his mother's good coffee?

The back door opened and his father came through wearing black pants with a crease so sharp it could have sliced iron. He wore a gray dress shirt, collar open, and his shoes were polished to a gleam as usual. His father never skimped on the details.

"You okay?" Pop asked.

All it took was that simple question and Frankie's head exploded. No, he was not okay. He was exhausted and his father could get to the bottom of it with a few phone calls. "That effing blockhead. I think he's behind these dognappings."

Pop scrunched his face. "What the hell are you talking about? Who's a blockhead?"

"Neil. The guy with the square head that I met at Petey's. I knew he looked familiar, but I couldn't figure it out. This morning, he cruised by Lucie and me when we were walking one of the dogs. You think that's a coincidence?"

"Hey." His father held up his hands and took a step forward. "Settle down."

"Someone has been boosting these dogs to steal the collars and coats Lucie is making. And I think Neil is behind it. Why the hell else would he always show up where Lucie is when she's walking the dogs?"

His father's face turned to steel. Finally. He was getting the point and maybe they'd find some answers.

"Frankie, what are you doing? You can't make an accusation like that. This guy Neil, he's a good earner. You're going to get him in a jackpot."

Frankie shook his head so hard it should have flown off his head. Of all the crazy things. When did his father develop dementia? Maybe it wasn't dementia, maybe it was something else, but he was not connecting the dots.

"Pop, listen to me. Please. I need you to look into this. I've seen that guy before. I'm not sure where, but I've seen him. The other day he wouldn't look at me and he wouldn't tell me his name. Why is that? He knows I've seen him somewhere he shouldn't have been. And now, with him showing up at the Lutz's this morning, it's too convenient."

A whistling started in Frankie's head, and his father's face went from cold steel to piping red-hot. Thank you. He was finally getting it.

"You're out of your mind," Pop shouted. Frankie's head snapped back. *Whoa.* Never had he spoken to him this way. Beyond that, how could he not understand Neil was behind this? Or, was he trying to save himself because he'd lost control of a crew when Joe Rizzo put him in charge?

"Me? I am *begging* you for help. Lucie is in trouble. She's carrying pepper spray, a stun gun and who knows what else. She's already zapped someone with that thing. Sooner or later, she'll get hurt. Do you want that to happen? Can you live with knowing you could have helped and didn't?"

His father scrubbed his hands over his face. "How the hell did you get in the middle of this?"

As if that mattered. "I love her. I'll do whatever I need to for her. Including going to Joe."

There. He'd said it. Threatened to go over his father's head.

Pop's eyes turned black. Hard. Frankie shoulders flew up. It had been years since they went at it and the dread assaulted him like bad booze.

"Pop, all I've been asking for is help. If you can't help me, I'll find a way. Please, help me figure this out."

Mom came through the back door carrying a grocery

bag. She glanced at Pop then her gaze shifted to Frankie, and her face split into a smile. "Frankie!" She set the bag on the counter, rushed over and pulled him into a hug. "What a nice surprise."

"Hi, Ma." He hugged her, closed his eyes a minute and let her happiness settle him. No matter how old he got, he wanted his mother happy.

"You should have told me you were coming. I'd have made you a nice lunch."

"It's too early for lunch," his father said.

"Still. I could have done *something*."

"It's okay, Ma. I can't stay. I needed to talk to Pop and I think we're done." He turned to his father. "Are we done?"

Hesitation hung heavy in the air, and Pop's gaze bounced between his wife and Frankie.

"Give me some time. I'll talk to Neil."

Frankie nodded. "Thank you." He could have gone on about how he appreciated it and he knew it was a lot to ask, but that was stupid. His father owed him this. He owed Joe Rizzo this.

Frankie turned to his mother. "I owe you a dinner. How about Friday night? Just the two of us. We'll go out somewhere."

"I'd love that." She turned to his father. "Do you mind?"

"No. Go have fun. You're always saying you want more time with him."

Frankie checked his watch. "I have to go." He kissed his mother's cheek then turned to his father. "Let me know what you find out."

"Yeah, I'll call you."

With that, he walked out. No shoulder pat. No handshake. No nothing. Frankie wondered if he knew his father at all.

LUCIE PULLED HER HELMET OFF, SHOOK OUT HER HAIR AND spotted Frankie standing in front of Rizzo's Beef waiting for them. He stepped over, wrapped his arms around her and nuzzled her neck.

What a greeting. But something wasn't right with him. His energy usually came in buckets, but now there was a heaviness she didn't understand.

"You okay?" she asked.

"I'm good. Happy to see you. Everything quiet?"

Joey swung his leg over the scooter seat and stretched his long arms. "We've gotta figure out this dognapping thing. The scooter is killing me. These bastards weren't built for people my size."

She ignored the complaint and released Frankie. "What did your father say?"

"He's gonna talk to Neil. See what's up."

"Listen," Joey said, "this Neil, he's dumb, but I don't see him being subversive. He doesn't have the guts to go against my father."

Frankie held his palms out. "My dad says he's a good earner. Somehow he's involved in this diamond thing."

Joey shrugged.

"Why else was he riding around the block at the exact time Lucie was there?"

Stepping closer, Joey glanced around at the pedestrians scattered along the sidewalk and, in a low voice said, "I didn't say he wasn't working for someone else. I'm saying he doesn't have the cojones to do it himself. I wouldn't be surprised if Mickey is behind this. He's always resented my dad."

"Why?" Lucie asked. They both looked at her. They'd

probably forgotten she was there. Joey and her father never talked business around her and this definitely fell under the business category.

Joey remained silent.

"No way," Lucie said. "You are not clamming up now. You're talking about something that involves me and I'm entitled to know."

Frankie and Joey exchanged a 'we're-stuck-humoring-her' look.

"Mickey wanted to be underboss. Dad gave it to Frankie's dad after the other guy...uh..."

"Lambed it?" she added. She wasn't stupid; she paid attention to the news. Three years ago, the supposed underboss of the family took off for parts unknown to avoid a RICO conviction. The FBI continued to search for him, but he was doing a fine job of staying unfindable.

"Yeah. Anyway, Mickey's been pissed off about it."

"Enough to do this?" she asked.

Joey shrugged. "Who knows? Maybe he hid the diamond in the house hoping the feds would find it."

Could be. Ro always said the guy was crazy. Rumor was he'd killed twenty-two people. Lucie didn't want to mess with him.

Or the statistic.

———

LUCIE WALKED THROUGH HER MOTHER'S BACK DOOR AND heard a male voice coming from the living room. She spun to Joey. "Were you expecting someone?"

He cocked his head to listen. "No."

He pushed by her and right on his heels followed him

into the living room, where their mother entertained none other than Detective O'Brien.

An immediate sickness slammed into Lucie as she locked eyes with O'Brien. He stood to greet them, his smile fast and loose. A man merely stopping by for a chat.

"Ms. Rizzo."

"Detective." Lucie slid her gaze to her mother, who remained seated and completely unruffled. Maybe this wasn't bad.

"I wanted to check on you," O'Brien said. "Make sure everything's been quiet."

*God, don't let him spill the beans in front of Mom.* To her left, Lucie was aware of her mother's eyes on her. The woman, after years of being surrounded by law enforcement, knew this detective sitting in her living room might as well have been a neon sign signaling a problem. Lucie would have to fess up. Partially. She shifted to her mother. "I had a problem with one of the dogs. Detective O'Brien helped me."

"Un-huh," her mother said, and the tension in the room swelled. With no other options, Lucie faced O'Brien. "This is my brother, Joey."

Joey nodded, but didn't offer his hand. He hated cops.

"Okay, then. Detective O'Brien and I will talk outside."

Once on the sidewalk, she spun to O'Brien. "I never told my mother about the dognappings. I didn't want her to worry."

"I gathered that. I didn't say anything. We've been making small talk for ten minutes."

Lucie snorted. "She didn't offer you any cake?"

"Actually, she did. I declined. She said she'd wrap a piece for me."

"That sounds like her. Is there an update on the case?"

"No. Sorry. I was working another case on the South Side and figured I'd jump over here and check on you."

"You could have called."

One side of his mouth hitched up. "I could have."

She'd bet this man was a charmer when he wanted—or needed—to be.

A car horn beeped and Lucie turned to see Ro's Escalade come to a stop in the middle of the road. She lowered the passenger window. "Who's the hunk?"

*Welcome to Franklin, Detective.* But O'Brien apparently liked being called a hunk by a beautiful woman because he cracked up.

"I love this town."

"This is Detective O'Brien from the Chicago P.D."

"Oh." The word came slowly.

"I know," Lucie said. "Hard to believe. He helped with the dogs and came to check on me."

A car pulled behind Ro and honked. She opened her window and stuck her head out. "Slap yourself!"

Lucie grinned at O'Brien. "In case you were wondering, her husband is president of the town council."

With the honking driver sufficiently reprimanded, Ro spun back to them. "I need to go, but I have an idea for a coat. I'll call you later."

Lucie waved as Ro sped off. "That was my best friend. As you can see, this town has its own set of rules. You either work with them or you get out."

"Which do you do?"

"I'm straddling the line."

The front door opened and Joey stuck his head out. "You need anything?"

Her brother wanted nothing more than to be rid of the detective. "I'm fine."

ADRIENNE GIORDANO

Joey threw the door closed and the *thwack* tensed Lucie's shoulders. O'Brien shifted and Lucie saw his sidearm tucked under his jacket. Maybe she could borrow that? Whack her brother over the head with it?

"I should go," he said. "Let me know if you have any more problems."

"I will."

He headed for the battered Crown Vic at the curb.

Between him and that nice Officer Lindstrom, Lucie was starting to like cops. Her father would have a heart attack. The front door opened again and, thinking it was Joey, Lucie whirled. Her mother. Darn. *Lucie, you have some 'splainin to do.* She drew in a long breath and took the first step toward the house.

"What's going on?" Mom wanted to know.

Lucie pushed by her. "Come inside and I'll tell you."

After parking at the dining room table and giving her mother the diluted version of *random* dogjackings, Mom stayed silent, her eyes focused on Lucie. She didn't look convinced. She'd known about the first one from the dinner with Frankie's family, but Lucie had kept the others to herself.

"Mom?"

"That detective is the one working the case?"

"Yes."

"And he thinks this is part of a show dog ring?"

"Maybe."

After a long moment of staring at each other, Mom's face hardened. Her mother worried, always, but this was something else. This stone exterior was anger that ran hot and deep and something inside Lucie's head snapped.

All this time she'd been avoiding telling her mother about the dognappings and diamond, but what if, by some insanity, her mother knew something? Could her mother somehow be involved in this? No. Couldn't be.

Lucie rubbed her fingers against her temples.

She forced herself to look at her mother, the woman who had always been so supportive and consistent in all the ways that mattered. Then fear took hold and Lucie's resolve collapsed. "Mom? Do you know something about this?"

Please let her say no. *Let her be the person I've always thought she was and not be involved in one of Dad's harebrained schemes.* The clock *kerplunked* on the hour and her mother shuddered from the sound. She cleared her throat and her eyes got a little droopy. Lucie's heart slammed, the pressure expanding, more, more, more, until her chest got tight enough to blow apart.

"I think so."

## 17

_____

The pain in Lucie's chest felt like an ax whacking at her. Her mother, the moral compass of the family, might be involved in this diamond mess.

"You know about the dognappings?"

Her mother gasped. "Absolutely not. I would never have allowed that."

Lucie slapped both hands over her face. *I don't understand.* They had to start at the beginning. It was the only way. She pulled her hands away and focused on her mother's eyes. "Did you know I found a diamond in my craft stuff?"

Mom's gaze held. "You used one?"

*Cripes.* "I used it on a test coat, but disregarded it because it was too big. We've been assuming there are more since the dognappings haven't stopped. I guess, since you asked if I had used *one*, we were right."

Her mother nodded. Two and a half weeks of trying to outsmart dognappers and keep it from her mother and the woman knew all along. Worse, she'd allowed Lucie to be put in danger. How could she do this?

"You have no idea what I've been through. Three of my dogs were kidnapped and two others had attempts made. Then there was the theft at Sammy's and Frankie's concussion."

Her mother flew out of her chair, ran to Lucie and threw her arms around her. "I didn't know. If I'd known, I would have stopped it."

The agony in Lucie's chest grew. "Please, tell me about the diamond. Frankie, Joey and I have been insane over this."

Pulling back, Mom drew a long breath and held it for a minute. "There are more. I don't know how they got into your supplies. I spotted them a few weeks back when I brought laundry into your room."

"How did you know they were real?"

Mom put her head down, cupped her hands over her eyes. "I've seen them before."

*Oh, no.*

"Are they Dad's?"

"No."

"Then whose?"

A loud clomping sounded on the stairs and Joey swung around the banister wearing a fresh set of clothes. He combed his fingers through his damp hair. *Must have showered.*

"That cop leave?" he asked.

"He's gone." Then wondering if she should clue Joey in on this conversation, Lucie glanced at her mother, who inched her head back and forth. Lucie looked back at Joey. "Are you going out?"

"Yeah. I'll be back later." He smacked a kiss on Mom's cheek and left.

"Thank you. I'm not ready for him yet."

"But you're ready for me?"

"I don't have a choice. Not with the dogs being stolen and Frankie getting hurt. That's gone too far."

This didn't sound good. None of it. Lucie sat back, settled herself in for a ride she wasn't sure she wanted. "Tell me."

Mom pressed her hands as if in prayer, holding them in front of a tight mouth. She closed her eyes, made a humming noise. "It'll change everything. Maybe it's selfish, but I want you to see me the way you always have."

And Lucie wanted to die. Maybe, just maybe, she'd idolized her mother to impossible standards.

Mom held her head higher. "I like being the dependable parent."

"You think that will change?"

She smiled in that pitiful way people did when they knew they'd reached an impasse. "I know it will."

A spool of navy thread sat on the table and Lucie reached for it, unwound and rewound it. She could leave right now and never know what her mother had done. Not knowing would probably be much easier.

But that wasn't Lucie's way. She needed to analyze facts. She needed to absorb those facts. She needed to understand.

"Mom, it can't be any worse than what Dad has done."

Her mother nodded and slid her shoulders back. "The beginning goes back twenty years."

Twenty years. How could that be? "The diamonds have been here twenty years? How did the feds not find them when they searched the house?"

"They weren't here for twenty years. They must have been put here after your father was arrested."

"Do you know who put them here?"

"I believe I do."

"And?"

Mom closed her eyes again and the sight sent a stabbing pain up Lucie's spine. This would be bad. "Mom, please."

"Al Falcone." The words came in a rush, as if she hated the taste of them and needed to spit them out.

Lucie sunk into her chair while a vision of Frankie's face flashed in her mind. "That can't be." Tears filled her eyes.

All this time Frankie had been going to his father, asking for help and his father was already involved? How? Why?

"I don't understand," she said. "Are you holding the diamonds for him? Why didn't he just ask you for them back rather than steal my dogs?"

"He doesn't know I have them. He obviously thinks you have them."

Frankie had told his father they had one diamond. Mr. Falcone must think she used the others and didn't know it.

*My God.* "Are they stolen?"

"I believe so."

Lucie slammed both hands on the table. "Tell me the truth."

"Twenty years ago, your father and I went through a rough patch. He was gone all the time, doing who knew what. People started to gossip. I knew what he was, but I hated the snickering. I know you understand that."

"Absolutely."

"You and Joey were six and nine. You wanted your father to be like the other dads. The ones who went to parent-teacher conferences and school functions. Particularly, Joey. He needed his father. Plus, the two of you were fighting all the time and I was tired and lonely. I wanted some peace. I didn't mean for it to happen, but one day a man started paying attention to me and, well, I *liked* it. He complimented me and wanted to spend time with me where my husband didn't."

*Oh, no.*

Mom's shoulders collapsed. "Please don't hate me."

"You cheated on Dad?" *Holy smokes.* That took a set of brass ones.

"I'm certainly not proud of it, but yes, I had an affair. The guilt was horrible, but the love that man had for me was remarkable. It sustained me."

And suddenly, Lucie saw her mother through the haze. Somehow, she understood. She understood her father had not been easy to live with. She'd experienced it herself and couldn't imagine being married to the man.

She reached for Mom's hand and squeezed. "I could never hate you. I love you. Who was the affair with?"

"Bob Martin."

The only Bob Martin Lucie knew was the goofy guy who owned the meat store on Franklin Avenue. "*Butcher* Bob?"

"Yes."

Her mom had done the nasty with a guy in a bloody apron. "Wow."

"It started out innocent enough. I'd go into the store and we'd get to talking. Before I knew it, we were having coffee and then...well..."

Lucie held up a hand. "Got it. Skip the details."

"We used to meet at the motel off of Janes Avenue."

"Oh, Mom, not the love-thy-neighbor-here place." *What a cliché.*

"It was the only place we wouldn't be seen. None of our friends would be caught dead in that place."

"For good reason."

"Anyway, somehow Al found out about us. I don't know how. Bob certainly wouldn't have told and I was too terrified of what your father would do. To this day, I don't know how Al knew. He stopped by the house one afternoon during the summer. Your father was out and I was in the yard with you. Al told me he knew about Bob, and I was terrified he'd tell your father. I knew I was betraying your father, but I couldn't help it. Bob had a normal life, wanted someone to live that normal life with him. I had your father and his carousing and the police knocking on my door at all hours."

Lucie took a second, let it all seep in. Every disgusting detail. Her father obviously didn't know about this because Bob would most likely not be among the living. Or he'd be in a wheelchair.

Which he was not.

How many times had Lucie walked into that butcher shop and made small talk with the man who'd done a horizontal mambo with her mother?

Mom let out a long breath. "Al told me he'd keep my secret, but I had to help him. He and your father weren't close back then and I never saw the Falcones much."

"What did he ask you to do?"

"I had to accept a package he'd send from England."

"England?"

"You probably don't remember, but the Falcones went on a family trip to London that summer."

"Did you ask him what the package would be?"

"No. I didn't care. All I wanted was to make sure my children grew up with their mother. At the very least, your father would have made sure I never saw you and Joey. I couldn't live with that. At that moment, I knew I'd do whatever necessary to keep you."

"So, you accepted the package?"

"Yes. It was a shoebox, but it had some weight to it. I

wanted to see what was so important that he'd threaten me with it."

"You opened it?"

Mom nodded. "Yes."

"Let me guess. The diamonds."

"The box was filled with jewels. I panicked. I don't know what I expected to see, but it wasn't that. I should have known better than to open that damned package. It's haunted me for years. Anyway, I sealed the box and turned it over to Al. He asked me if I'd opened it and I said no. I lied."

"And that was the end of it? He took them out of the house?"

"Yes. Until three weeks ago when I saw them sitting on your work table."

Lucie sat in a stunned state of hyper-analysis. Questions warped her mind. *How did they get there? When did they get there? Why now?* She mentally sorted the possibilities into manageable piles. That would be the only way to attack this. One element at a time. The diamonds had to be first.

"We can assume the diamonds are stolen," she said. "Do you know from where?"

"No. Obviously England. I wasn't supposed to know what was in the box. I never asked questions. Nor did I want answers. All I knew was my children were with me."

"I don't understand why, after all these years, Frankie's father hid the stones here? Could Dad be involved? Maybe Mr. Falcone was hoping the feds would find them and blame him?"

Mom shook her head. "I doubt it. The FBI tore this house apart when your father was arrested. All the boxes in the attic had been overturned."

Lucie remembered it. The place looked like a war zone after a bombing.

"I had to clean that mess. There were no diamonds. I think if the FBI had seen the stones they would have known they were real."

A valid point. "The stones had to have been put there after Dad was arrested. Mr. Falcone, for whatever reason, suddenly needs a safe place to hide the jewels. He has an emergency key for the house so he goes into the attic, comes across my craft stuff and hides the jewels there. I haul the box down and start creating my accessories and wind up using one of the diamonds. He must have flipped when Frankie told him about my trunk shows. He probably came looking for the jewels, but I'd already cleared out what was in the attic. Why wouldn't he have just taken them from my room?"

"I switched them with fakes. He probably came looking for the bag in your room, but only found what I'd put there."

"So you have the real ones?"

"Yes. *I* took the real diamonds. I must have done it right after you used the one stone. I swear to you, Lucie, I didn't know you'd used that stone. I never wanted you or Joey involved. You could be charged with a crime. I panicked. Then I got mad because that man still had power over me. I hid the real stones. For a change, I wanted *him* to panic. I wanted him to feel what I've been feeling. For once, in this crazy, misbegotten life, I'd have control."

Mom played tough, holding her head high.

"You should have told me. I could have helped. Joey could have helped."

"I couldn't take the chance on something happening to either of you. It was my problem."

"Yeah, but now it's *our* problem and I need to figure a way out of it."

*Which probably includes telling Frankie his father black-mailed my mother.*

---

AFTER SPENDING AN HOUR IN HER ROOM SEARCHING THE internet for London jewelry heists, Lucie entered the Coco Barknell headquarters, a.k.a. the dining room, and found her mother hand stitching a black leather coat adorned with a faux fur collar.

She cleared her throat as the pungent aroma of coffee smacked into her. Mom's coffee made Mr. Atlas look weak. "Hi."

Mom set the coat down, smoothed it against the table, and then brought her gaze to Lucie. "Hi."

And there it was. The invisible barrier of a bag full of precious stones lodged between them.

Heaven help her. Lucie wrapped her hand around the back of her usual chair, pulled it from under the table and sat.

"Mom—"

"Lucie—"

She bit her bottom lip while Mom fiddled with a spool of inky black thread.

Lucie held out her hand. "You first."

"I'm sorry I didn't tell you about the stones. If I had known what you were going through, I would have told you."

Her mother had been the dependable parent for twenty-six years. Nothing would ever make Lucie believe otherwise. She reached across the expanse of the table. "I know."

Mom gripped her hand, nearly breaking her fingers. "Ow," Lucie cracked and her mother snorted a laugh.

Nothing like a little humor to lighten the tension.

"You okay?"

*Not so much. No.* "I don't think so. I lost my job, was forced to move back home and now I'm dealing in stolen jewelry. I can handle the job loss and moving home. The stolen jewelry has me hugging the edge."

*Check the penalties for unknowingly harboring stolen diamonds.*

Lucie couldn't think about that. "Mom, I should be down at police headquarters trying to clear myself. I can't do that though. Not with you being involved."

"All I wanted was to protect you and Joey."

"I know." Telling her mother she was a fool would not help matters. Somewhere in her mother's mind, she'd been able to justify helping Frankie's father commit a crime. All to save herself and her children. Maybe Lucie would have done the same, she didn't know.

"Here's what we'll do," Lucie said. "I just researched jewelry thefts. There was a big robbery at an English castle around the same time Frankie's dad shipped you the package, but we need more information. Unfortunately, that's going to require Frankie's involvement."

"No."

"Sorry, Mom. He's already involved and he'll get suspicious if I suddenly shut him out. Plus, it's his father. He has a right to know."

"Lucie, please, don't tell Frankie about the affair. Please."

Did she have the right to let her mother's secret out? Did it even matter anymore? Lucie jammed the heels of her hands into her gritty eyes. Her shoulders must have weighed a hundred pounds. She pulled her hands away. "I'll do my best to keep the affair out of it, but hearing this about his father will be devastating. If it will help him to understand, I'll tell him. He's entitled."

Her mother nodded.

"I need those stones, Mom."

"No."

Was that invisible barrier between them expanding? Had she ever argued with her mother? Really argued?

Probably not.

"I understand what you're doing. Protecting us is who you are. But this time, there's no way around me having those stones. Whoever is snatching my dogs thinks I have the diamonds. I can keep you and Joey out of it if they continue to think that."

Manipulating her mother's emotions might be the crummiest thing Lucie had ever done.

Call it collateral damage. Joey was already on the government's radar, and any hint of a jewelry heist would intensify that interest. Her mother would sooner drop in front of a bus than have one of her children be accused of a crime they didn't commit.

*Four, three, two, one...*

"Fine. I'll tell you where they are, but if you want them, I'll get them for you."

One thing was obvious. They weren't in the house.

"Where are they?"

"At the bank. Aunt Tillie's safe deposit box. I didn't know where else to put them."

The *bank*. Lucie hesitated, let the idea sink in. She and her mother had both hidden diamonds in safe deposit boxes. Great minds? Possibly. At least the dognappers couldn't get to them. Not unless they robbed the bank. Even if that happened, they'd need the box keys. Well, they could break into the house, trash the place, find the keys and *then* rob the bank.

*Wow.* What was up with Lucie's imagination?

She shook it off. "At least I know where they are. We can work with that."

For now.

---

Dead tired from her mother's recent revelations, Lucie walked through Frankie's front door prepared to tell him about a castle in England. A banner day all around.

She found him at the kitchen table reading the newspaper. He wore a stark white undershirt, his favorite blue basketball shorts and his coffee brown hair zigzagged into a wonderful mess.

"You okay?" she asked.

"Yeah, I had a headache. Came home early and napped. What's up?"

He shifted sideways to face her and Lucie took a moment to savor the crazy hair, the sleepy eyes, the crease from the sheet running down his left cheek. The simplicity of it calmed her, but now it was time to break his heart.

"We need to talk."

He blew air through his lips. "That's never a good sign."

She slid into the chair next to him. A good way to do this didn't exist. She dug her fingers into her forehead until the pressure penetrated her skull.

"Luce?" Frankie pointed at the sheet of paper in her hand. "What do you have there?"

"An article I found on the web."

"About?"

"A jewelry heist in London."

"*O*-kay."

He held his hand out and Lucie contemplated crumpling the page, forgetting the whole thing and finding another way. This piece of paper might as well be a guillotine slicing through their relationship. The world's largest paper cut.

Too late. She could see Frankie gliding his shoulders into the ready position.

"Let me have it," he said.

He had no idea what she was holding and the stillness saturated the space between them. *Forget the whole thing.* And yet, she couldn't. Even if Frankie would never know, *she* would.

And that was enough to destroy them.

She handed him the article. When he began to read, she went in search of the photo taped to his bedroom mirror. By the time she returned, he had finished skimming the article and she set the photo on the table. His eyes flicked to it before looking up at her.

"And what?"

She gestured to the photo. The one of Frankie and his family standing in front of a church in London. The day before the castle was robbed. "Did you see the date on the photo?"

"No, Luce. Just because you pull a story off the web doesn't mean my father had something to do with it. That's crazy. He loves you. He loves your father."

*Not enough.*

"You think this is a coincidence?"

He stared at her. She stared back. Finally, he flicked his finger against the page. "This article says two men on a tour of the castle hung back from the group and when they were alone in the gallery, they overpowered the guard and escaped with three million dollars' worth of stones."

"Yes. I researched other similar thefts. At the time, inadequate security made this common with privately owned castles that were turned into museums. Realistically, any average person with enough nerve could have pulled this off."

"Meaning it would have been easy for my father, with his vast criminal background, to do."

*Deep breath.* "I'm telling you what I know." She jabbed at the article. "This is what I know. I came here to share it with you so we could get to the bottom of it."

"You have one diamond. We can't find the rest. You think my dad snuck into your father's house, hid one diamond and not the rest?" He laughed, but the sarcasm of it could be felt in the next state. "He's not that stupid. Even if he was, where are the rest of the stones?"

"My mother has them."

Frankie shot from his chair, sent it flying backward against the cabinets and Lucie flinched.

"How the hell did *she* get them? Is she telling you they're my father's?"

"She found them in my craft stuff and, not knowing that I had used one, switched them with fakes. She didn't want me to get caught with them."

Frankie crossed his arms. "She admitted this to you? Out of nowhere?"

"Of course not. O'Brien stopped by the house to give me an update and my mother figured something was wrong. I had to tell her about the dognappings. I could tell by her reaction she knew something."

"And?"

"And she told me she had the real ones."

"Where did they come from?"

She pressed her lips tight.

"Come on, Luce. How does she know they're his?"

"I can't say."

Apparently, that answer wasn't flying. Frankie slammed his hands on the table and sent the leftover pop in his glass splattering. His hands stayed connected to the table, and he flexed and unflexed his fingers.

Moving slowly, she placed her hand over his. "I'm sorry. I knew this would be hard."

He stayed silent, his head drooping toward the table. Clearly, he wanted to fight the realization that his father had done this, but he didn't know where to begin.

After a moment of blazing silence, he looked at her with stormy eyes and she understood, down deep, she understood the rage brewing inside him.

Their fathers had disappointed them in horrible ways.

"I don't understand how your mother knows my father did this."

This wasn't fair to Frankie. He was a journalist. He liked facts—and these facts concerned his family. "My mom said your father asked her to accept a package he would ship from England, and she did. When she opened the package and saw the stones, she got scared. She sealed the box and never told him she had looked."

"And your mother didn't tell your father about this package?"

"No."

"Why?"

"I can't say."

He dropped his head and let out a huff.

"I'm sorry."

"For what, Luce? For not trusting me enough to tell me

what you're holding back? Or for accusing my father of lying to me when I asked for his help with the dognappings?"

"I'm sorry for all of it. I didn't know what else to do, so I came here, hoping we could put our heads together."

Frankie straightened, closed his eyes and his mouth started to move. Talking to himself. He held up a finger. "Let's back up."

"Fine."

"Even if my father did this—and that's a big if—why would your mother be involved?"

A reasonable question that he had a right to have answered. The life now pitted her mother against Frankie's father and, with Frankie's ironclad loyalty, Lucie didn't foresee a good outcome. Twenty years' worth of deception had landed between them. Someone around here needed to be honest.

"Twenty years ago my mother had an affair."

Frankie's head snapped back. "No way. Saint Theresa?"

"Yes. With Butcher Bob."

He burst out laughing. "Butcher Bob? You're kidding?"

"No. She told me. That's what started this whole thing. Somehow your dad found out." Lucie hesitated, put herself in Frankie's place and tried to imagine hearing about her parent's filthy blackmail scheme.

My God. She couldn't get away from the people in this life. How did their bad decisions constantly bring her to a dark place? For years she'd been trying to run, and somehow, she always wound up being reduced to Lucie Rizzo, Mob Princess.

And Frankie never understood her aversion to it. Maybe now he might.

The air in Lucie's body evaporated. She slapped a hand to her chest to get something, anything, moving.

Then, for some reason, her mind flashed to her missing spreadsheet. Frankie's father was probably the one who took it. Obviously, he'd used his key to enter the house and hid the bag of stones there. What was to stop him from coming back and grabbing her spreadsheet?

*Bastard.* The stolen dogs, the Sammy Spaniel robbery, Frankie's concussion. His own son. The man was a monster.

Boiling hatred of the life spewed inside her and burned every inch. These damned twisted people. "*Your* father put this whole dognapping mess in motion."

Frankie, trying to maintain his go-to-guy persona, folded his arms and leaned against the veneer cabinets they'd repainted together. He'd picked a chocolate brown because he thought it was manly. Manly. Thinking back on it, maybe she should have taken that as a sign she'd never live here with him.

On top of those manly cabinets, they now had stolen diamonds and the fact that his father had put her family in harm's way. The legal implications of harboring stolen property aside, how could she get beyond it all? How would she ever again be able to share a meal with the man knowing what he'd done?

And suddenly, the pressure in her chest erupted. Her heart was literally coming apart and the sharpness of the pain cut into her, forcing a low moan in her throat. She loved Frankie and now it was done. Over. The decision finally made because his father could only think of himself, and not about his son or the people his son loved.

"Hey." Frankie snapped his fingers in front of her. "You okay?"

No. She wasn't *okay*. She and Frankie could battle a lot of things, but this one? No chance.

She glanced up, saw the concern in his eyes and realized

that once again he had become wedged between her and his family. She wouldn't ask him to choose. She loved him too much for that. Besides, even if he chose her, she'd have to live with the idea that his father had done this to her. Their children would never know their grandpa because she would refuse to let him be part of their lives.

No win. Not even close. She would have to deal with this alone, because telling anyone what Frankie's father had done would only cause more hardship. Her father was absolutely out. Who knew what he would do? Particularly about his wife's affair.

Then there was Joey. He'd go insane, and she couldn't risk the type of violence that might employ. Not with Frankie caught in the crossfire.

The complications ran deep and left a hollow cavity where Lucie's stomach should have been. She fisted her hands and her nails bit into the soft flesh of her palms. The prickling brought tears to her eyes. She blinked. Once, twice, three times. Still the tears. *Dammit.*

Then she was in Frankie's arms, sobbing against his chest, her heaving gasps tearing through her, leaving the emotional ruin of her life in a sloppy heap. Finally, the release. "How can this be happening?"

"I'm so sorry," he said over and over again.

She knew it was true. Frankie didn't apologize unless he meant it. And really, it wasn't for him to apologize. *He* wasn't the one who had literally left her holding the bag.

And yet, here they were, and she had nothing to say. It was all too muddled. She had to think.

In one giant step, she backed away and swiped her palms across her eyes to blot the tears. More fell. She hated it. Hated the weakness. "I have to go."

"Luce—"

She put up a hand. "I'm sorry I ever involved you in this. I have to figure out what to do."

He grabbed her before she could scoot out. "Luce, wait. *We* will figure it out. I promise you."

No. They wouldn't. She turned back to him, looked into those dark eyes that had always been part of her life, the lean, angular face that had captured her heart at fourteen and then again at twenty-three. So many years together, first as friends, then as lovers. Now it was over. She'd never be able to look at him and not think about what his father had done. Frankie's loyalty would drive him to find a way to make peace, but in the end, that loyalty would keep him from completely taking her side. And they'd be back to the same old issues.

She squeezed his hand. "I love you, but I need to do this alone."

"Luce," he said, his voice more determined. "It's a shock, no doubt, but we'll get through it. Don't throw everything away."

Silly her, but she wasn't the one throwing it away. The crazy people in their lives did that. No, this way of life would never fit. Enough was enough.

If she wouldn't make Frankie choose, she had to. She slid her hand from his.

"I can't do this anymore."

## 18

"**D**ammit!" Frankie roared, the pressure behind his eyes so fierce he pushed his fingers into them and miraculously found no blood seeping through.

Lucie had just walked out of his house—probably his life—and he wasn't even sure he understood why.

He stuck his bare feet into running shoes and ran the three blocks to Petey's.

"Ho!" Jimmy said when Frankie stormed through the door. "You're a mess, kid."

Ignoring the comment, Frankie, hands on hips and his breath coming in bursts from the sprint, turned to his father. "I need to talk to you. Outside."

Pop stood, motioned Frankie to the door and followed him to the sidewalk. Not wanting to risk being overheard by any listening devices planted outside Petey's, Frankie turned left and they strode in silence for a solid block.

Their steps chewed away at the cracked concrete as cars ambled by. Feeling secure that they'd walked far enough, he stopped.

"Straight out. Did you plant stolen diamonds in Joe Rizzo's house?"

As expected, his father's face, lit from a street lamp under a darkening sky, remained impassive. Nothing. Frankie waited. One of them would have to give in. Dad stood on the sidewalk, completely at ease after Frankie had just accused him of being a thief.

"What, Frankie?"

Bingo. Evasive action. A non-answer to a simple yes or no question. Suddenly, the frustration and exhaustion from the past weeks curled inside him, shifted to a slithering rage that consumed him. His father had lied.

"All these dognappings. You putting me off when I asked for information. It's making sense now. Guess what? Theresa found those stones and hid them."

His father held up his hands. "Whoa."

Whoa nothing. Frankie was beyond that. "You stole those stones and hid them in Joe's house. In *Joe's* house!"

His father held his arms out in a, who-me? gesture. "Frankie."

Frankie stepped back. He had to. Never in his life had he thought about putting hands on his father. Never. But the fury inside scrambled his brain and thoughts of pounding on the man railed at him.

He bit down hard, sucked the cold evening air through his nose and closed his eyes. "Tell me what you did."

"Hang on."

He opened his eyes. "No. Tell me. Because from where I'm standing, it looks like you lied to me when I asked you for help. Worse, you put Lucie in danger."

Silence stretched between them and the relationship Frankie thought he had with his father began to crumble.

Frankie waited. His father finally shook his head and peered at the sidewalk.

"There's no way around it," Frankie said. "Not if you don't want me taking a bag of jewels to the cops."

That got his father's attention. He looked up, his eyes burning into Frankie's. "You'd do that? To your own father?"

"If you brought this mess to Lucie, yes, I'd do it."

His father stayed quiet for one, two, three seconds. "I hid them there."

The whooshing of cars on the street, the awning of the hardware store flapping overhead, a bus horn, all amplified inside Frankie's head and he pressed his fingers against the throb. As sure as he had been that his father was guilty, he wanted him to deny it. Wanted him to explain this insanity.

"You robbed that castle twenty years ago? You've been hiding those stones ever since?"

"Frankie—"

"Answer me."

"Yes."

"You and who else? The article Lucie found said it was two men."

"The guy you asked me about? Neil? I did it with his father. His father died last year, told Neil where his share was."

"Does Joe know?"

His father snorted. "No. It was a side job. Neil's father came to me with the idea. The castle had just been turned into a museum and didn't have good security. We jumped on it and split the stash."

A fierce thought slammed into Frankie. "When we were there, in London, you had me hold a box closed while you taped it. You told me they were souvenirs you were sending

251

home. Did you have me help you pack those diamonds? Your nine-year-old son?"

No answer. He'd take that as a yes. His father had made him an accomplice. At least in Frankie's opinion.

Frankie folded his arms as the last of his adrenaline rush faded and the cold air blasted his bare arms and legs. *Forgot a jacket.* "You robbed the place, blackmailed Theresa, *then* twenty years later used a house key Joe trusted you with to hide the stuff?"

Silence.

"When did you hide diamonds?"

"After Joe got locked up, I figured the feds would come after me next and since they'd already searched Joe's house, I thought my share was safe there. All I needed was to hang on to the stones for a while longer. I've been holding them, letting time pass so when I fenced them no one would remember the heist. The cash from those jewels would be a nest egg for your mother and me."

"Don't think you'll play me by bringing Ma into this."

"Just give me the bag and I'll put it somewhere else."

Frankie spurted a laugh. *Classic.* "What am I supposed to tell Lucie?" He held his hands out and in a singsong voice said, "Gee, honey, this has been a whole misunderstanding. My father broke into your house, hid the stuff, terrorized you and now I need the bag. Oh, and don't tell your father."

"How much does she know?"

"About your involvement?"

His father nodded.

"All of it. Theresa told her when a detective working the dognappings came knocking on their door. You didn't count on Theresa finding the diamonds and holding out on you. She's had them the whole damned time. Lucie used *one* stone on a test coat. She never even sold it. Theresa found the rest and swapped them with fakes."

His father poked a finger at him. "Talk to Theresa. Get the bag and tell her you'll take care of it. Leave Lucie out of it."

As if. And that quickly, he understood Lucie's aversion to this life. Maybe Frankie had been walking around with blinders on, but he'd been happy not knowing. This kind of betrayal though, how could he ignore it?

"I can't get my head around this. You ordered Neil to kidnap those dogs? To steal from Lucie's clients?"

"I didn't have a choice. You told me she was selling the accessories. I went back to the house and the jewels were gone. I had to make sure she wasn't selling them."

Frankie's vision blurred. He tapped his fingers against his thigh. "I told you she wasn't selling them."

"Hey, you said you found one stone. I figured she sold the rest and didn't know it. I couldn't take a chance."

"How'd you get her client list?"

"When I was looking for the stones I saw the report on her desk."

He bent at the waist to keep from pulverizing his own father. Sickening. All of it. This is what loyalty got him. Despite what his father did for a living, Frankie had trusted him to take care of loved ones. Instead, he'd walked all over them. Including Frankie.

"You were going to keep at it until you got everything back?"

"Unless we came up with another idea."

Frankie turned toward the street, stared across at the three-story building fading into darkness and wondered what the hell he'd say to Lucie. She had already figured it out, but he hadn't wanted to believe her. Now he had his father's admission.

And what about Joey? He would have to know. Frankie's chest caved in. All these people knowing upped the risk of Joe finding out, and he would demand some sort of retribution. This ridiculous scheme could put an end to Frankie's fathers' life. He turned back. "Where's Neil in this?"

"He's helping me get my stuff back. He's got his father's end and could go to prison for it."

"Tell him to back off Lucie's dogs. She never used any of those stones on her accessories." The irony of it finally hit him and he let out a sarcastic laugh. They were stealing dogs for no reason. "I can't believe you did this."

"How the hell was I supposed to know Lucie would lose her job and start making dog accessories? At the time, it was golden."

"Yeah," Frankie said. "At the time. Now it's a mess. And Lucie is in the middle of it."

---

LUCIE KNEW JOEY HAD RETURNED HOME. SHE KNEW THIS because he made sure to stomp his ginormous feet when he came in. To give it a little oomph, he slammed the back door hard enough to rattle the windows. And she heard all this from her bedroom.

For the love of God. The events of the day had already sucked every ounce of energy from her. Facing Joey couldn't possibly trigger further damage. She closed her laptop and headed downstairs for a cup of tea.

By the time she got to the base of the stairs, he was in the living room.

"You look like hell," he said.

Forget the tea. She so didn't have the energy for this. "Thanks so much." She turned back toward the stairs and the quiet of her room, where she could decide how to get her family out of this without hurting Frankie.

But then Joey's hand clamped on her shoulder and he spun her around. "What's wrong with you?"

*Ha!* That question would take waaayyyy too long to answer. Lucie stared into his eyes and hoped he wouldn't make some sarcastic comment that would cause a fight. With Frankie not here to mediate, it would be a bloodbath.

Without warning, the realization of living without Frankie slammed into her and the pressure behind her eyes built. *No.* She couldn't cry anymore.

"Whoa," Joey said. "What is *wrong* with you?"

"Back off!"

"Screw you. I've been busting my butt helping you."

To hell with him. The tormenting tension coiled and her brain went silent for a minute. She went up one step so she'd be eye to eye with Joey. Maybe blasting him would relieve some of the pressure. "I've thanked you a hundred times. What do you want from me?"

His head snapped back an inch and she felt her temper slowly unwinding. "You're not the one who lost a coveted banking job. You're not the one who has had dogs stolen. *You're* not the one holding stolen jewelry. Oh, and by the way, you flaming jerk, Frankie and I are done. Caput."

Joey folded his arms. "You two break up constantly. And you don't know that diamond is stolen."

The hell she didn't. She mirrored his stance. "You don't know what you're talking about."

Lucie blinked a couple of times, but didn't say anything.

"If there's something else, you'd better tell me."

With his hot head, he'd be the last person she'd tell. She spun away from him "Go away, Joey."

"Yeah, sure, great. No problem. What do I need you for? I'll run down to Petey's and ask Frankie's father what that blockhead has to do with a diamond being in our attic."

"No!" Lucie tore down the steps and followed him into the dining room. Joey stopped short and she plowed into his back. Her gaze shifted to the pile of fabric on the table waiting for her attention. Coco Barknell. The start of this whole thing. A bitter taste flooded her mouth.

"Son of a bitch," Joey said. And then, with tiny movements, he turned to her, his body moving ever so slowly while the gears in his brain clicked into place. He set her with an icy stare. "Frankie has talked to his dad all along. What aren't you telling me? What does Al Falcone know about this? And is it going to piss me off?"

The last morsel of Lucie's energy fluttered away and she dropped her shoulders. What a mess. Joey was the last person she wanted involved in this. He was too high-strung, too ready for battle, but from his bullying stance, she knew he wouldn't give up. With him already suspicious, he'd create more chaos.

"Three seconds," Joey said, "and I'm going to Petey's."

*Dammit.*

"One...two..."

Lacking a white flag, she waved her arms in front of her face. "Stop it. Please. Give me a minute."

Maybe two. Or maybe two *thousand*. Not that it would ever be enough. She pulled one of the dining chairs and dropped into it before looking up at him. "Promise me you won't freak out."

"Yeah. Good luck."

Figures. She shifted from him, fiddled with a piece of

fabric and wondered at the sudden calm inside her. Had she given up? Or did the fight just not seem worth it? Drawing a breath, she set the fabric down, smoothed it flat and turned back to her overbearing brother. In Frankie's absence, she'd have to do this.

"I'm going to tell you what I know. You are *not* going to lose it. If you do, we'll all get hurt. Including Mom. If that's what you want, go ahead...blow your stack. But I believe you're a better man than that." She flopped both hands out. "It's up to you."

———

TEN MINUTES LATER, JOEY STALKED THE LIVING ROOM, HIS yelling bouncing off the walls while Lucie sat in her chair watching the tirade. And she'd conveniently left out the part about Mom's affair. Sooner or later, he would question why their mother felt inclined to accept a package from Mr. Falcone, but for now, he was too busy storming about the diamonds being hidden in their house.

The back door opened and Lucie spun to see Frankie, still wearing his shorts and T-shirt—*he must be freezing*—step into the kitchen. She launched herself out of the chair before Joey spotted him. Who knew what would happen with this absurd level of tension.

Frankie looked at her with those deep brown eyes that reached inside her and the temporarily dormant ache in her chest suddenly pummeled her.

"I guess you told him."

She waved a hand in the direction of the screaming. "He was threatening to ask around. You should probably go until he calms down. He's not mad at you, of course. But the situation is...*awkward*."

"Awkward?"

"Look who's here," Joey hollered when he caught sight of Frankie.

Frankie glanced over Lucie's shoulder. "Stop acting like a moron and we'll talk. If you can't do that, screw yourself."

*Bam!* Joey shut up. Gotta love that Frankie. He had a way with people.

"*You* go screw yourself," Joey said, his big feet eating up the space between them.

With her hands on her brother's chest, Lucie gave a push. "Knock it off. No one here is to blame. Let's sit down and talk. I'll make some coffee."

As much as it shredded her emotionally, she needed Frankie right now. If nothing else, he always brought order. The fact that she'd spent the afternoon bawling was an obvious indication of her need for help.

Her brother headed back into the dining room.

Frankie squeezed her arm, but she didn't want him touching her. His touch reminded her of too many nights spent together. If she had to move on, she couldn't be thinking of those things. She patted his hand and slid from his grasp. His hand remained suspended in midair. Their eyes met for a second and she saw the sting of rejection fill his eyes.

Yes. They had both been gutted.

"We'll talk later," Frankie said, clearly not willing to give up on them. "Let's work on the problem with the stones."

"Excellent idea," Joey fired.

"Shut up," Lucie and Frankie yelled.

But Frankie wasn't done. He walked into the dining room, Lucie tight on his heels, ready to bust up a brawl. He pointed to a chair. "Joey, sit and be quiet for five minutes."

The two of them did that stare down thing men did until Joey, probably exhausted from his tantrum, sat.

"Luce," Frankie said. "I'll help you with the coffee." He held a hand for her to go first and then followed. "You okay?"

She grabbed the coffee pot and held it under the faucet. "I'll live."

"Good." He jerked his chin toward the dining room and leaned in close enough that his breath brushed her cheek. *Could he not step back?* "We need to keep Joey focused."

"Always a challenge." The metal coffee canister sat on the counter and she doled out a few scoops then flipped the switch on the pot. "But if he can stay on course, he'll be able to help me. And I need help. I mean, it's not like I can go to the police. I have a vision of my mother's mug shot and it's not amusing."

"Nobody is going to jail. Where's your mom?"

"Bingo night at church."

"That's good at least."

"This is ironic," Lucie said. "The one time I want my father's help and there's no way to communicate without the authorities listening."

"Yeah. And *my* father is definitely out."

Propping a hip against the counter, she sighed. "Wouldn't it be nice if we could return the stones? Just take those suckers back?"

Frankie rolled his eyes. Lucie puckered her lips. Was that a joke? She wasn't sure. The thought had to have come from somewhere, right? And considering she was a firm believer in the universe sending messages, maybe this was a message.

Why couldn't they simply return the stolen jewels?

Frankie, seeing her hesitation, grunted. "You can't be serious."

Boosting away from the counter, Lucie went back to the dining room where Joey sat like a bad boy in time-out. "What if we returned the stones to the castle they were taken from?"

"Come on, Luce," Frankie said from behind her. "How are we gonna do that? We can't walk in there and drop them off."

Lucie angled into the chair across from her brother. "Of course not. We'd have to come up with something. All I know is that it would get stolen property out of our possession."

This felt foreign to her. Lucie had always been the rule follower in the family, never taking chances or disobeying superiors. She was the good girl. And yet, here she was, trying to figure a way to unload a million dollars' worth of stolen jewelry. Not to mention the stash Neil had. Somehow, this wound up in her lap to fix.

And she'd do it. If only to save her mother from hardship.

Assuming Frankie would fight her, Lucie turned to Joey. There was nothing he loved more than conflict. "What do *you* think?"

He shrugged his big shoulders. "It's nuttier than a fruit-cake, but why not?"

*Pay dirt.*

"*What*?" Frankie hollered.

"You got a better idea?" Joey showed an amazing amount of restraint.

"Why don't we just ditch them somewhere and let the cops figure out where they came from?"

"No," Lucie said. "I want to return them to the owners. That's the right thing to do."

The more she pondered this idea, the better it sounded. "Frankie, I know it sounds impossible, but why couldn't we go to London and just check it out? See the layout of the place. Maybe we could wear disguises or something. I saw a post on the website about a charity function in a few days. That gives us all day tomorrow to get there and, if we have time, we could check the place out. We can buy tickets for the event and one of us could sneak off and leave the bag where the family would find it. Then we walk out and disappear."

Joey nodded. "It has possibilities."

He probably just wanted to be rebellious, but what did she care as long as he agreed with her?

"Assuming I would even agree to this crazy idea, that only takes care of my father's end. What about Neil? He has the other half of the stash." He turned to Lucie. "You gonna go after Neil next?"

With Neil being so intimately involved in terrorizing the dogs, that wasn't a bad idea. "I'll deal with that later. Neil's part of all this is not in our possession. Let's get rid of the stones we have."

Frankie clucked his tongue. "What if we get caught? They probably have security cameras. Even with a disguise, we run a good chance of getting nailed." He stopped, ran a hand over his mouth. Thinking.

Yesterday, she would have reached over, entwined their fingers and snuggled into him while making her point. That was before she knew what his father had done. Damn these people and this life.

"We should check it out."

ADRIENNE GIORDANO

Frankie stared into space. "I don't know. It might be worth a trip."

"Exactly."

Joey slapped his hands on the table and stood. "Good deal. You two take care of it."

"Right," Frankie said, not sounding convinced. "I'll tell my boss I have a family emergency. They always love that. Last time it happened, my father's picture wound up on the front page. My emergencies are good for business."

"Wait." Propelled by a blast of panic, Lucie jumped from her chair. "Frankie and I broke up. We can't do this together."

*No. No. No.* She could not spend time alone with Frankie. He'd try and talk her out of the break-up and, right now, she needed time to strengthen her resolve for living without him.

The afternoon crying jag had convinced her she needed to distance herself from the chaos of the Rizzo world. The latest plan for moving downtown while building Coco Barknell had already been hatched. Money would be tight, but she could do it. It would put enough separation between her and the life. The life included Frankie and she needed to find a way to survive the loss.

Mucking things up even more was the money he'd loaned her. She would pay that back as soon as she was able because a clean break is what she needed. No questions asked.

"I can't spend that kind of time with Frankie." She turned to him, hoped he would understand. "It would pulverize me."

"Boo-hoo," Joey—Mr. Sensitivity—said. "I'm not going to England. Besides, who knows if the feds are watching me? You don't want to risk that."

Frankie grinned. "I have to agree."

*Jerks.* Both of them. Even if they were right about Joey's involvement drawing unnecessary attention. She'd have to suck it up. Along with everything else.

Lucie puffed up her cheeks and blew air. "I want the window seat."

## 19

———

Kildare Castle, a stone mammoth of a building, sat on five hundred acres of lush green parkland. Lucie yearned to step off the cobblestone drive and collapse on the thick grass.

The castle had been turned into a museum, but the Kildare family descendants still occupied part of the home. The residence would be the key to Operation Reverse Diamond Heist.

On the far left, a sentry tower rose high in the air, and Lucie lowered her head and pulled her jacket closed at the neck. This fifty-degree day felt more like twenty degrees, but Lucie knew that was just fear freezing her blood.

She had donned a long blond wig for this tour and hoped to avoid drawing attention, but Frankie, despite the thick black eyeglasses, still looked like a hottie. Could he not tone that down somehow?

Trees lined the long drive, offering barely a glimpse of sunlight as they walked along. They had been forced to park in the remote lot for security reasons, and with each step they came closer to the three-story archway leading to the castle's entrance.

Had this been where Mr. Falcone entered?

She glanced left to the gardens. Thousands of tiny white flowers swayed in the brisk wind. For a moment, she wished she'd brought a camera. The beauty and tranquility of those flowers could sustain her for days.

Lucie tilted her head back and wondered what it would be like to live here, where no one knew her name.

"You ready?" The smooth baritone of Frankie's voice tore away a chunk of her already battered heart. How would she ever live without that voice? Without him? The finality of it seemed way too severe. Limbo. Again.

She smoothed her hand down the front of her jacket and, given the cooler temps and her freezing body, she wondered how her hands could be sweating. Stress. Boat-loads of it. That's how.

The only good thing about this trip was Frankie's insistence on chartering a private plane. After all, how would they get a bag full of stolen jewels through airport security? *Yeesh.* Still though, she took a few minutes to appreciate the luxury of flying on a private jet for the first time and couldn't find a whole lot wrong with it. Well, aside from the hot diamonds and Frankie covering the cost of the plane. Her tab with him was growing. Not a good way to leave a relationship.

Lucie focused on the castle in front of her. At any other time, she'd be lost in fairy tales and knights in shining armor. The only thing shining in her head now were the bars that would lock her into a cell if they got caught. She hefted her tote bag a little tighter to her body. "I'm ready."

Frankie rested his hand on her shoulder as two middle-aged women strolled by. "Chill out. You're holding that bag so tight someone is sure to search it. You should have left it behind."

Lucie eased her grip. "I couldn't leave the diamonds in the hotel. You never know, the maid could have gone through our stuff and found them. Then where would we be?"

"Out a million dollars?"

*Imbecile.* "Let's just do this."

He shrugged. "We're taking the tour. No big deal. A couple of tourists out for the day. Don't look guilty."

Two minutes later, they strolled to the enormous stone archway where a woman wearing a polo shirt and khaki pants greeted them in what had to be the thickest British accent Lucie had ever heard. Lucie stared at her for a second trying to decipher the words.

"The tickets," Frankie said. Of course, he got it. The Frankie Factor.

They stepped through the doorway into an alcove and found a table with detailed maps of the public areas of the castle. The private rooms were outlined on the map, but the spaces remained blank.

"Luce, you've got to relax. You completely froze back there."

"I couldn't understand her. I was translating in my head."

Frankie, Mr. Calm, laughed.

The interior door opened and a man with gray hair— what there was of it anyway—and a few extra pounds under his castle-issued polo shirt greeted them. "Welcome."

Lucie froze again. The weight of this little charade bounced off the man's pleasantness and smacked her upside the head. She'd never be a good thief. The Catholic-Italian guilt would kill her first.

"Hello," Frankie said.

"I'm William. The tour will begin in ten minutes. Please come in and browse the main hall."

"Uh," Lucie said. "Thank you."

*Way too loud.*

Frankie squeezed her arm and unleashed the Frankie Factor smile on the man. "We'll take a look around. Thanks."

A redheaded woman of man-killer caliber wandered over from a painting she'd been analyzing and glanced at Lucie. Then she moved to Frankie where, as usual with all women, her gaze stayed focused. Even with the damned nerdy glasses, he still had the touch.

Unable to stop herself, Lucie glanced up at Frankie, who simply nodded at the woman and shifted his eyes to the curving staircase ten feet in front of them. *Good boy.* Lucie threw her shoulders back. Even if he wasn't her boyfriend anymore, at this moment, they were pretending to be a couple.

The woman smiled at Lucie and moved to the far side of the room. *Yeah, you'd better move on, sister.*

Next to her, Frankie's breathing mingled with whispers from the twenty people scattered throughout the foyer. Classical music floated in the air and, although not a classical fan, Lucie found the soothing strings settled her nerves.

She glanced around the intricately carved stone pillars that shot three stories high and admired the architectural details and arresting images of angels sculpted into the walls. A man, his back to her and wearing a newsboy cap, stared at one of the giant pillars.

Frankie perused the map.

"What are you looking at?" Lucie asked.

He flicked a finger against the page. "I'm trying to figure

out where we're going to put the—" he paused as a woman walked by.

"Yeah. I get it," Lucie said. "I thought we were just having a look today?"

"We are. Probably."

Why did she think her plan of attending tomorrow night's thousand dollar a plate charity function would be altered?

"Frankie?"

"What?"

"Don't do this to me."

A guy in his twenties squeezed behind Lucie and she stepped an inch closer to Frankie to whisper in his ear. "We have a plan. A plan we spent a lot of money on. Let's stick to it."

"Good morning, all." William the tour guide called. "I will be leading you through the tour, but feel free to stop and enjoy the lovely artifacts preserved by the Kildare family. Keep in mind, if you choose to meander you will miss the wonderful narrative. We will start with the room you are standing in. This is the main foyer and these columns were erected in 1602. They were hand carved by a local mason. During that time..."

Lucie tuned William out and concentrated on Frankie, who still had his eyes on the map.

He tapped a finger against the map. "This could be the spot."

She glanced down. The dungeon. How appropriate. The group surrounding them began to move, but Frankie pretended to analyze a painting. "Stay here a second."

The last of the group wandered by. "Let's at least stay with the group," she whispered. "Even if we hang back."

No sense in calling attention to themselves right out of

the gate. She stared at the map. *Hey, now.* "Next to the dungeon. That room is marked private. If there's a doorway, we might be able to stash the stuff there. It looks like the only place that has some sort of direct access to the private areas of the castle."

"Okay. I see what you're saying. We can check it out."

Thirty minutes later, after visiting the marble-encased ballroom and the library's massive two-story bookshelves, Lucie stepped into the dungeon. At the front of the pack, she could hear William talking about the stone walls in the stairwell.

Cool air enveloped Lucie and she breathed in the unexpected floral scent. Who ever heard of an air-freshened dungeon?

At the bottom of the stairs, the arched stone doorway led to a corridor roughly twenty-five feet long. The only available light came from iron sconces perched over cutouts in the walls where various forms of torture implements were displayed. She imagined herself chained to the wall, blood oozing from her skin. *God, what were they doing?*

Several people in the tour group took advantage of the wooden benches lining the walls and Lucie considered joining them before her legs turned to jelly.

According to William, the doorway on the right led to what used to be holding cells, now converted to the Kildare family's private wine cellar.

Frankie grabbed Lucie's hand. "That's it."

She hefted her tote bag higher on her shoulder. "*Could* be it."

Insanity. They should stick to the original plan. But this *could* work. And she was never one to run from an opportunity.

The tour group shuffled ahead to an area where prisoners had been restrained by irons. Lucie gulped the pool of spit in her mouth.

Four steps later, they slowed as William spoke of the open doorway that led to the wine cellar.

"This is as good as it gets," Frankie said. "There's a camera on the wall to the left. Have you noticed all the doorways leading to the private areas have cameras?"

Nope. Hadn't caught that. *I'm a horrible thief.* "That's a problem. Then again, I've got this crazy wig on."

"*I* barely recognize you."

"I'll wait until the camera points the other way and head down the hall."

Frankie's head swiveled back and forth, examining the various torture devices on display. "If you want, I'll duck down the hallway and drop the bag in the wine cellar. Let's hope there are no security guards watching monitors somewhere. If the cameras are just recording, we'll be able to get out of here without a problem."

His only disguise was a baseball cap and the stupid glasses. "No. I'll do it."

The tour group moved from the doorway leading to the wine cellar. Frankie motioned Lucie to one of the torture devices on display. "Let them get ahead of us. I'll hover here while you dump the stuff."

"Right. If anyone comes by, distract them."

Frankie leaned down and hugged her. "You'll be in and out before anyone spots us."

The way he hugged her, so tight and strong, made her realize she wasn't the only one suffering through this ordeal. He had finally gotten to that place of disillusionment she'd reached years ago. That black, lonely place where disappointment in her father ran so deep it became part of her soul.

When he finally backed away, he wore the Frankie Factor grin. Lucie closed her eyes, slowly let out a breath. She could do this.

For the love of Pete. She'd be a terrible, just horrible criminal.

Frankie, tired of waiting, tugged on the tote bag containing the diamonds. "I'll do it."

"No!" She'd never be that much of a wimp. "We're in this together."

"Atta girl."

Right. "We'll wander up and I'll duck into the doorway."

Within seconds they reached the arched doorway where only a red rope stood sentry. A chill prickled Lucie's arms. At least if she got caught she wouldn't have far to travel to be restrained. *There's a thought.*

"You ready?" He asked.

*No.* "Yes."

They held back a second longer while the tour group marched down the hallway reviewing various torture devices. Lucie heard something about finger removal and wiggled her digits to make sure they were all intact.

Frankie continued his exploration of the displays and she moved to the doorway. One step over the rope and she'd be in.

The camera above hummed as it swiveled and Lucie glanced up. Pointed the other way. *Go!*

She hopped over the rope, tore down the hallway and found a glass-paneled door leading into a wine cellar bigger than her mother's first floor. Holy smokes. These people liked their wine.

The door had an L-shaped handle, rather contemporary for a castle. Wow; what a bizarre thought that was. What was she doing?

Fixing a mess. That's what.

Using the hem of her shirt as a glove, she pressed down on the handle. Nothing.

Locked.

*Dammit.* What now?

The gurgling hysteria tearing her stomach apart surged up her throat. *Calm. Stay calm and think.* She could abandon this plan and run back down the hall before anyone spotted them.

But then they'd have to try again at the event tomorrow night and Frankie was probably right about the massive security.

*Think, Lucie.*

Who would carry a key to the wine cellar? Staff and family members. Would there really be that many keys? Ridiculous. Not everyone would carry a key, but they might all need access.

*Go with that.* Lucie turned and spotted a shaft of light from a doorway a few feet down. Would there be a key hidden there?

Why not?

Holding tight to her bag, she ran to the doorway and peered in. The small room held a chair and a simple white desk with a drawer. She could leave the bag here.

No. Anyone, like her, could wander in and grab the jewels. She needed the key to the wine cellar.

She stepped into the room and, once again using her shirt, she opened the drawer. Nothing. She dropped to her knees, looked under the edges of the desk. Nothing.

An ancient chair made of wood so thick Joey could use it to bash heads sat next to the desk. She crawled to it to study the underside. Nothing.

She caught a gleam from behind the desk. A hook holding a key.

Had to be for the wine cellar.

Abandoning her worry about leaving a print, she grabbed the key. She'd just wipe it clean like they did on television. Who knew if that even worked, but she had to get moving.

A voice carried from the opposite direction of the dungeon and Lucie froze. "We'll need four bottles," a woman with a thick English accent said.

Oh, no. Someone needed wine. Lucie hung the key back on the hook and spun. The echo of heels on the tiled floor grew closer and a rioting panic boiled her cheeks. *Hide.*

But where? She couldn't step into the hall and there certainly wasn't any place in this tiny room to hide. Behind the door. She'd likely get caught, but she'd risk it. She heard Frankie do a loud *ah-hem* from the dungeon, said a quick Glory Be and jumped behind the door, smashing herself against the wall as if it would swallow her and offer protection.

The English woman stepped into the room and Lucie held her breath. *Not a sound, not a sound, not a sound.*

"Why is this door open?" a very American sounding male asked.

"It gets jammed," the woman replied. "We told Mr. Habers about it and he's coming 'round to have a look."

Lucie heard a shuffle and the two left. She released a silent breath as her heart banged. She couldn't move. Not yet. Not until they brought the key back.

A long two minutes later—Lucie had counted in her head—the voices drifted closer again.

"I'll put the key back," the man said. "I hate leaving this door open though. We'll have to shut it."

*Please don't let him see me back here.*

And then everything slowed as the clink of the metal key being replaced vibrated off the stone walls and a big meaty hand wrapped around the edge of the door just inches from her nose. She pulled in her stomach, imagined herself shrinking and willed her body to be still.

The door swung away from her and caught at the jamb before the man forced it shut.

Lucie bent at the waist and drew three long breaths. Way too close.

She was so not cut out for this.

*Get moving.*

Once again, she grabbed the key from the back of the desk and placed her ear against the door, checking for the distant click of the woman's heels. Quiet. Good. She pulled on the door handle.

Nothing.

She tugged again. Nothing. Trapped. Seriously? She placed one foot on the wall, held the door handle with the other and pushed off with her foot. Not even a budge.

A vision of her fingers being removed flashed in her mind. Damned dungeon. *Don't think about it.* She wouldn't panic.

"Luce?" Frankie whispered from the other side of the door.

*Thank you.* "What?"

"What are you doing?"

She rolled her eyes. "Having my nails done."

"What?"

"I'm stuck!"

"Uh-oh."

No fooling. "You push from that side and I'll pull."

"Okay. On three. Ready?"

Lucie propped her foot up again. "Yes."

*One, two, three.* She pulled with every bit of strength she could summon. Two seconds later, the door flew open and Lucie sailed across the tiny room. Rather than take a face plant, she twisted and—*boom*—her left shoulder bounced off the wall. She landed on the tiled floor with a whoosh.

"Ow!" Pain rocketed through her backside.

Frankie stepped into the room, grabbed her hands and hauled her up. "You okay?"

She nodded. "Let's just do this."

She ran back to the wine cellar, inserted the key into the lock—*score*—opened the door and tossed the tote bag.

Wait! If the camera recorded her with the tote bag and then without, they'd know she was the one who'd left it.

Not good.

She entered the wine cellar and her skin puckered from the chill of the refrigeration. She removed the gallon-sized bag of diamonds from the tote and tossed them back on the floor. Good enough.

With swift movements, she locked the door, wiped the handle and key and ran back to the storage room to replace it.

At the hall entry, Frankie grabbed her arm before she stepped in front of the camera.

"Listen for the swivel. There. Go."

Lucie hopped over the red rope, heard the hum of the video camera and glanced up. Aimed right at her. Panic ripped into her. Was the camera on her when she stepped over the rope? She couldn't worry about it now. She watched the camera swing away from the entry and waved Frankie over the rope.

"Let's get out of here."

He slid his arm around her and squeezed. "You okay?"

The feeling of his hands on her brought instant calm to her shattered nerves. She loved this man and their world was screwing everything up. "I'll be fine when we're on a plane home."

"Not so fast," a hushed voice said from behind them.

*Caught.* Lucie reached for Frankie's arm, squeezing with such intensity he winced.

"What are you doing here?" he whispered.

She tore her gaze from Frankie and looked over her shoulder at the man with the newsboy cap she'd seen in the main hall. The dim light forced Lucie to lean forward for a better look and, three seconds later, the realization of who this man was hit her. His plain beige jacket and dress slacks screamed I'm-trying-to-blend, but Frankie's father always did have a sense of style.

Mr. Falcone, the security camera to his back, looked at Lucie first and then his son. "You idiots."

But Frankie wanted no part of that and took two steps toward his father before Lucie grabbed him. "Don't freak out in here." Heck, usually it was him doing the warning.

"What are you doing here?" Frankie repeated.

"What are *you* doing here?" Mr. Falcone slid his eyes to Lucie and whispered. "Where are my diamonds?"

For the first time since this dognapping ordeal started, she was in control and the perverse pleasure warmed her. "Locked in the wine cellar down this hall."

Mr. Falcone made a move around them and Frankie blocked him. "Don't do this. We're getting the Rizzos out of this. Joe will never have to know. Leave it alone."

A moment of steel-jawed tension pulsed between them and Lucie began to flop sweat. Fabulous.

Finally, Mr. Falcone stepped back. "I didn't chase after

you to let you give them back. Of all the stupid things, Frankie."

Lucie gasped at Mr. Falcone's vicious tone. She shouldn't have been surprised after what she'd learned about him. Regardless, they were wasting time.

They'd been down here almost ten minutes. Someone was bound to come along.

"We need to move," she said.

Frankie grabbed his father's elbow and half dragged him to a display. Something that looked like a life-sized set of salad tongs. What the heck did they use those for? Lucie leaned back and glanced down the corridor as the camera swiveled away from her. They needed to wrap this up and get out. No telling if they had people manning those cameras.

And then, her bladder filled like a water balloon attached to an open faucet. Was the flop sweating not enough?

Frankie, in a very Frankie move, stepped closer to his father, their noses just inches apart. Lucie held her breath. Their profiles—the long, straight nose, the angle of the jaw —were so similar, she could have been looking at an aged progressed photo.

"You've done enough," Frankie said. "Keep moving and I might forgive you."

Was he really speaking to his father this way? This is what the situation had come to. She should have been happy, ecstatic even, because all along she'd wanted Frankie to separate himself from his father. To take her side. Somehow though, this seemed wrong. All wrong.

She put a hand on his arm. "This is over. Let's just get out of here."

"Lucie," Mr. Falcone said.

The sound of her name coming from his lips fried her and she poked a finger at him. "You shut up."

The stern look he wore had probably sent many men to their knees, but Lucie's fury ran so hot she was immune. This man had tormented her for weeks, not to mention what he'd done to her mother. Being disrespectful was the least of the damage Lucie sought.

"I haven't been hiding those diamonds all these years to let you give them back." He snatched her arm and squeezed. "Where's that damned key?"

The camera hummed again and Frankie stepped sideways to block it from capturing his father's hold on Lucie. "Let go or I walk out of here and you never see me again."

The un-Frankie-like violence simmering in his voice wasn't helping her back teeth to stop floating. Good Lord, she had to pee.

He stepped closer to his father. "Am I worth what's in that bag?"

Mr. Falcone had the nerve to laugh. At his own son.

Enough of this. Lucie elbowed them both away. "Knock it off. We're all leaving here."

Voices from the stairwell carried through the narrow hallway and a couple with two young children stepped into the dungeon. Lucie, Frankie and Mr. Falcone huddled around the salad tong display and played tourist.

Could there be a bathroom down here?

Frankie blasted the woman with the Frankie Factor smile and she returned the gesture. "We've seen this before," she said to her cohorts. "Let's get to the next area."

All four filed passed and Lucie crossed her legs. *Really have to pee.*

She went up on tiptoe and put her lips to Frankie's ear. "Let's just leave. There's nothing he can do."

He nodded. "You're right."

With his attention focused on his father, he said. "Even if he finds the key, he'll have to explain to my mother and sister why I refuse to see him."

Mr. Falcone gritted his teeth and Lucie imagined those pearly whites snapping under the stress. Thirty years from now—if he lived that long—he'd be an old man with shifting dentures who could have been her father-in-law.

"You would do that?" Mr. Falcone asked Frankie. "Over money?"

"I should be asking you that."

*Touché, young squire.* Lucie stood a little taller as her heart flip-flopped. After all the fighting and breaking up and getting back together, Frankie might finally understand her yearning to be more than Lucie Rizzo, Mob Princess. And all it took was a couple of dognappings, a concussion and stolen jewelry.

"What's it gonna be, Pop?"

Lucie glanced at Frankie. "I could always ring up Detective O'Brien and tell him about this. Or, better yet, the local police. I bet they'd love to hear this story."

"There's a thought," Frankie said.

"Wouldn't Neil *love* that?" she added.

Mr. Falcone drilled her with another hard stare. "Don't be stupid, Lucie. You've got a lot to lose."

"But not nearly as much as you. I can't imagine my father would be very happy about this. You know what a temper he has. Then there's the whole messy legal aspect." She shifted around him and stood next to Frankie, but she wasn't done yet. This man needed to pay. And she was just the girl to make that happen. "I could *crush* you with that bag. Or, we can all walk out of here and forget the whole thing. I'd say that's fairly generous of me considering what you've put me through."

Mr. Falcone shifted his gaze to Frankie.

"Don't make me choose, Pop. You won't like it."

And Lucie knew it was over. For once, Frankie had sided with her.

"I have to pee," she said as they pushed through the door leading out of the dungeon. Frankie kept an iron grip on his father's elbow as they walked and Lucie picked up the pace.

Like a beacon, the restroom sign flashed into sight. *Thank you.* She turned down the corridor and sprinted.

"Luce? Please."

"Sorry. Gotta go." Did he think she wasn't just as anxious to get away?

Well, some things couldn't wait.

"Hurry," he called from behind her.

Two minutes later, after the longest pee of her life, she emerged from the restroom to see Frankie and his father waiting for her. In silence, they all walked out the main entrance to the long driveway that had led them in.

Once they were out of earshot, Frankie said to his father, "How'd you know where we were?"

"Your mother told me you were going on a trip. The timing was strange for a vacation. I wanted to see what you were up to."

"I didn't tell Mom where I was headed."

"Cell phone," his father grumbled. "My guy at the P.D. has a friend at the phone company."

Frankie halted. *Uh-oh.* To remind him she was there, Lucie clasped her hand over his. She, of all people, knew the hurt that came when a parent proved to be a disappointment.

"Stay focused on what's next," she said.

He drew a long breath and closed his eyes. "Right. We get him back to his car, get his stuff and he flies back to Chicago with us."

"That's a plan."

As much as the idea of being in Mr. Falcone's company infuriated her, they couldn't risk him trying to steal the diamonds back. He'd caused enough trouble over these past weeks. Lucie would never forgive him.

Never.

Particularly because the other half of those stolen jewels were somewhere and she knew who was responsible.

These damned people. All she wanted was a respectable life and this is what she got. Shoulder-deep in stolen jewels.

---

A BANGING ON THE AIPORT'S SINGLE BATHROOM DOOR sounded and, like a springboard, Lucie shot off the toilet. For God's sake. Why couldn't she take a pee in peace anymore?

All she wanted was a few minutes alone before they boarded the plane and the only place to find it at this private airstrip was the miniscule bathroom the pilots used.

"Luce!" Frankie banged again.

She yanked her pants up, washed her hands and ripped the door open. She loved this man, but the damned building had better be on fire.

He dragged her into the outer room where the attendant had abandoned the news to chat with their pilot on the tarmac. "It's on the news. The stones. The owner can't believe it."

On the television, a reporter doing a live feed from

Kildare Castle was delivering the details of the recently discovered bounty.

Frankie jerked his chin to the television. "They're questioning all the tourists who bought tickets with credit cards."

"Good thing we paid cash," she quipped, but her head began to pound. What if the camera had caught her going down that hall?

"The Kildares will have to give the insurance company part of their money back, which we didn't think about, but hell, Luce, we got rid of the stones."

They had actually pulled it off. It wouldn't right the wrong, but at least the stolen merchandise was out of the hands of innocent people.

"Do they have any idea it was us?"

"Don't think so. No one has come forward about seeing anything."

She dropped into one of the two metal-framed chairs. Could it really be over? It would seem so, but they needed to get out of England. No sense hanging around. She could follow the story on the web. "We should get out of here. Fast."

## 20

————

Two days later, Lucie arrived home at three-forty-five after walking the dogs. With the stolen jewelry no longer in her possession, she had taken the bold step of not only walking alone, but going back to her original, time-efficient route. The emotional freedom of it, the mental peace, allowed her to feel like herself again.

She settled in with her laptop at the dining room table to review the inventory for the Frampton's order. Good progress had been made and she needed to log each item. Her mother had separated everything into large bins stacked in the corner of the room. A bin marked Coats sat at the top and Lucie hauled it to the table.

The front door opened and she turned to see Frankie come through.

"Hey," he said.

She smiled. "Hi. Look at what we've created. This Frampton's order might be the start of something. For the first time in a long time, I'm excited."

"Does that mean you're staying in Franklin?"

Lucie made a huffing noise. She hadn't thought about living arrangements. "I guess it does. For now."

He grinned, pulled her out of her chair and wrapped her in a hug. "Good for you, Luce. I'm proud of you."

Slamming her eyes shut, she concentrated on breathing. How did he always know exactly what she needed?

Because he loved her. Over the years, they had learned to tune into what the other needed. He was definitely better at it, but maybe that could change. Despite the craziness of their families and the fact that his father had put her in danger, she loved him.

All this time she'd been blaming him for being born into the life, asking him to change, to do what *she* wanted. He deserved more than that. And she'd give it to him.

She backed out of his grasp, but held onto his arms. "Thank you. I needed to hear that."

She waved a hand toward a chair, and Frankie dropped into it as if the world had pushed him there. He'd been through a lot these past days.

"How are you?" she asked.

He shrugged.

"About your father, I mean."

"It is what it is."

What a typical male non-answer. Lucie snorted. "Silly me, I expected you to talk, but then I remembered that men don't talk, so I guess I will. You're in a bad place. Your father disappointed you. I've been in that place. I'd love to say you'll get over it, but you probably won't. You *will* learn to deal with it though. I promise you that. I'll do whatever I can to help you."

He waggled his eyebrows and she rolled her eyes. Always with the sex.

"Actually," he said, "I'm not even in the mood for sex."

"Lordy, it *must* be bad then."

"I'm so pissed I can't even look at him. All I want is a meatball sandwich from Petey's, and I can't go there because I'll see him. I'm so filled with...with...I don't even know...that I'm not sure what I'd say to him."

"I know." She squeezed his hand. "It's like someone drilled a hole in your chest and scooped out part of you."

He blew air through his lips and started tracing imaginary lines on the table.

And then she remembered something her mother had said to her a few years back when she and her father were fighting like rabid animals. At the time, the words didn't seem like much, but over these weeks, she had come to understand the importance of them. "Frankie, our fathers, in their own way, love us. They simply make bad decisions. We don't have to embrace their choices, but we need to live our own lives. I'm hoping you and I can do that together."

Frankie's fingers stilled on the table and he glanced up at her. The silence of the room lingered.

"Luce, what my father did will always sit between us. I hate that, but if I turn away from him, my mother will be devastated. I can't do that to her. She doesn't deserve it. For all the loyalty I've given everyone, I feel like the schmuck now. I don't know where I go from here. I have to figure out how this thing with my father and your family will play out. And I want you to help me. I *need* you to support me, Luce."

A month ago, she'd have walked away. She'd have left Frankie, like she had done many times before, to figure it out on his own. Now she wondered if she'd been fair to him and that cinched her chest. Agonizing pressure. Her desire to prove she'd risen above the life almost cost her the love of a good man. An exceptional man.

She linked her fingers in his. "You stood by me through

all this craziness, even going against your father. I love you for that. And for so much more. I don't have to like what your father did, but I'll learn to co-exist with him. I'll do that for you."

He bent over, dropped his forehead against her hand, still linked with his and breathed out. "Thank you."

Slowly, she combed her fingers through his hair and rubbed. "To prove how serious I am, I'll do one more thing for you."

He bolted upright and the spark in his eyes made her smile.

"I'm listening," he said.

"I will go to Petey's and get you a meatball sandwich."

He grinned. "You hate Petey's. It must be love if you're willing to go that far."

He had no idea. "Yes, I believe it is."

## 21

On a bright sunny day the following week, Lucie hurried the girls along. It was close to lunchtime and her schedule was beginning to unravel.

The girls, however, must have sensed her angst and refused to poop.

"Come on, girls. Cut me some slack. We've been out here thirty minutes."

Josie looked at her, blinked twice then stuck her nose to the ground to continue the search for that perfect spot.

Lucie sighed.

A battered Crown Victoria came to a stop and double-parked. Oh boy. She knew that car.

Detective O'Brien emerged.

"Ms. Rizzo, how are you?" A smile eased across his freckled face.

Was he looking for her? He stepped onto the curb and reached to rub under Fannie's jaw.

"Hello, Detective. I'm fine. What can I do for you?"

"I'm on my way back to HQ and saw you. Figured I'd check in. Everything been quiet with the dogs?"

She nodded. "Absolutely." *Now that we've returned part of the stolen jewelry.*

"Glad to hear it."

"I'm still working the dog theft ring case, so if you ever need anything, be sure to give me a call."

What she needed was for him to arrest a blockhead named Neil and find the rest of those hot stones. Knowing Neil had gotten away with the remainder of the jewels, not to mention tormenting her by stealing the dogs, was chewing at her a millimeter at a time. Pure torture. She'd love to see him suffer for it.

Maybe she'd give the good detective the 4-1-1.

Then again, hadn't her father always taught her not to be a rat? A snitch? A fink? Yes, he had. But he also taught her not to take any crap, and the way Lucie saw it, Neil had dished out a whole lotta crap.

Her hands started sweating. What was with the flop sweating all of a sudden? She bent low to pat the girls and then straightened. *Dirty rotten staller.*

"I'll let you get back to work," O'Brien said.

He stepped off the curb, but turned back. "By the way. I saw footage about some diamonds that were returned to a castle in England. The guy caught on tape has a strong resemblance to Frank Falcone. You know anything about that, Ms. Rizzo?"

Lucie's brain exploded into a flurry of thoughts. Had he seen her on the tape? Was he playing with her? No. If he had proof, she'd be in handcuffs.

"Detective, I don't have a clue what you're talking about."

He ran his tongue along his bottom lip while a grin played peek-a-boo. "That's what I thought. Like I said, if you think of anything, you give me a call."

Once again, he moved to leave. *Tell him about Neil. Get rid of the guilt.*

But she wasn't sure she could do it. Somehow, it seemed a betrayal of her father's rules. Then again, what about her own betrayal? Didn't that count for something? Didn't she have the right to see her tormentor punished?

O'Brien stopped at the back bumper of his car, and waited for a bus to go around.

"Detective?"

She met him at the curb.

"Something wrong?" he asked.

Lucie inhaled, letting the moist lake air fill her lungs while Josie squatted to poop. Must be a sign from the universe that all was well.

"Ms. Rizzo?"

She smiled. "I can't help you with the castle incident, but I know someone who can."

The End

# EXCERPT OF KNOCKED OFF

Book two in The Lucie Rizzo Mystery series:

Lucie paused in front of the Lutz's garage while the door made its ascent. The heat from the tiny cobblestone driveway scorched right through the bottom of her sneakers, and she rocked back on her heels. For what this brownstone cost, the driveway should have come with air-conditioning. After all, Chicago in August? The humidity alone could suffocate her.

Once the door silently halted, Lucie pointed toward the interior door. "Stay alert, Lauren. This is where it gets tricky."

The newest part-time member of Lucie's dog walking team studied the door and waited for instructions. Lauren seemed like a nice kid. Well, at twenty, she wasn't really a kid. Lucie was only six years older. Still, Lauren was new to Coco Barknell and needed to understand the intricacies of working with the dogs.

Particularly this dog.

"The door," Lucie said, "is your friend. Otis is the deadly combination of a jumper and a runner."

Lauren scrunched her face. "What?"

"When you open the door, you have to do a body block so he doesn't squeeze through. He's an eighty-five pound Olde English Bulldogge. If you're not careful, you will either A) wind up flat on your butt with Otis on top of you or B) be chasing him around the neighborhood. I've done both and it's not fun. Plus, it'll destroy your schedule."

And with the number of clients Coco Barknell serviced in a day, the schedule was the Bible. As happy as Lucie was about the growth of her dog walking and upscale-dog accessory business, she hated turning the dogs over to others. Of course, she'd done a thorough background check on Lauren, but these animals were almost her babies and she couldn't trust just anyone with them.

Lucie stepped to the door and planted her feet, weight on her heels. "Are you ready?"

"Ready."

Lauren smiled and maybe that smile had a bit of lady-you're-a-fruitcake in it, but the first time Otis did one of his Underdog leaps, she would learn.

Lucie opened the door and the howling began. "Hi, boy," she said, her voice firm and level, no excitement that would cause a doggie mindmelt. "I'm coming in."

Slowly, she inched the door open and slid through with Lauren bringing up the rear. Otis did his normal jumping and Lucie steadied herself for the onslaught. "Off!"

Finally, he sat, but he tracked Lauren with his eyes. Then —*here we go*—unable to withstand the pressure of a new person in his space, he leaped, his long tongue flying in search of a cheek to lick.

"Off!"

But Lucie would never be Cesar Millan when it came to making Otis understand who the alpha was. That was Joey's specialty. It helped that he was six-foot-four and weighed somewhere in the vicinity of two-thirty.

"Sit, Otis," Lauren said, her voice calm, yet assertive in a truly enviable way.

Otis sat.

Cripes. Nothing like the newbie showing the boss up. "Perfect," Lucie said. "He likes you. Come in and I'll show you where his leash is."

Dressed in micro shorts, a tank top, and sneakers, Lauren epitomized the wholesome, yet sexy college co-ed. Her heart-shaped face and long blond hair only added to the morphing of girl-next-door and sexy vixen. If Lucie wasn't careful, the girl might drive Coco Barknell's male clients insane.

But the risk was worth it. So far she'd been a responsible employee who showed up on time, ready to work.

Lucie led her through the kitchen to the utility closet, strategically placed in a nook between the kitchen and the adjoining dining room. Otis's leash and various other dog supplies—poop bags, treats, shampoo—were all stored there and it made Lucie's life a whole lot simpler. Too bad all her clients weren't this organized.

"Whoa. Is this an Arturo Gomez?"

Lucie turned and spotted Lauren a few feet away studying the new painting near the dining room entrance. Lucie had seen the painting for the first time last week and marveled at the rich tones. She'd been drawn to the woman's long, auburn hair cascading over her shoulders as she concentrated on the lute in her hands. The deep red of her dress brought out the smoky archway behind her, and Lucie imagined music echoing off the stone on the surrounding walls.

They shouldn't be snooping, but the painting was right there. Plus, Lauren was an art history major and probably couldn't control herself. Lucie decided to let it go. Except the schedule was quickly falling apart.

"I don't know who the artist is, but the leash is in this closet."

Ignoring her boss, Lauren inched closer to the painting. "I did a paper on Gomez once. Pure genius at Renaissance."

"Uh-huh," Lucie said.

"It might not even be a Gomez, but it looks like one. I don't think this would be an original though."

Lucie rolled her eyes. The only fake thing in Mr. Lutz's world were his wife's boobs. And those had probably cost a fortune. The man never did anything on the cheap.

"If this is a copy," Lauren said, "it's amazing."

"Lauren, we need to go."

The girl straightened up. "Right. Sorry. I've just never seen one in a private collection. I remember something weird about Gomez's paintings and how they were sold. I could be wrong though. I'd love to know where he got this one."

Lucie knew exactly where Mr. L. had gotten it. She'd introduced him to Bart Owens, an art gallery owner who was also a Coco Barknell client. Mr. Lutz had mentioned he wanted to invest in art. Lucie connected him with Bart, and next thing she knew, Bart offered her a finder's fee for the sale of the painting. And all she'd done was make an introduction. If the amount of the finder's fee were any indication, that painting was most definitely an original.

After that hefty commission, Lucie—a business owner with escalating expansion expenses to deal with—found herself dropping Bart's card off with every client she serviced.

Lucie reached into the closet for Otis's leash. "I think it's an original. Here's the leash. Always grab a few of his treats. If he gets loose, it's the only way to lure him back. He's a sucker for peanut butter. Trust me, you don't want him to get loose. He's an animal."

At the sight of his leash, Otis leaped, knocking Lucie back a step, but she held her hand out. "Yes, baby. I know. It's Lucie time."

When Lucie shoved the leash at her new dog walker, Lauren tore her gaze from the painting. "Sorry. I promise I'm not this flighty. It's like meeting my favorite celebrity. Total fan-girl here. Would you be able to find out the name of this painting for me? Would that be okay?"

She looked back at the painting with a wistful longing and something in her expression reminded Lucie of herself at twenty. She'd been at Notre Dame back then and dreaming of a future in banking. She'd worked hard, graduated with honors, and landed a job as Mr. Lutz's assistant at one of the city's top investment banks. During that time, she'd lived her dream of being more than mob boss Joe Rizzo's kid. In the world of investment banking, she'd moved beyond the title of mob princess.

For a little while.

Being downsized had certainly humbled her. Reminded her, as if she needed reminding, how easily life could change. It had also busted her back to living in her parents' home.

That aside, she was now living a different dream. Building her own company. Who would have imagined her little side business of making high-end dog accessories would take off? But take off it did.

In a big way.

Now Lucie, along with her mother and her best friend, Roseanne, had a major department store pressuring them for more dog coats and collars. The faster they made them, the faster they sold and Lucie's panic meter had shot to the red.

All in all, a nice problem to have considering she could still be unemployed, but as with any growing business, time had become scarce. Speaking of...

Lucie checked the time on her phone. Eight minutes behind.

If they didn't make up some of that eight minutes, by the end of the day, it would be an hour. "Let's hit it, Lauren. Plenty more dogs to see today. I'll ask Mr. Lutz for the title of the painting."

**Want more? Don't miss the next Lucie Rizzo mystery.**

# A NOTE TO READERS

Dear reader,

Thank you for reading *Dog Collar Crime*. I hope you enjoyed it. If you did, please help others find it by sharing it with friends on social media and writing a review.

Sharing the book with your friends and leaving a review helps other readers decide to take the plunge into the nutty world of Lucie Rizzo. So please consider taking a moment to tell your friends how much you enjoyed the story. Even a few words expressing what you enjoyed most about the story is a huge help. Thank you!

Happy reading!
Adrienne

# ACKNOWLEDGMENTS

To my dear friends, John, Mara and Josh Leach and Cindy and Kevin Palmer, thank you for allowing me to use your beloved (and hilarious) dogs as characters. Otis, Josie and Fannie made this book a joy to write.

A huge thank you to Dianna Love for her continuous generosity and support. You're the best! Thank you also to my critique partners, Kelsey Browning, Theresa Stevens, Tracey Devlyn and L J Charles for your constant patience while doing revisions. Frankie and Lucie have finally made their debut and you were all a part of it. Thanks also to Amy Atwell for the early critiques and fantastic title suggestion. Milton Grasle, thank you once again for helping me brainstorm an action scene. Margie Lawson, your input on this story helped me get it ready for publication and I'm grateful for all you've taught me. Gina Bernal, thank you for always making the editing process a joy. To Judy Beatty, thank you for turning copy edits around so quickly!

Finally, to my husband and son for always making me laugh and giving me a daily reminder of what a wonderful gift love is. And, of course, I must thank Buddy the Wheaten "Terrorist" Terrier, who gives me unconditional love and a stream of great material to use in my stories.

# ABOUT THE AUTHOR

 **Adrienne Giordano** is a *USA Today* bestselling author of over twenty romantic suspense and mystery novels. She is a Jersey girl at heart, but now lives in the Midwest with her workaholic husband, sports-obsessed son and Buddy the Wheaten Terrorist (Terrier). She is a cofounder of Romance University blog and Lady Jane's Salon-Naperville, a reading series dedicated to romantic fiction.

*For more information on Adrienne, including her Internet haunts, contest updates, and details on her upcoming novels, please visit her at:*

www.AdrienneGiordano.com

agiordano@adriennegiordano.com